- Acknowledg

Without help and encouragement from ___ would never have written, or if I had ___ have published, these tales. In no particular order muchas gracias to: John Clevenger, Pam Pryzbylo, Billy Finn, Luigi Chiarani, Paul Maritz, David Lundquist, Zola Stoltz, Tim Roska, Dori Vialpando, Tadeo Poderes, Chris and Kathleen Talbot, John McAfee, Bill Cummings, Kenny Brown, and John Kemmeries. Much gratitude to the Circuit Writers of Portal, Arizona. Thanks to Gordon Stitt for many great photos.

ISBN 0-9820703-0-6 Paperback
ISBN 0-9820703-1-4 Hardcover

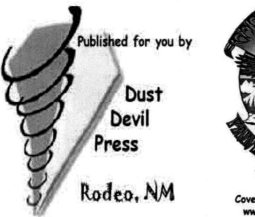

Published for you by

**Dust
Devil
Press**

Rodeo, NM

Cover art by David Lundquist
www.EagleEyeStudio.com

Cover Photo by Jim Afinowich
Nevado de Tuloca Zinantécatl- Central Mexico Highlands

Tales From The Wild Blue Yonder
Living Dangerously
By John Q. Olson

This book is dedicated to all the Earthlings who wanted to fly, but found it too difficult to learn, or too expensive, or too complicated with stupid rules and regulations. The author considers himself very fortunate to have discovered flight when few of those factors were an issue, and blessed to have taken wing with alacrity. May you all experience plenty of vicarious thrills right here, within these pages... C'mon up!

This book is also dedicated to Billy Pilgrim, who taught me that life is not lived chronologically.

TABLE of CONTENTS

This morning at 3:15 Wilbur passed away, aged 45 years, 1 month and 14 days. A short life full of consequences, an unfailing intellect, imperturbable temper, great self-reliance and as great modesty. Seeing the light clearly, pursuing it steadily, he lived and he died.
  --Bishop Milton Wright May 1912

> They all went to Mexico
>   Buenos días got to go
>   Tengo que obedecer mi corazón
>   They all went to Mexico!
>   --Santana

Desperados for México or,
South With The Wind

MAY-hee-ko" hollered Maynard, pointing at the horizon off the starboard bow of the Ford-From-Hell. He pronounced it "MAY-hee-ko", as I'd taught him and repeatedly assured him that so would the natives. "Sure don't look nothin'like the brochures B'wana, nothin' at all. No swaying coconut palms, no snow-capped volcanoes, no señoritas in skimpy bikinis. Maybe we should just point this wagon elsewhere B'wana. I hear Miami Beach is nice this time of year."His name isn't really Maynard and mine, isn't really B'wana. I call him Maynard for his remarkable likeness to my childhood hero: Maynard G. Krebs, TV's first beatnik. Maynard calls me B'wana since I'm in charge of this safari and we are headed deep into foreign lands.

"Still not too late to turn us around," continued my compadre. "Party down some on Sixth Street in Austin and sell off some of these here gliders. I think this wagon handles better when we're not so damn top heavy."

We had pulled off the pavement on a dirt wide spot for a final pit stop before turning south the last few kilometers to the Mexico border. Due to a strong north wind we were forced to piss in a southerly direction or soil our britches.

"Old MAY-hee-ko!" hollered Maynard again, and pointed south with his pecker in hand. Sure enough: somewhere in

the low-lying saline scrub off yonder lay the Mexican border-
as vague as my destiny and yet the subject of my
considerable stress. Distress I should say. On the stereo the
Eagles were singing a sweet tune:

> *Desperado*
> *Why don't you come to your senses?*
> *You been out ridin' fences*
> *For too long now!*

"Don't start on me Maynard," I said. "The dye has been
cast. You know if I ain't in Xochitenango by this time next
week my good name is mud."

"Hoe chee what the...?" puzzled Maynard above the tunes.
"I just hope I can say it by the time we get there." He grinned
his Maynard grin at me and wagged off the last few drops. A
large raven was trying to beat to weather just over our heads,
but was getting nowhere. As we watched, the bird gave up
the fight with a loud "craw", cranked a turn downwind and
disappeared in a flash. I was in a hurry to get my show
through the border and wished for a moment I could be that
crow. Even the wind seemed in a hurry to get to Mexico.

> *Oh you're a hard one*
> *I know you got yer reasons,*
> *These things that are pleasin' you*
> *Will hurt you someday!*

"Check the oil would you Maynard, while I check the tie-
downs. Just try to make yourself useful for a moment can't
you?" I really wanted to hog-tie him up on the roof rack, up
with the wings where he couldn't be seen or heard, but how
would that look to the Federáles in Laredo when they got to
poking around my load, if I come driving up with a big hairy
gringo lashed to the roof rack? I was zipping up my fly when I
next heard Maynard's cackle around front of the Ford.

"Check it out B'wana!" he exclaimed. He was looking upwind now and examining something in the same general
direction as Canada. Then I spotted it too.

"I'll be dipped in shit, B'wana" hollered Maynard. That's
another thing I admire about him- his ability to turn a colorful
phrase. "Talk about some bad timing." Maynard checked
traffic- nothing coming as far as a Texas eye could see- and

strode out onto the highway. "Talk about yer poor timing," he hollered again. "This may be a pretentious omen B'wana, I say we go no further."

"Omens are not PRE-tentious Maynard," I said over the wind. "Maybe POR-tentious. But not PRE-tentious."

My amigo lifted his slack-jawed face at me. "Whatever, I say let's turn this show around B'wana. It's an omen!"

Now I too was standing on the wind-lashed Texas blacktop peering at the pavement: a possum had passed over here some few days ago and had some bad timing, indeed. The critter was flattened spread-eagled and squished down to about the thickness of a corn tortilla in the center of the highway. Some very determined bottle flies were trying to nest in his rotten flesh in spite of the odds and, in fact, there were maggots burrowing their nasty way through the carcass. But what really impressed me, and had left even Maynard speechless was the yellow stripe running almost perfectly through this poor critter's carcass. It appeared that the county paint crew had recently been at work on this lonely stretch of road. Whether or not they'd noticed the flattened marsupial, they'd sure enough painted a perfect line through his back. Sort of a final indignity of man toward beast, I guess. Maynard turned his grin upon me once more.

"Portentious, pretentious... It's an omen for sure B'wana!"

The "show" of which Maynard spoke is Safari Sky Tours: a Mexican hang gliding vacation for gringo glideheads. This would be my third southerly sojourn with a stack of ten hang gliders from Pacific Airwave in Salinas, California. Rolling back on the highway now my determination to see this trip to its conclusion had flagged only momentarily at the sight of poor Mr. Possum pancaked on the pavement. As our self-appointed chronographer and photographer, Maynard had sprawled himself up-close and personal with the beast and recorded for posterity the creature's last stand. Then we pulled back on the highway.

"What was all that fuss back there?" asked a yawning Cheap Steve as he emerged from the plywood and wire cage which is the Ford-From-Hell. Cheap had acquired a bottle of florazepan somewhere, and brought it along for the trip. We'd be driving for about four days straight and I guess Steve wanted to catch up on his sleep. Fatigued and uptight though I was, I didn't want him behind the wheel. Like the wings stacked on the roof, he too, was essential baggage- just not quite so precious.

"That was 'Possum Plays Dead' take number seven three five," spouted Maynard.

"Huh...?" muttered Cheap. He looked like hell in my rear view mirror and I again bemoaned the fact that his presence here was necessary, at least through the kilometer 18 checkpoint below the border. After that I could jettison his ass.

"Huh?" Never known for his eloquence, Cheap was downright monosyllabic under the effects of a narcotic downer. "wha... who... where are we?" he muttered.

"Third stone from the sun," hollered Maynard. He'd stuck a new cassette in the stereo and had to yell over Jimi Hendrix, "Planet earth, western hemisphere, North America, State of, formerly Republic of Tejas!" He pronounced it as TAY-haaz, as I'd also taught him.

"Still?" pondered Cheap. "We were in Tejas yesterday."

"If that don't narrow it down enough we got us an E.T.A. of about fifteen minutes to the border Steve." I yelled. "Get your shit together and have your passport handy. And for Chrissake keep those pills on your person will you? Or throw 'em out the window if you wanna do me a real favor." Not that I was at all worried about Steve taking illegal prescription drugs to Mexico. Who takes buns to the bakery? The Feds at the border would be much more interested in guns and ammo, and the Ford looked capable of transporting a small arsenal. In fact the Ford looked like a rolling battlewagon. There was war fermenting with the Zapatístas in the south; the Feds on the border were reported to be jumpy.

"You want me to declare my pistol B'wana?" asked Maynard. He was stroking an air guitar and mouthing Jimi's " 'scuse me while I kiss the sky."

"Oh gimme a break Maynard" says I, exasperated. I knew he wasn't really packing a heater- that none of us were. Guns are highly illegal in Mexico. Only last month an assailant had gunned down Luis Colósio in the streets of Tijuana, the

handpicked next-President of Mexico, and there were reports of tension and hassles all along the border. "Throw that hunk out too will you?" I chided him. For all of Maynard's peace-nik looks, I knew him to be an accomplished shooter and that he'd agonized over bringing his piece to Mexico or leaving it home. In the end, hang gliding had won out. Even more than blasting things full of holes, Maynard loves to fly.

"And if any of these guys wanna know how many gliders we're hauling...?" I queried them. There were ten gliders on the roof rack but they were double-bagged to look like five.

"Cinco," returned Cheap Steve, who fancied himself the linguist of the bunch. 'Cinco' was indeed correct- we would tell the Feds we had cinco hang gliders. This was the most eloquence I'd heard from Steve since leaving El Paso about twenty hours back.

"I say we stop for some televisions, too" said Maynard. "Kinda take some heat off these here wings, B'wana. I hear them Federáles like televisions." This was a topic with Maynard ever since the afternoon we'd spent bundling the gliders together and slipping the giant condom-like bags over them, hiding ten wings to make them look like five. Bagged up like that, it took two strong gringos to hoist them overhead for loading atop the Ford's wing rack. Maynard wanted to know why all the secrecy and fuss. "Imagine showing up at the border with ten televisions," I'd explained. "You just can't convince the Federáles that you're goin' down to Mexico to watch a bunch of tube. That you're going down to the beach to relax and drink tequila and watch CNN. They just won't believe us. They'll insist on import duties 'cause they figure- you show up with ten televisions- it's because you're a television salesman and they want their cut." As Mexico's top smuggler of foot-launched soaring wings, I could ill afford import taxes, which, for sporting goods like hang gliders is one hundred percent. "So, we'll double-bag the gliders and pray to avoid inspection." I concluded.

That got Maynard started, again: "Maybe you should consider TV tours instead of hang gliding tours B'wana. That's it! It's BRILLIANT! You could convince large groups of gringo couch potatoes to come down south and vege out. There's gotta be more couch potatoes around than glideheads B'wana. Much more profitable. Plus- TV's just gotta be safer than hang gliders. A LOT safer."

There was truth indeed in Maynard's words but, "Too late to change plans now amigos," I said. "We're going hang gliding Maynard, just like we've been planning all these months. We're gonna slip them surly Bonds of Earth amigos, we're gonna make circles!" Visions of dust devils and high cloudbases danced in my head. "Now- do me a favor and keep your mouths shut." Navigating through the streets of Laredo, the Ford turned the last corner and there ahead lay the chaos of the Mexican border. Six months of planning and scheming came down to these next few minutes or hours and my stress level was about to max out. "And nobody speak Spanish! Got it?"

"Sí señor!" came Maynard's reply.

My border apprehensions were unfounded as we all successfully acquired our tourist cards and I my vehicle permit without hassle. The bureaucrat Federále in his official blue Federále uniform had been exceedingly bored with the procedure, he yawned twice as he stroked an old Smith Corona, and banged up the necessary documents. Papers in hand, we offered a quick 'thank you', and climbed back aboard the Ford.

"That was just too easy, B'wana," said Maynard. "Why all the fuss, anyway? I told you we shoulda brought some televisions. What will we do when we can't fly, huh? Answer me that B'wana."

I glanced briefly at Maynard. "We ain't completely through yet Maynard," says I. Putting the Ford in gear I swung out into the chaotic streets of Nuevo Laredo- finally on the Mexican side of the border. "We still gotta pass the 18K checkpoint," I said.

Maynard's head was swiveling back and forth, taking in the sights. "Well... it looks pretty Mexican out there now, B'wana," he observed. The Ford eased through a crowd gathered around a street-side taco stand, and was temporarily engulfed in fragrant smoke. "Smells like Mexico too!" he added. "MAY-hee-ko!"

"Brraggh," intoned Cheap Steve. "Lard and dead cow!" Among Cheap's other contributions to humanity, he also preached vegetarianism.

"There's an Aduana checkpoint at the kilometer 18 and that's where we really enter the Mexican interior." I pointed out. "Keep your fingers crossed but so far, so good."

"Aduana?" inquired my amigo.

"Customs, Maynard." I clarified. "Aduana is Spanish for customs. Nothing is certain until we get past those guys." The Ford rolled south with gathering momentum and we soon left the tight sprawl of the Mexican border town behind. My thoughts were focused on the up-coming Kilometer-18 checkpoint. "Let's hope they're too busy to hassle gringos," I muttered.

The Ford was stuck behind a plodding and odiferous truck full of live chickens, the flying feathers from which left a sort of pleasant, if smelly, white Mexican blizzard in its wake. Then the road widened to four lanes and soon the checkpoint rolled into view, where the Ford joined a short queue of traffic headed for the interior. The gringos rolled up to a traffic light set at arm's length from the final stopping line. The idea is that you roll to a stop there and push the button. If the light comes up red you are forced to pull in for 'inspection'. If, however you are lucky and you get a green light, you're good to go- a sort of Mexican lottery if you will. Braking to a stop, I

said a silent prayer to the Sky Gods.

Pushing the button, I hoped for the best.

Bingo! Got that green light, baby!

I stepped on the throttle and the Ford-From-Hell lurched south. There was nothing between me and a winter of tropical skies and sweet señoritas now except a stout brown

Federále lounging against the station wall. As the Ford accelerated we must have caught his attention, because he stepped casually out into my lane and gestured me to a halt. I considered running his sorry ass down for a brief second but thinking of a life spent in the Mexican federal prison system, and balancing that notion against a winter of Flying Nirvana, I stepped on the brakes instead of the throttle. The Ford-From-Hell groaned to a halt only fifty feet beyond him. The border guard sauntered over to my window and hitched up his trousers.

"Donde van ustedes?" he demanded. Where are you going? He stuck his head completely into my window to get a good look about, tilting it this way and that. I could suddenly smell his sour breath, see the blackheads in his swarthy complexion and the waxy buildup in his ear. Difficult to pretend I don't understand; just play stupid I remind myself, and shrug my shoulders.

"Buay-knows know-chay," I spouted with a weak grin. Clearly, it was not 'know-chay' as a hot sun shown down from a cloudless sky and a bead of sweat clung to his brow. I said it anyway, to indicate what a stupid gringo I was. "Buay-knows know-chay, seen-your!" Good night sir!

The Fed stood back and stared suspiciously at me for a moment, and then proceeded around to the stern of the Ford. I could see him now in my rear-view mirror, studying my load of gliders. He raised a finger and began counting, "Uno, dos, tres, cuatro, cinco, hmmm..." Then he peered through the cage of the Ford at Cheap Steve's dusty visage and Maynard's grinning mug and counted us gringos, "Uno, dos, tres!" Next, he strode back to my window and said, "Porque las bolsas señor?" What are those bags, sir? I had to play stupid again, and just grin and shrug.

"You speak Eeenglish Seen-your?" I asked, and I grinned some more, trying to act cool and calm. I really didn't want him to decide I'm a wise guy. The señor stepped back from my window and motioned that I should exit my vehicle. Uh oh... not good! But with weak knees and mounting unease I did as he instructed. We stood behind the Ford as he gestured at the ten hang gliders stuffed in five bags and mostly concealed under the Ford's custom wing-smuggling tarp.

"Estos, que son?" he inquired. These, what are they?

I played stupid once more as the señor asked his question again, this time with a gesture towards the gliders. Saying nothing, I turned to the Ford and grabbed a Hang Gliding magazine I'd kept handy for this possibility. Handing the magazine to the señor, I turned the page to show a glider in flight. It was a photo of another gringo- Kenny Brown- soaring the dunes at Marina Beach. I could even recognize my friend's face and his silly grin.

"Oh, sí, sí sí!" declared my Federále with sudden insight. "Sí, sí, son papalotes!" he said nodding enthusiastically. Yes, yes, they're kites! He spread his arms like a bird. He flapped them feebly as if in flight a couple times, and glanced up at the Heavens Above. I nodded and grinned in agreement and enthusiasm. Turning back to the Ford now he frowned and pointed once again: "Uno, dos, tres, quatro, cinco," he counted, and then turned back to the gringos. "Uno, dos, tres. Porque?" *Why have you five papalotes when you are only three gringos?*

I allowed him to go through the routine twice before I registered a look of vague comprehension. "Oohhh," says I, the big stupid gringo. "You mean... why are we only three gringos... but we have... five kites?" The señor frowned and nodded his head, crossing his arms over his chest. We were starting to look like crazy gringo papalote smugglers. Maybe he really had something here... A Big Haul? A contraband of kites? It was the critical moment, my time to shine or suffer failure. They just couldn't turn me back now, nothing could stop me now!

Spreading wide my arms like wings and rising on my tiptoes I decided this had better look convincing. "That's easy seen your," I explained, "because we crash a lot, kaboom!", and I pretend-crashed into the dusty Mexican dirt at our feet, adding some throaty sound effects of pain and disaster to embellish my point.

The old señor's brow unknit with a sudden look of surprise and delight, "Oh sí sí, sí, señor. Porsupuesto!" he said, happy now. "Comprendido!" *Yes, yes, yes sir. Of course! I understand now! The loco gringos have come to Mexico to kill themselves!* Spinning on his heel and turning his back to more urgent matters, he gestured benevolently with a hand. "Pasa les, pasa les!" he dismissed us: "Bienvenídos a México!"

My legs still felt weak as I jumped back into the Ford-From-Hell and stepped on the gas, headed south for who-knows-what adventures, towards a promise of sunny winter days, ripping thermals, high cloudbases, cheap cervesa and fragrant, willing señoritas.

"We're outta here B'wana!" rejoiced Maynard as the throttle pinned him back in his seat. "MAY-hee-ko here we come! WAHOOO!"

My Señor Will Be Very Angry! or Another Mexico Welcome

It was sure good to be back at El Peñon. Walter steadied the wing and took four giant steps. He pushed off and sailed clear, into the sky. He let out a 'Whoop!' of joy and dug into the house thermal. While he climbed out, he watched as Mork launched too.

Together they worked the lift to the top of the thermal. It was still very early in the Mexican soaring season. Cloudbase was low and the lift was weak. But the whole season lay ahead. Walter felt like the luckiest gringo in all of México. Having topped out in the thermal together, they headed over the back towards Las Peñitas, several ancient lava domes that stand sentinel over ripe fields of milpa. The local farmers were just beginning the harvest, so there were few fields available for landing. Walter and Mork didn't care though: there was always the soccer field- the gancho de fútbal. The field was really quite tiny for a landing area, which made it an extra-satisfying place to land.

Walter, being the first to leave launch, was also the first to arrive over the field. He worked his way down to a pattern altitude and then flew a down-wind leg. He turned base and calculated a final that would bring him low and hot over the soccer goal. He cleared the goal and skimmed the field. His landing was lined up very nicely, all he had to do was to dissipate energy and time the flare. It was going to be a beautiful no-stepper, like getting down off a barstool.

Suddenly, Walter felt an unusual FLICK on his wing. In his peripheral vision, as though someone had cracked a whip, Walter saw a line being snapped. *WHAT WAS THAT?* he thought, but there was no time for more. He flared the glider to a stop and settled gently to earth. He kept running off the field however, aware that Mork was hot on his tailfeathers. He carried the glider under giant shade trees and dropped it there. He quickly un-clipped and stepped out to see what had happened.

There, in the middle of the soccer field, suspended just above head height, and much to his consternation, a piece of electrical wire had been strung across the soccer field. It was gray Romex electrical wire, the type of cable used to wire houses, and it was now thrashing wildly, a sort of crack-the-whip caused by Walter's contact. It was attached at one end to a powerpole and at the other it disappeared through the window of a nearby shack. It had been strung there illegally and must have been hung up there sometime since Walter's departure the year before.

SHIT!

Walter looked back on final approach and, sure enough, here comes Mork! He was on the same line as Walter had just taken, but maybe a little higher. He had no idea about the wire either, which still bounced wildly from Walter's encounter with it. The Romex had hit Walter's wing just on the upper nose wire, which had deflected it over the wing, causing little effect. But if the wire got under Mork's wing, it could be disaster! Certainly, it would lead to broken tubing, at least.

There was little Walter could do to warn his amigo however. If he should run out on the field he would just distract the flyer. If he ran out on the field waving his arms what could his buddy do, go around? If he ran out and yelled a warning, Mork wouldn't hear him anyway. He could only pray that his amigo saw the line, and that he too got under it, or flared short. A certain amount of luck would be involved- if Mork encountered the wire on a down-stroke he would certainly hook it. But if he happened to time it as it bounced up he might just slide right under. As a bizarre counterpoint to the scene of impending disaster, Walter realized that there was music, Mexican radio music, floating merrily from the window of the shack where the cable led, a Mexican polka.

> *Hey, baby, que paso?*
> *Thought I was your only vato*
> *Hey, baby, que paso?*
> *Won't you give uno beso?*

As Walter stood dismayed, Mork hit the wire. His glider nose just barely slid under it and he lucked-out, sending the wire over upper rigging, just as Walter had done. As the wire was lifted over the wing again, it cracked the whip once more. At the same time as Mork flared to a stop, there was a loud CRASH from the nearby shack, and the music suddenly ceased. Mork stood in the middle of the soccer field and looked around, astonished. Walter ran over.

"What the chingada?" asked Mork. "What was that?"

"You just hit a powerline," replied Walter.

"A WHAT?" said Mork in disbelief.

"A chingada piece of Romex actually," said Walter. He couldn't believe it either. "They must have strung it up last summer, while we were gone." It was a typically Mexican move. These people knew the gringos loved to land here, that they would certainly return someday and when they did they were certain to encounter the wire. But did they CARE?

Hell no. And, of course, the wire was an illegal hookup.

"Shit!" said Mork.

"¡Mierda!" said Walter.

The gringos began to bag their wings. Several local kids came out to visit. They, at least, were glad to see the gringos return. It gave them something to relieve the boredom and tedium of life at Las Peñitas.

Walter noticed a woman approaching from the direction of the shack. In her hand, she carried an AM/FM cassette recorder- a ghettoblaster. The handle of the machine was broken off and the cassette door dangled by a wire. She proceeded straight to Walter and explained, bashfully:

"Ustedes rompieron mi grabadora." *You have broken my recorder.*

She carried the antenna in her other hand and held out the smashed music box as evidence. It must have been wired directly into the bandito piece of Romex. This would explain why the cable had been run illegally and haphazardly across the soccer field, and also why the music stopped suddenly with a crash when Mork hit the cable; he had pulled it off the shelf.

Walter pointed at Mork. "Es su culpa," he offered. *It's his fault.*

The woman timidly faced Mork. "You broke my recorder," she accused him, in Español.

Mork looked incredulously at the seõra. She was clad in a threadbare cotton dress and flat shoes, a tired apron draped around her neck. A colorful piece of ribbon held back her silver hair, a testament to a hard life of toil and sweat. There had been music though, for a little while anyway there had been plenty of music until... this gringo.

"Sheesh," said Mork turning to Walter. "Do you believe this?"

"Hey man, you broke her music," laughed Walter. "What you gonna do now?"

"Oh that's ridiculous. The chingada wire might have KILLED me!"

"I think you exaggerate amigo. Might have broke yer glider, yes. Yer neck, unlikely."

The peasant woman took one small timid step towards Mork, and held out the cassette player like exhibit uno. "Mi señor seria muy enojon," she explained. *My husband will be very angry.*

"Shit," said Mork. "What should I do?"

"I guess you just bought a ghetto blaster," laughed Walter.

"But you hit the wire too, didn't you?"

"Maybe, but there was still music playing after I landed. *Hey Baby que paso...* Then you came along and knocked it off the shelf, or whatever."

"Shit!" said Mork. He walked over to the señora and took up the broken remains. He examined it briefly and tossed it in the back of the truck. "Di le a su señor que lo compro uno de nuevo hoy," he said: *Tell your husband that I'll buy a new one today.* At that news the peasant lady nodded with thanks and mumbled something only she understood. She turned away and walked back across the soccer field and into her shack.

> Hey, baby, que paso?
> Thought I was your only vato
> Hey, baby, que paso?
> Please don't leave me dis un poco
>   -Freddie Fender

Sunset on Playa Paraíso or,
A Gringo Gets His Gecko

Waves tossed the shore, the sun was setting, and the gringos were getting drunk, glad to have survived the journey thus far. They had left Valle de Bravo two days earlier, and driven hard for the border with Guatemala. There were two 'muscle' trucks following Walter, and they too, were full of gringos. Walter was glad to have the support. At one point during the journey, Walter's caravan was joined by a Green Angel riding herd and an ambulance bringing up the rear. It just doesn't get any better than that while traveling in Mexico.

But this evening was for celebration; the trip south was near an end. From here it was only one more day of travel through the Guatamela border at Tecun Uman, along the low-land jungles, and then up to the high alpine lake of Atitlan. They found a popular seaside restaurant and made themselves at home.

There were two pilots from Colorado, Kevin and The Kutcher. Walter didn't know the origins of The Kutcher's name, and he didn't inquire, but the Kutcher was regarded as a slightly unstable Vietnam vet. *Let sleeping dogs lie*, he thought. Kevin, at least, seemed a normal sort for a glidehead.

There were also three kids from Kitty Hawk, in North Carolina. They drove their Dad's new Chevy Suburban, and otherwise traveled in style. As pilots, they seemed pretty green. Dave was their leader and did most of the talking. Tommy didn't say much. Will said nothing at all. He was a gangly kid who seemed painfully shy. In the two weeks or so that Walter had known Will, he had said nothing to Walter beyond a simple "Uh huh" or "Uh uh". Not exactly an outspoken sort, he was happy to let Dave do the talking.

Traveling in the Ford-From-Hell with Walter were Danny and Denny, gringo flyers extraordin-air. Danny had plenty to say, and kept Walter informed of all developments.

Tonight they sat in the tropical breeze and ordered cocktail de camarón, cocktail de pulpo, ceveche and filete de pescado. It was a sumptuous repast, washed down by mucho cervesa and tequila. As the sun set, the naked overhead lights came on in the restaurant. There were Mexican families dining also, but no other gringos for miles in either direction, they had just come too far south.

Dave noticed them first, "Check out the lizards!" he said. They were tiny lizards, attracted to the bugs who flew around the light bulbs. They waited patiently on the ceiling and walls, stalking their tiny prey.

"Those are geckos," said Walter.

"Whatever," said Dave, "they're really cool." One of the critters darted along the wall and skarfed up a bug. The geckos had sticky little feet that allowed them to scamper across a vertical surface. They could even scamper along upside down with ease. The gringos, unanimously, liked the geckos. Danny stood on a chair and chased a gecko, turning the tables on the poor thing.

The hunter had become the hunted.

The gecko saw the gringo coming, and dove off the wall. Landing at Danny's feet, he scampered away across the floor. The gringo gave chase, but the gecko scooted under a nearby table. Danny was forced to give up the chase and focus on another gecko. More tequila arrived at the table, and the hunt was postponed in favor of inebriation. There were cheers of "GUATEMALA!" and "ATITLAN!" The gringos knocked back the fiery swill.

Danny continued his hunt, and soon caught an unlucky gecko. He held it up by its tail, but the critter simply left his tail behind, leaving Danny with nothing but the wiggling appendage. He tossed it off among drunken laughter and sought another, whole gecko. He stood on a chair again and this time caught the tiny beast, carefully. He held it up like a trophy, made a dare: "I've got ten thousand pesos for anyone who will swallow this gecko," he offered. "I double-dare ya!"

Amid the howls of disgust and delight, Will stood wobbly from his seat and uttered the first complete sentence that Walter had heard him say during their entire brief acquaintance.

"Make it twenty thousand and I'll DO it!" he said. This elicited more cheers and taunts. "Twenty thousand, twenty thousand," came the refrain. "Twenty Thousand!" A paltry sum, actually, at the exchange rate of three thousand pesos to the dollar, this amounted to about seven bucks. Twenty thousand would buy a case of frosty. Mexican cervesa, however...

"Twenty thousand, twenty thousand!"

The pesos were quickly laid out on the table. The other diners had noticed the fuss, probably didn't quite understand exactly, but when Will held that startled gecko over his head and stared it down, when he opened his maw wide and waggled his tongue, there was just little doubt what would transpire next; the gringo slipped the gecko into his mouth, and swallowed.

"Gulp!"

"Bwaaa ha ha ha!" screamed the delighted drunken gringos. The Mexicans quickly gathered up their small children, keeping them close should the foreign devils design to eat other, more precious, creatures. The gingos slapped Will on the back, by way of congratulations.

"I can feel him wiggling around my throat," said Will, wondrously.

"Ha haa!" cried Dave. "Here, wash him down with some cervesa."

"Wait!" cried Danny, who always had a better idea... "I'll give you ten thousand more pesos to puke him back up, alive!"

Will's cheeks bulged slightly, as though the mere thought had caused a gag reflex, but he simply held out his hand and said, "Put yer pesos where your mouth is." It seemed he was becoming, with each drop of tequila, a bit more brave, a bit more eloquent.

The foreign crowd loved him. The locals weren't quite so sure. Danny pulled a wad of peso notes from his pocket and slapped a ten thousand note in Will's hand. Will secreted the bill in his shorts and stuck his finger down his throat. He hunched over and gagged a few times and the gecko hit the dirty floor in a pile of spittle.

It sat there, bewildered by its strange journey for a moment, and then scurried off towards safety, leaving a trail of Will's drool behind.

The place went wild. As the gringos all slapped their new hero, the Mexicans gathered up their kids and belongings and sought the nearest exit. They had some concerns about what might come to pass next, guessed Walter.

The gecko resumed his hunt, no worse for his journey.

Slide Mountain Hazard or,
Fire in the Sky

"**C**lear!" On the south launch, Rooster bailed.

"Clear!" On the east launch, Mork bailed.

"Outta here!" Way over on the north launch, Terry bailed.

Walter was number three in line now, front and center, on the east launch at Slide Mountain. He picked up his wing and took two steps forward to close the gap that opened when Gordy stepped over the guardrail after Mork bailed. Gordy didn't bother to set the wing down on the cliff side of the rail. He just steadied the wing, pointed the nose down the steep slope, went for it.

"Clear!" he hollered.

It was May 23, 1985, 11:54 AM, Primetime at Slide Mountain, and the bailage was in full swing. Like lemmings, the glideheads bailed right, left and center. Slide Mountain was happening. Each flyer, locals only, peeled for the clouds overhead with graceful turns, climbing out like colorful buzzards, on white-knuckle rides to the clouds. The sky was filled with the chatter from a dozen two-way radios; a good time was there for all!

Walter was number two now, and he watched Airwreck step up to bat. Over the guardrail Airwreck's wing was caught by the thermal and lifted awkwardly. A helpful launch crew grabbed a wire and brought the wing back to level. With a cautionary "CLEAR!" Airwreck took three hard steps and bailed too, leaving Walter number one, east launch, front and center, Slide Mountain.

It was as he picked up the wing to step over the guardrail that he noticed something amiss; his flight deck was disturbingly quiet. Usually the variometer, an optional piece of electronic equipment that most glideheads consider essential for thermal flight, would be making at least some slight chirping noise at this juncture, but all was silent from Walter's flight deck. So, before jumping the guardrail, he set the wing down and checked the unit. The display was dead... Shit! He shut it off, waited for a few seconds for a reboot, and then turned it on again. The battery status was briefly displayed and... sure enough... it was dead. Shit and two!

"What's the hold up?" The query came from one of the Beck brothers, notoriously pushy and shovey, who was lined up behind Walter. Beck was number two now, he was suited-up for the clouds and sweat etched his Vuarnets. He was not in a loitering mood.

"Ahhh... my flight deck ahh... is dead I guess."

"Screw the flight deck," demanded Beck. "Just bail. Yer burnin' daylight dude!"

"Ahh... well," said Walter, hesitant to follow such hasty advise. If he got out there, hucked himself off the cliff, and then discovered that he really had no functional variometer, he would be behind the eight ball right from the git-go. He just wasn't that confident in his own thermaling ability without some electronic help. "Ahh... how about I... just step aside and... and let you push?" It was standard launch etiquette. Beck didn't even reply. He just picked up his wing and held it impatiently until Walter cleared the hell out of the way. Advancing forward when Walter was clear of the launch, he stepped easily over the guardrail to the precipice, steadied the wing and felt the launch-cycle for a moment, and then hollered the Slide Mountain launch mantra of the moment:

"CLEAR!" he cried, and with his toes making tiny puffs of dust in the dirt, he was gone.

Walter set his wing down beside launch and appealed to the crowd in general. There were plenty of tourists watching the action, yakking excitedly with each other, pointing and craning their necks at the clouds above, and taking photos of tiny specks in the sky. There were also a few more glideheads making hasty preparations to bail- the Late Crew. "Anybody spare a nine-volt battery?" he yelled.

The nine-volt is that small rectangular battery with both terminals protruding from one end, and it is the battery of choice amongst the glideheads. It was what would get Walter's flight deck up and singing once again.

I've got one Walter," came the reply. Kelly Hatfield was stuffing battens as fast as he could- a bit behind schedule. He tossed a fresh package of two Energizers at Walter, who offered to pay for them at a later date. "I gotta bail!" he explained. But the explanation was unnecessary.

"Just keep 'em both 'till I see you next," Kelly offered. And then, "Get high, go far!"

Quickly, Walter replaced the dead battery in his flight deck and checked the results; all systems GO. He dropped the other battery in his Levi pocket and then hastily, without much more thought, he stepped over the Slide guardrail himself and BAILED!

Several other flyers were mixing it up out front and a few had sunk below launch and were attempting to dig it out over the Knobs. Walter proned-out in his harness and prepared for battle. The day was pregnant with promise, but there would likely be some wrestling in an attempt to get skyed-out. He settled into his cocoon, gripped the bar evenly, and waited for that first welcome tug on the nose.

But suddenly he noticed something strange; something painful in his groin... Something stinging him or... or burning him. Something HOT... in his groin. Or was it stinging? Whatever- definitely not a normal occurrence, what the hell was going on?

Confused, trying to stay focused on the task at hand, Walter lifted a leg out of the harness and gave it a slight shake. The burning/stinging went away. Relieved, he rested back in the harness and made a turn, concentrating again. Almost instantly, the burning/stinging was back again, only worse now...

YIKES! What the hell?

Puzzled, Walter again lifted his leg from the harness and gave it a good shake. Once again, the pain vanished. He relaxed once more in his harness, concentrating on flight again, only to again experience the same nasty burning sensation.

What the HELL?

This time, Walter tried to ignore the pain. It was really only discomfort anyway, he was losing altitude with his struggling, he really must concentrate on the task at hand...

AAHHHWWW!

What the...!

By lying back down in the harness Walter was suddenly stung again, as though by a hornet or a scorpion maybe... Something terrible. Or maybe he was being burned by...

By the battery?

No!

What?

The Energizer?

That must be it. The Energizer was getting hot for some strange reason. But how could it be getting hot? I must concentrate on flying! The battery cannot be getting ...hot. Forget it!

Oh, but it is, it is! The battery is getting HOT! How could it be getting hot? The wing swung wildly this way and that as Walter grappled with the obvious, the ridiculous, the unlikely...

THERE IS A BATTERY DOWN MY PANTS. THE BATTERY IS GETTING ME! HOW... CAN... THAT... BE?

Out of the blue it dawned on him- he must get that friggin' battery out of his trouser pocket somehow, but laying in the harness as he was it would not be easy. The Energizer must be contacting something... that was it! The Energizer was contacting some coins in that same pocket! It was crossing a quarter or... or a penny! Yes, a penny is copper of course- a great conductor. Maybe if I can just shake it around a bit it will lose contact? Walter again lifted his leg from the cocoon and this time wedged his hand down between the harness and his pants, gave his leg another good shake. He could feel the battery and the change down there too. But the wing was knocked about by the thermal turbulence and he had to grab on with both hands again. It is difficult to fly a hang glider in turbulence anyway, but with just one hand- for more than a moment or two- it is quite impossible with any precision.

In fact, it was going to be damned hard to get that battery out of there at all, and live to tell about it. But he must, oh he MUST!

EEEYYYOOOWWW that's REALLY GETTING HOOOOOOT!

Walter was plummeting out of the sky now. Rooster, Mork, Gordy, Napper, Beck- they were all becoming tiny dots of Glory overtop the mountain while Walter was plummeting, plummeting into Washoe Valley and ignominy. He dug a hand down into the harness, almost made it TO the pocket, but not anywhere IN the pocket... Almost got to the pocket, but the wing was standing on a tip, slipping... plummeting...

Desperately, he wrenched his hand out and grabbed on to fly again. The wing pulled massive 'Gs' as it wanged level once again, but the flyer was almost completely indifferent to the wing now...

"AAAHHHOOOOWWWW that's TOOO DAMN HOOOOOOOT!"

Walter soon determined that if he flew in a semi-prone position the heat did not contact his leg. It was more bearable, but also a horribly uncomfortable way to fly. Maybe the best solution was to fly as quickly as possible down to Washoe Valley and land? Give up on the flight to idiocy.

Maybe throw my parachute? That wouldn't help, he would still be burning...

GET THE DAMN BATTERY OUT OF MY PANTS!

HOOOWWW?

It's TOO HOT!

Desperately, determinedly, struggling for control, struggling for a grip, Walter shoved his hand down his pants, tearing his knuckle on a Levi's rivet. He shoved his fingers and then his hand into his pocket, and felt something blazing hot- the Energizer and a pocket full of change. With the glider stalled badly off on a tip and plunging wildly out of the sky, Walter tore the terrible contents from his pocket and, without a hesitant thought, gave it a heave into the Wild Blue Yonder...

"SSSSSHIT!" That was one Energizer Walter was glad to get rid of!

"What's goin' on down there in Valleyland Walter?" came a query over the radio. It was El Gallo's voice. "Nice up here at cloudbase," he taunted.

In the background of the transmission Walter could hear Rooster's flight deck squawking a merry tune just to spite him: *weeneeweeneeweeneewenee!*

Spent, he settled back into his harness- there was no terrible stinging/burning now, only exhaustion, a couple of skinned knuckles, and a shaken confidence level. A bead of sweat dribbled down the inside of his Ray Bans, inside his flight suit was steamy like a sauna. He leveled the wing and began searching for any little scrap of lift, anything going up, please! He was quite low as a result of his ridiculous ordeal, gazing at the parched flat valley land, rather than the lofty High Sierra over Lake Tahoe.

There was some catching up to do...

Flight will free Man from the remaining chains, the chains of gravity, which still tie him to this planet. It will open him unto the Gates of Heaven.
    -- Wernher von Braun

Flying is more than a sport and more than a job; flying is pure passion and desire, which fill a lifetime.
   --Adolf Galland

ShowTime at Sun 'N Fun or,
A Splotch In the Ol' Logbook

The largest airshow in the World, Sun 'N Fun, was in full swing when I wheeled out the SAMBA from Don's hangar at South Lakeland airfield. The morning fog was burning off nicely, and it looked to be a good day for a fly-in, and the estimated one hundred thousand people who would attend.

The little SAMBA trike was very sweet in the morning sunshine, but was still a fairly new commodity to me. I had only a few hours of flying the pretty little soaring trike. I was very comfortable with the TOPLESS wing- it was really just a fancy hang glider after all. But it was the Zenoah G-25 engine that was still sort of a mystery. No matter, I was happy just shoving out and aiming my wagon for the show at Paradise City. I fired up the engine and let her warm up.

When I arrived at Lakeland-Linder airport for the show, I landed very short on the runway, and rolled to a stop with no brakes at all. I had just enough time to hurry to the briefing tent and get a coffee and donut. I got my briefing pass and headed back to the SAMBA, excited about flying the morning parade.

Parade is the only time during the show when only the ultralights are flying, and when we are allowed to fly over the main runway, and all that expensive hardware parked on that apron.

This morning was very pleasant, and as I walked I talked with Leonard, who is a Sun 'N Fun veteran of many years, and was also planning to fly the ultralight parade. As we walked the field he warned me: "Lots of dew this morning." He certainly was right. Our feet were already soaked with dew; it sparkled in the grass and over everything in central Florida. Then Leonard warned me: "Your brakes won't work on wet grass you know."

I wasn't paying much attention. "Yea," I replied. As a desert pilot I should have paid more heed. 'Dew' was just not part of my flying lexicon. Leonard jumped in his trike and I jumped into the SAMBA. I pulled the recoil start, and blazed off into the sunrise. When I got settled in the sky and following all the other funny-looking machines around the parade route, I reached over to the dangling VG string and cinched-up the crossbar to tension the sail.

I had a delightful morning ride with a dozen or so other ultralights and an otherwise empty sky. The SAMBA performance amazed me once again. I flew the parade pattern two or three times and then decided to land. Looking back, I realize that I made three mistakes on that approach, which added up to big embarrassment.

First, I left the wing on full tight geometry. This means the TOPLESS was in glide mode- tightened up for maximum glide.

Second, the idle on that Zenoah engine was set a little high, or maybe the throttle was a little stuck. In any event I was still getting a small amount of push even at idle.

And three, I hadn't taken Leonard's advice to heart.

Anyway, coming in to land I set up a little long, looking at mid-field for a touch down. I figured there was certainly plenty of room to get the little trike stopped if I landed-mid field. But when I pulled the nose down to shorten my landing, that little trike just went gliding- it didn't come down as planned at all!

I see the end of the runway, but I still figure I have plenty of room to spare. Finally I get the gear down on the runway, but I have to cheat and plunk the wheels down with a little extra airspeed. I immediately step on the brake, but I don't feel much effect. I glance at the front wheel and notice- to my dismay- that the front wheel is locked up. Dew is splashing off the tire like the bow wave of a boat.

The trike is NOT slowing down!

I reach the kill switch and shut off the motor. This helps a little, but now the end of the runway at Paradise City is looming foremost in my brain. I try turning the fork to aim away from disaster, but this makes no difference, the trike keeps making a beeline for the ditch!

I abandon the pegs now, and place my heels firmly on the ground. This helps a little too, although I feel as though I am stepping on ice. Suddenly, everything is in slow-motion, and I see several spectators standing along the fence that borders the runway; some are aiming cameras at me. There is a volunteer from the flightline standing at the end of the runway in his orange vest. He sees me coming and dives out of the way...

The end of the runway is approaching, and I put everything I've got into standing on my Nike brakes. I strain at the lapbelt and wonder if I have time to release it and bail out. I am not going fast now, maybe I can grab the trike as I bail, and slow it down? But there is no time, I strain some more and now my feet start digging into the wet Florida turf.

Here comes the end! The end is a muddy ditch, with cattails sticking up. I'd flown over this same ditch many times, but never paid it much attention. The ditch is about ten or twelve feet deep, looks to have a couple of feet of mud at the bottom.

The SAMBA is very slow now; I've almost got it stopped. But not quite. As the nose wheel drops over the edge, I'm moving at a snail's pace. But that's too much, over the edge I go, the trike makes a terrible sploshing sound as it buries its nose in the muck.

I pop the lapbelt buckle and crawl out of the trike. I'm standing in knee-deep muck, cattails, leeches, snakes and bugs. I crawl up the bank of the ditch and spot Chaz, standing there with a dismayed look on his face.

"Ole!" he says. "What the hell are you doing?" Chaz was monitoring the end of the runway. It was him I saw in the orange vest, it was he who dove out of my way.

Then, another voice, a spectator running across the field with a camcorder held over his head.

"I got it all on video," he hollers. "I got it all on video!"

"Chaz," says I, "can you get me outta here? Please?" Chaz called for a golf cart. We hitched a line on the SAMBA, and with several other volunteers pushing on the golf cart, we pulled it from the muck.

So much for ShowTime.

Beto Makes His Point or,
No Time For Polite Conversation

"**M**ucho gusto," said the gringo. "¿Tu hablas Inglés?" My old amigo-from-way-back John Clevenger was determined to practice his Español during his Mexico vacation, and learn as much as he could. Clev walked up to shake Beto's hand now. Leaning on the truck under his reflector shades, his ballcap turned backwards and baggy trousers, with his FEAR THIS tee-shirt and his ear ring, Beto looked like a Y2K José Cool. He pushed off the truck with an elbow and sauntered over to meet the gringo, and shake his paw.

A simple 'Yes' or 'No' answer from Beto was really all that was required here, but it was too much to ask. Typical of many teenagers, asking Beto a simple question often just resulted in more questions, not answers. Of course, Beto was way too cool to admit that his English was nearly nonexistent. In the days following this initial encounter between my old friend Clev and our driver Beto, we would not hear more than a handful of Inglés from him, most of it tired and worn-out four-letter words. Right now Clev wondered if maybe Beto had not heard, so he repeated, "¿Tu hablas Inglés?" he asked again.

Beto dropped back a step and examined my old amigo Clev with a sidelong glance and a bit of a smirk. Then he stated two words very simply: "Bill Clinton," he said. Actually it sounded about as foreign, as... SPANISH as could possibly be, the syllables bursting from Beto's lips with a hard Latíno accent; it came out more like Beel Kleen-Tone-ah, and it amounted to the bulk of Beto's English vocabulary.

There was little doubt is WAS English though, with a hefty Mexican flare, and Beto then used a little body-language to make sure we had the same Beel Kleen-Tone-ah in mind. To punctuate his point he reached out about waist-high with both fists as though grabbing some imaginary buttocks. Then, with a quick three-stroke, he rocked his pelvis forward and his elbows back. For emphasis, Beto added his best Beel Kleen-Tone-ah facial imitation, casting his glance skyward in ecstasy.

For Beto anyway, this is exactly what our President was about.

Clev's jaw dropped at this sudden insight and his eyes bugged for a moment. He turned to me with a look that mixed surprise with equal parts delight and dismay. A verbose and enlightened sort, this was one of the few times I have ever seen my friend at a loss for words. He just laughed instead, and tried a quick three-stroke pelvis rock a few times himself.

"Beel Kleen-Tone-ah," he agreed. Quite obviously, Beto speaks Inglés...

Revenge of the Electra Flyer or, Cowboys Go Flying

Walter rolled into Randolf, Utah, looking for launch. It was obvious from ten miles out where the flying was, an awesome ridge rose up from the edge of town- looked to be two thousand feet high and quite precipitous. For hucking yourself off, it looked promising indeed. Better yet, a westerly was blowing straight in. Passing the Randolf Post Office near town center, Walter noticed Old Glory standing straight out and proud, pointing the way to the ridge.

Wahoo!

Just a few days before, he'd met some other glideheads who'd just come from Randolf and raved about the flying. "The Crawfords" was how they called the place. "When you get to Randolf," they'd explained, "just turn right and go through town until Main Street turns to dirt and heads up them mountains," or some such advise. "You can't miss," they said.

Walter stopped off in town and bought some essentials for spending a night atop the ridge, a six-pack, some dogs and buns, some potato salad and a candle to read by that night, then hopped back in the van and sped for the summit. The dirt road switched-back several times on the way up, but was in excellent shape. Easily topping the ridge, the road split to run north or south along the top.

Hmmm. Which way to launch?

The road south appeared a bit more heavily-traveled, so Walter spun the wheel south. Over a crest and down the other side and quickly he noticed a side road headed straight for the west face. Glancing that way, he spotted a pickup truck and a hang glider set up alongside. What great luck!

Walter approached in his van and was greeted with a friendly wave. A windsock had been erected atop the ridge and it stood ripping in the wind. Redtail hawks soared above. The place was happening, booming!

"WHEEOOHEE!" cried one of the fliers as he stepped from his wagon.

"WHEEHOOWW!" yelled the other. "She's a crackin'!" He grinned at Walter, showing a missing tooth. His cowboy hat blew off, revealing a knobby head. "We're gonna SKY OUT today boys," he exclaimed as he gave chase. "Big dogs!"

A family of rooks crabbed by overhead, muttering their imprecations at the Earthlings below. "Caa caa CRAW!" they called. They did a few loops and barrel rolls and generally cavorted above our heads, showing off.

The cowboys had a sorry-looking old Electra Flyer Cirrus 5b, a rather antiquated design, into which one of them was stuffing battens. The glider had seen better days.

Quick introductions were made; these were two local cowpoke brothers from a ranch in the valley below, Wayne and Duane, both decked-out in button-snap western shirts and neckerchiefs, western vests and turquoise, Levis and cowboy boots, looking much like they'd just stepped out of Gunsmoke Episode #77— Festus Goes Flying. Duane had traded his cowboy hat for a red helmet in anticipation of a flight, and it perched atop his head incongruously, like a silly beanie. Wayne clutched his bonnet to his head against a strong wind. They were new pilots they explained, but had flown the Crawfords before. "Sled rides," said Wayne, the friendly one.

Walter quickly jumped to set up his Comet, not wanting to miss the fun, and as he performed a preflight the Flying Cowpoke Brothers carried that Cirrus 5b to launch. The glider showed signs of advanced ultraviolet damage and sail rash and had seen plenty of hard duty. From Walter's perspective the downtubes had a distinct pretzel look about them. Walter kept his eye on them, not wanting to miss the launch.

When at a new, unfamiliar site, goes the collective wisdom, *watch the locals.*

So... he watched as the brothers carried the glider quite a ways down the slope. Then they set it down on the base tube and Duane clipped his carabiner into the hang strap. So far so good.

Next, Walter could see them discussing the situation as the glider flapped and flailed and tried to fly in the strong lift, but their words were blown away, gone with the wind. Then it appeared that maybe Duane decided to wait for something; a lull? For the wind to die or to straighten up? For a better cycle? It wasn't obvious... Maybe he just had a sudden urge to pee.

In any event, at Duane's directive Wayne lowered the nose on that big ol' glider, dropping it into the ferocious wind, until the noseplate touched the ground.

Now, all the textbooks you read are always preaching that the force of the Wind increases exponentially or logarithmically or some such crap. But Wayne and especially Duane learned a quite different lesson just then, a lesson much more profound... Right there atop the Crawfords, the cowpoke brothers in a blink of an eye, learned that the force of the Wind depends entirely on how much you oppose it. Because, next thing they knew those squiggly tired old downtubes collapsed under the opposition of the wind, just gave up the ghost, the both of them at once, and that big ol' Cirrus 5b flattened Duane in a heartbeat. For a split second he was visible only as a vague lump doubled up under the sail, and in the next heartbeat, while a startled and dismayed Wayne watched helplessly, the wind got UNDER the nose and ripped poor Duane right off the ground for a double-whammy. Right before their eyes Duane did the rag-doll at the end of his suspension like some hapless rodeo buckaroo, and then smashed back atop the broken glider like a demented turtle. It flipped again as Wayne gave chase, this time smashing Duane into the hard dirt atop the Crawfords for a double-double whammy.

For those of you who need a bit of hang gliding theory to understand what had just happened well, hang gliders are made of cables and tubes forming numerous triangles. Wherever the component is loaded under tension, it can be made of wire cable. Wherever the component is loaded under compression it must be made of tubing, and as long as that tubing remains straight it can withstand loads. But the tubing on the Cirrus had been bent several times and then straightened by... well... by someone. It worked just fine until it suffered a tremendous load there on launch, and then it gave with a snap. When the triangle failed the whole wing lost its structural integrity and became like a leaf in the wind.

The glider flipped a couple more times, each time flinging Duane into another whammy like a mismanaged marionette, before it migrated out of the strong laminar wind, where Wayne finally leaped atop it and got it under his control. By now, Walter had dropped his glider in the lee of his truck and run to assist.

"OH SHEEEEIT!" howled Wayne as though wounded. "SHIT HOWDY DUANE! YA BROKE THE GODDANG KITE!"

"UNG...UNG...OH!" was the only answering sound from under the fabric. "UH... UH...OOOUH..."

Together, Walter and Wayne unclipped the carabiner and lifted the wing off Duane, who still lay curled up in a ball. "Duane Goldang it. You broke the goldang kite!" hollered Wayne. He seemed to be oblivious of the gravity of the situation, so to speak. His only concern was for the broken tubing and sailcloth trashed at his feet. Disgusted, he kicked some dirt at his wounded brother.

Meanwhile, Duane gasped for air. "Fuf fuff fuff!" he groaned and then finally spoke, "SSSSSSSHIT!" he said. "My... my belt buckle my belt buckle."

"Chuck yer belt buckle alright," howled Wayne, who had no lack of air whatsoever. "Where we gonna find some'a these here tubes huh? Answer me that."

"I... ahh... I... think it cut me...," wheezed Duane, "...it cut me in two. Ohh...UUGGHH!" He writhed in pain, made a weak attempt to rise on an elbow, spat some blood into the wind.

"Shoot," said his brother Wayne, and he walked off in disgust.

Next, Duane spit a bloody tooth upon the ground. "Pahtooie," he moaned, "Oh God! Help me outta this here harness, will ya fella'?" he pleaded to Walter. "I gotta... get... gotta get outta here." Walter did as bid, unhooking him and helping him painfully to his feet. "Oh God," he proclaimed. "Jesus H...!" He stumbled, bent and leaning heavily on Walter's shoulder, towards the sun bleached '56 Chevy

Apache that could only be theirs. Blood trickled from his nose and mouth. He clutched at his middle and popped the buckle of his belt. It was one of those large rodeo-trophy type of things, a nifty oval plate about the size of a small sauté pan. The metal looked very sharp to have been bent over, bent doubled-up over.

Duane ripped the belt and buckle from around his waist and just tossed it to the ground. He reached the truck and threw open the door. He crawled moaning into the passenger side and lay down. "Lordy," he moaned. "Get me down ta Doc Wilson's. I think I'm fixin' ta die!"

"SHEEEOOT!" scoffed Wayne from over by the wreckage, "I see'd you hit harder n'at comin' off a bull. Don't be such a wussy!" But Duane inched himself painfully up in the driver's seat. Clutching his middle with one hand he pulled the stick into neutral with the other, just sucked it out of gear really, and let 'er start rolling away from launch, back down the road, towards the civilization, the hospitalization, in the valley below.

"AW SHIT!" cried Wayne as it started to move. He was speaking to Walter now. "Cain't NEVER have no fun with that boy," he grinned. He lit out then, sprinting as best he could in his Tony Lamas he chased down that Chevy and jumped on the running board just about the time Duane popped the clutch. The truck lurched and rattled down from launch and disappeared between the hills, leaving Walter behind with the wreckage of that Cirrus 5b. Last he saw of the cowboy brothers Duane was leaning in through the window, swatting Wayne with his hat.

In one of his rare moments of discretion and restraint, Walter bagged his wing, content to wait for more locals, for... OTHER locals, to show up and show him how it's done on a windy afternoon in the Crawfords.

Let this serve as a lesson for us all: hang gliding IS a dangerous sport.

The Comandante Gets His Gringo or, Busted... on an Easter Morn

Standing on the hot sunny beach with the toes of his spit-shined boots just out of reach of the gentle Baja surf, Guaymas Aeropuerto Comandante Jesus Maria Ortez Garcia Marquez de Martini of the Policía Federal de México was pissed. So angry in fact, that the veins in his forehead and the tendons in his neck bulged with anger and frustration. Tiny specs of saliva spouted from his lips as he let go a string of maldiciónes, and generally behaving like a dangerous Mexican volcano, about to blow. He could have ordered his men to open fire, should have ordered his men to open fire in fact, he might have brought down the gringo's strange flying contraption as it took off along the beach, put an end to this whole miserable affair. But ¡no! Somehow, caution had stayed his hand. There were other sunbathers and recreators after all, frolicking in the surf. He just couldn't bring himself to give the order. His job, his position as Comandante, already jeopardized by this flying fool as it was, might indeed be lost if one of his mens' rounds had missed the loco gringo and found its mark instead in a recreating beach goer.

"¡Me llevo la chingada!" he cursed. *¡I'll get the fucker!*

As he stood there gazing in anger along the beach, the early morning sun illuminating the scene with a ferocious glare, his head thumping with an equally ferocious hang over, he watched the gringo cut a graceful, arching, climbing turn over the gentle surf and headed back the way he'd come. It might have been a beautiful vista under different circumstances, and for a moment he prayed perhaps the gringo had heard his curses and decided to surrender himself up to the Federáles right then and there, him and his strange, illegal, avioncito.

But the gringo did not land, no. Instead he made a low pass over the water and waved to the folks as he passed by, zinging along in easy gunshot range grinning like a damn... ¡pendejo! The sunbathers and the swimmers all waved back, and the Comandante again held his temper in check. The gringo kept going, sailing gracefully by just above the waves, and soon becoming a tiny dot in the blue sky, heading in the direction of the old CATCH 22 movie set and yet another runway, the same runway from which the Comandante had just returned, in a previously futile attempt to ground the chingada gringo, FOREVER! Another attempt gone bad.

¡Pinche gringo chingada cabron!

"¡Jamás!" he hollered, raising a clenched fist. *Nevermore!* He spat on the ground and cursed again. Every time he and his hombres appeared to be closing in on the gringo, he flew that funny looking machine to some other beach or strip or golf course or just a patch of damn desert scrub somewhere. ANYWHERE! Seems like you could land that contraption anywhere. HE could anyway.

Last night he had hidden at the country club. He knew it was the chingada country club, but in spite of his mens' best efforts they had failed to locate where the gringo was hiding his funny-looking flying machine, and they'd had to abandon the search at darkness. Then, this morning, he had been rustled out of a warm bed, an inviting bed, a bed full of sweet fragrant Margarita and her enormous nalga, just as he was about to put it to her to in the harsh morning sunlight, Margarita, just the thought of whom put him in a rut like... *como un toro...* by a phone call detailing that the gringo and his strange aparato could be apprehended, that very moment, on the beach in front of the Club Med Bahia San Carlos. So, instead of making love to dulce Margarita, and proving once more that he was the most macho of her lovers, rather than working her into the bellowing slut that she was, he'd been forced to pull on his trousers and go off on this...this... wild gringo chase.

But that too had backfired. No sooner had he and his men arrived to nab the gringo at the spacious Club Med resort near the end of Bahia Bandoleros, but there he goes again, flying back down the playa, back towards San Carlos. Now, having chased him back into town and lost him yet again, the Comandante gave up the futile hunt temporarily, with a vow to catch the gringo some other day... Oh, he'll catch him all right. Just a matter of time... And when he does *iMadre de la chingada!* He will toss the gringo in the carcel and throw away the llave...

iMadre Mio! The gringo will never see his contrapción again... iNunca jamas!

But mañana was Domingo de Resurrección, the most Holy of days on the entire Holy Mexican calendar, and decorum demanded that he would have to spend it, or most of it anyway, with his señora and his family. What he should do is he should run straight back to lovely Margarita and fuck her good one more time is what he should do, take out his frustrations on her ample bottom. Then he could get good and borracho tonight and have an excuse not to want to do the wife- he would be too cruda. She was like fucking an old sow anyway. He would simply pass out on the cama, and dream of his novia. Madre de Dios but that was a good plan. That's exactly what I'll do he decided, and with a sudden conviction barked an order to his men.

"¡Vamanos caballeros!" he commanded. As they loaded into the black-and-white Federále pickup, he swore he'd get that gringo chingada chingadero. Perhaps not today, and probably not tomorrow, but soon.

¡Pronto!

Tonight would be for fucking and drinking and fucking some more. And tomorrow was a holy day, time to sleep late and recover. No not tomorrow... but soon. ¡Pronto! And when he did, that would be one sorry gringo.

Walter swung his TrikeZilla into a hard bank to larboard and kept the wingtip just inches off the water. He strafed the beach at the Club Med, but there was no one stirring this early on an Easter Sunday—not a single chingada gringo. *Difficult to make a peso around here*, he thought. ¡Chingada gringos! He savored that word again

¡Chingada'!

The expletive had recently been added to his Spanish vocabulary, and he liked the way it burst off the tongue. He'd soon noticed that the street Spanish he was picking up was loaded with this invective verb in many variations... chingada, chingadero, chingaso... ¡chinga te! For example:

¡Este chingada chingadero esta de la chingada! *This fuckin' fucker is fucked!*

Well, the chingadero gringos ought to stand in a chingada line to fly this chingada machine. Show 'em what flight's really all about.

¡Chingales!

He gunned the throttle and pushed up on the nose. Straight ahead lay the signature peak of San Carlos, twin peaks that the locals called Tetas del Cabra: *Tits of the Goat*. Walter leveled his wings and aimed for the gap between them. No matter how often he shot this gap, or circled out over a pink nipple, he never became bored with the exercise or failed to get a rush. Always, a tight little knot grew in his chest, a shiver rushed up his spine, and he was gripped with a mild vertigo as he looked down on their top-most rocks, splashed white by eons of buzzard shit, and glistening in the sun. Tetas del Cabra, indeed.

Squirting through the tits, shivering slightly with apprehension, the gringo pointed TrikeZilla over the perfect arching bay below and climbed through the sunrise. It was going be a hot one today and Walter was a happy gringo; just to be able to step on the gas and send his 'Zilla climbing above it all, free white and flying, to where the air was always cool, his troubles ne'r existent.

Speaking of cool, he thought, he better be cool... maintain his cool... for the eventuality of encountering his first local Federále. They couldn't be too happy about his aviating. He was sure to be violating Guaymas tower airspace, however far removed he had stayed. If he climbed high enough, he could just barely see the runways and the terminal in the hazy distance, and he could watch the arriving heavy air traffic in their pattern some miles away. He guessed that if he hung around long enough... it was only a matter of time. Maybe they were even now looking for him, moving in to nab him...? Might just have to force the issue somehow... Meet the man in charge and cross that puente. Maybe tomorrow I'll fly over there, he thought, give 'em a howdy...

¡Chingaderos!

Walter's welcome here in San Carlos had been a mixed bag thus far ever since the day he arrived. At the new runway, as yet unpaved, Walter had sold a couple of joy rides and made friends with a gringo who had a cooler full of chilly cervesa. Then, a pistol waving Yaquí in a confrontational mood had run him off! Walter couldn't be sure of course, weather or not the man held any authority other than the gun, but that was plenty. He'd left the strip and flown to the tenth hole of the Country Club San Carlos. There he'd managed to sell a couple more rides, during which time he rechecked the new airport and confirmed that the pissed off Indian and his pickup truck had disappeared. Maybe later he would return and try and sell some more rides. But then the manager of the country club had appeared on the scene in a golf cart and informed the gringo that if he didn't depart PRONTO, as much as he disliked the authorities, he would have to involve them in Walter's removal and arrest for trespassing. Walter offered to just bag the whole wagon and drag it off club property, but the gerente had conceded. "No, no, you can fly away," he said. "¡Vuela usted!" It was obvious he wanted to watch the funny-looking avioncito and the silly gringo take off into the Wild Blue Aca.

So Walter flew back to the abandoned airfield at the old CATCH 22 movie set that was close to the Club Med, and circled it a few times and then landed. But when no chingada gringo with their chingada pesos materialized he took off again.

He flew back to the condos at the end of the bay towards Guaymas, a place called Condominios del Mar. Here he was greeted enthusiastically by a man and his young son. Señor Gomez was the manager of these condos and liked Walter's wagon a lot. Walter explained that a trike was a three-wheeled power pack and pusher prop slung underneath a hang glider. He'd actually flown it down to the beach from Phoenix, where he'd built it himself, for the purpose of teaching an alumno in Hermosillo, another señor named 'Nacho" who was a hunting guide. Señor Gomez seemed quite impressed with this bit of info, so Walter further explained that he was vacationing now, spending Semana Santa as a flying tourist, and hopping a few rides to cover expenses. He took them both up for a flight in exchange for some Mexican hospitalidad, and Señor Gomez suggested that Walter should unburden his machine of all his luggage and camping gear in the bodega at the condos and fly more unencumbered.

The gringo took him up on it, and breakfast as well, fresh fruit and huevos rancheros and delicious fresh camarónes. Señor Gomez and little Daniél, it seemed, were quite enthused about Walter's sudden appearance.

Then he pushed his 'Zilla back to the beach and made himself comfortable in the shade of the wing with a tattered copy of Wind, Sand and Stars, settling down to await the gringos and their pockets full of pesos... He knew they would come, ¡chingaderos!

But shortly Walter's respite was disturbed by sound of a vehicle fast approaching from behind.

The black-and-white sedan, looking terribly akin to a California black-and-white, wound to a tortured stop amid a cloud of sandy dust on the far side of the beach, followed by a small pickup. Three menacing armed figures emerged from the squad car. Walter took the only precaution he could under such brief notice of trouble: reaching into the glove box on the 'Zilla seatframe, he pulled out the turban he kept there for occasions such as this and he pulled it over his head. The turbante was part of a Halloween costume Walter had purchased at Bailey's Food and Drug for $6.95. It was made of a stretchy gold lamé material and had on the forehead a large blue rhinestone, which Walter referred to as "mi safiro". Having recently learned about the Mexican radio cult-hero who is also known for a golden turbante, Walter was hoping to make the most of a good thing. In previous encounters he had learned that when things got tough in Mexico, or to get anything done in short order, just put on the turbante and a stupid grin and hope for the best. Always act grateful and show respect, under no circumstances act with fear.

So Walter kept the turbante handy. It was harmless, and had in fact been blown through the prop once with no damage to itself or to the prop. It fit easily in any pocket, and would withstand full speed, full throttle in the TrikeZilla, for the best effect of all— an eighty-mile-an-hour turban. Furthermore, as far as Walter could speculate, this was possibly one of only two such turbantes existing in all of México, or at least for many kilometros in any direction. This, and the one worn by the great Kaliman himself, El Hombre Increíble; Kaliman, who had been fighting crime and injustice in Mexico for some thirty years.

Now Walter shoved the turbante over his head and turned to meet his quarry, who were even now running awkwardly through the deep soft sand in their Gucci loafers. With a tight, sinking feeling in his rectum Walter figured it was Kaliman Vs The Comandante and his Henchmen. He prayed for the same sort of victorious conclusion that the Great Kaliman himself was known for.

Then the tranquility of the scene was transformed into a confrontation as a command split the coastal breezes: it came from the fastest Federále who was running through the sand at Walter and his 'Zilla.

"¡ESE AVION ES MIO!" he commanded. *¡THIS IS MY PLANE!*

This meeting had been pre-destined it seemed, ever since Walter's arrival in San Carlos, and the beach was as good a place as any for the face-off. At least there were friends here. Señor Gomez and his son would vouch for Walter's welcome if they'd just show up soon enough. But the Comandante did indeed look pissed off. His latino-brown skin was showing a red tinge of anger that matched nicely with his bloodshot eyes. Three-quarter scale compared to the big gringo, he moved with an agitation that was frightful. For a moment Walter thought he would actually swing a punch, and braced himself to take it. The Comandante, dressed in civilian clothes, kept hollering about the TrikeZilla, how the plane was HIS as of this moment, and that Walter would NEVER fly it again.

He listed the infractions that were among the obvious: that the gringo had no registration number, no radio, and that he was violating Mexican airspace. That he had filed no flight plan and was currently sitting on the beach, which is, of course, Federal turf.

His turf.

Walter felt a lump growing in his throat now too, and had a sudden urge to shit. He tried to look respectfully impressed and interested as the Comandante showed him a handful of snap-shots of other planes he had confiscated, apparently over many years. Most of the photos were old and tattered and sweat stained, but he must have quite a collection of ultralights somewhere, probably tied down on an apron, rotting in the sun. "¡Le tira por el CARCEL!" he roared. *¡I'm throwing you in JAIL!*

The two henchmen and a third man who was driving the pickup, were as big and gleeful as the Comandante was pint-sized and pissed. One of them approached the 'Zilla with some sort of paper in his hands. As Walter turned slightly, in an effort to keep them and the Comandante in his sights, he noticed the man held a sticker, about the size and shape of a bumper sticker. He peeled the back off the sticker and attempted to glue it to the cowling of Walter's Rotax 503.

"¡Deja me ver su licencia!" demanded the Comandante. *Let me see your license!*

Walter reached into his wallet and produced his Arizona Driver License, the only license he held. He handed it to the Comandante who gave it a glance and then, with exaggerated motion, threw it to the sand. He ground it into the dirt with his foot, and left it with the other litter scattered there. "¡Licencia pilotear!" he demanded. *¡Your pilot's license!*

Walter didn't have a pilot's license of course. He did have a stupid grin though, and offered it up now to the Comandante. "No tengo licencia, Señor," he stated truthfully. *I have no license, sir.*

The Comandante went momentarily ballistic and then stopped suddenly. "¿Y el plan de vuelo?" he inquired. *¿The flight plan?* A pair of plastic zip-ties dangled from the Comandante's belt loop, and Walter felt certain that at any length, he must stay out of the handcuffs. Remain calm, he told himself, like Kaliman. With much remorse, the gringo shook his head. "No tengo plan de vuelo, señor," was all he could offer, as if he should be filing a flight plan for every hop around the beach anyway, a ludicrous idea.

I have no flight plan sir.

The Comandante's henchmen were busy plastering their sticker to the engine cowling, but they had chosen a poor location. There was a small exhaust leak on the manifold and a slick of unburned oily fuel had accumulated on the cowling. As Walter kept watch they tried several times to smooth the sticker in place but the oil just would not allow let it stick. Finally, satisfied with their minimal efforts, and more interested instead in watching the drama unfold between their chief and the gringo, they turned their attention back to the confrontation. Perhaps they pictured themselves having their way with the gringo in some dim dungeon of despair.

They didn't notice then, as the bumper sticker was blown off the engine by the sea breeze, and landed on the sand. Another gentle puff carried it along to come to rest on the sand between the enraged Comandante and his out-of-luck gringo. A moment of hesitation passed between the two adversaries as they gazed at their feet, and studied the sticker. Walter finally got to read exactly what it said and his heart sank. It was just one word, a word which could nicely sum up the philosophy of the Mexican Federáles in general;

CLAUSARADO it read. *CONFISCATED*

A terrible dread engulfed the gringo, it was his worst nightmare, it was what all the other gringo trikers had told him would come to pass if he continued to wander about Mexico illegally. Well, maybe it was his *second* worst nightmare...

Suddenly, at the same moment, Walter and the Comandante both bent down to retrieve the sticker. They bonked their heads together sharply in the effort, and Walter, due to a considerable reach advantage, came away with the goods. The Comandante staggered back and held his already aching head between his hands. He screwed up his face in a hideous grimace, adding pain to the aggravation he already felt for the gringo. He let out an oath that Walter could not entirely translate, but which might have been his worst nightmare. They stood there faced-off for a moment while the gentle Mexican breezes washed over them, and then Walter did the only thing that came to mind. *How will it look back at the hangar if I come slinking home with my tail between my legs, and without my 'Zilla? What will they SAY?*

He took the sticker in both hands and looked at it once more: CLAUSARADO

He hucked-up a goober of saliva and spat on the back of the sticker, and then with exaggerated motion, he slapped the sticker on his own forehead. The spit and the sweat beading up there offered a bit of adhesion. The breeze helped too. Then he faced the Comandante and gave him his best expression of remorse. The Comandante looked back in turn and for just a moment, ever so slightly, the wind went out of his sails; he deflated.

His henchmen found somewhat more humor in the situation though, and began to chortle. They pointed to the gringo, standing there in his stupid gold turban and reading: CLAUSARADO. For a second Walter thought the tide was turning in his favor. Then with a renewed effort, the Comandante lit into the gringo once again.

"¡Ese avion es MIO!" he growled.

Comandante Martini began pointing at the black-and-white that had brought him out to this beach on Easter morning at 8 am. He was speaking such rapid-fire Español that Walter could understand only occasional words, none of which were reassuring. He gathered that the Comandante wanted his ass in the back of the squad car for transport to some Hellhole back in Guaymas. That was becoming clear. While Walter was in no hurry to get there, he also did not wish to aggravate the man any further. He also needed to do something with TrikeZilla or she would certainly be damaged, maybe destroyed, by mankind or Mother Nature. He turned towards the truck and tried to reason with the Comandante:

"Señor Comandante," he began. Their attention was distracted by the approach of Señor Gomez, manager of Condominios Del Mar, walking up the beach towards them. Señor Gomez and his ten-year-old son Daniél Jr., were coming out to fly again with Walter, and to take some photos of their idyllic stretch of beach from above. Walter felt some of the hostility of the situation evaporate as they approached over the dunes. It might have been wishful thinking but...

"¡Buenos dias, señores!" he greeted with forced optimism. "Muy buen dia para volar!" *It's a great day to fly!*

Daniél Jr. noticed Walter's turban and called out to him. "KALIMAN!" he yelled. He ran up and grabbed Walter by the leg. Comandante Martini pretended not to notice.

"Lo siento amigito, me llevan a el cárcel." Walter told little Daniel: *Sorry my little friend, they're hauling my sorry ass to jail.*

"¿De veras?" laughed Sr. Gomez. *Really?*

"Si entiendo todo, parece que sí," replied Walter. *If I understand everything, it appears so.*

"¿Por que?" inquired Gomez. *Why?*

Comandante Martini spun into the exchange like a sore tornado. "¿Por que?" he scowled, "¿PORQUE?" *¿WHY, WHY?* "¡Le digo porque!" *I'll tell you why!* And with that he started once again his litany of charges against the gringo. No license, no registration, operating commercially on Federal turf, and other digressions not fully understood by the gringo. "¡Plan de vuelo!" he kept yelling. "¡Plan de vuelo, PLAN DE VUELO!"

"Pero, Señor Walter," prompted Gomez, "¿No haz explicaste que estasiendo usted aqui?" *Haven't you explained what you're doing here?* Walter had to think about that for a moment. How would explaining that he was vacationing at the beach serve to help his cause? Martini was still agitated to the point of frenzy. Fortunately, Gomez took the initiative.

"Este Señor esta chambiando por el Grupo Zitur," he offered. *This gringo is working for Group Zitur.* The news seemed to stop the Comandante in his tracks.

"¿Quien?" he asked suspiciously. *Who?*

"¿Este señor," said Gomez. *This gringo.*

"¿Grupo Zitur?" asked Martini, astonished now and somewhat deflated.

"Es sierto," confirmed Gomez. *It's true.*

"Enceña a Nacho de volar," he finished. Walter was following the conversation with great interest. It was true, he was working for an outfit called Groupo Zitur and he was teaching Nacho, a hunting guide, to fly. But that was up north, near Hermosillo. So what? What news was that down here in San Carlos?

"¿El Nacho?" said Martini with an accent on 'EL'. *THE Nacho?* "¿Mi Tio Ignacio?" Walter thought they were perhaps the sweetest words he'd ever heard in the Spanish language, from any lips, and that would have to include Consuelo's luscious labios.

¿MY UNCLE IGNACIO?

"¡Sí!" confirmed Gomez, who had learned this from Walter just yesterday. "Esta volando por los cazadores, he explained. *Yes, he's flying for the hunters.* This was also true. Walter was training two pilots in Hermosillo to fly a TrikeZilla that their employers had purchased to survey game animals on their enormous ranchos. One of them was named 'Nacho', which Walter had only recently learned is short for 'Ignacio'. At this news Martini did an about-face on the Walter, his demeanor changing abruptly. With little hesitation he grabbed at the gringo's hand and started shaking it vigorously. He told Walter how pleased he was to make his acquaintance. Still holding his hand he led the gringo toward his pickup again, only this time he dragged him over to the helera, which he popped open to extract two chilly cervesa Pacificos. Before Walter really understood what was happening, he was standing there with beer in hand, talking about good ol' Tio Nacho.

The Comandante quickly drained the beer and cracked another. With a loud belch and a limp handshake he dismissed himself, and abruptly turned and barked to his henchmen, whose demeanors had also changed for the better. They were now enthusiastically helping themselves to the cold beer. "¡Vamanos caballeros!" he ordered. Everyone seemed quite happy now, including Señor Gamez and his boy and... slowly, the gringo. *Let's go!* Perhaps the Comandante has something else on his mind this Easter morning hoped Walter. Some more pressing activity.

Quickly, the Comandante and his men sped off in the squad car and pickup truck leaving Walter, Señor Gomez, and his young son standing on an again idyllic sandy beach, amidst the gentle breezes and the seagulls. Daniélito shook the gringo by the hand. "Can we go flying now?" he asked, his English perfect.

His father laughed, "That's all he's talked about since yesterday." They loaded up in Walter's TrikeZilla and flew away into the Mexican morning.

When we get to the place where the road and the sky collide
Throw me over the edge and watch my spirit glide
-- Jackson Browne

Pilgrim's Progress or,
A México Flying Adventure

Pilgrim stood before Walter and shifted nervously back and forth on his feet. Pilgrim was the only pilot who showed up for flying Safari Sky Tours that week and Walter found himself grateful for small blessings. Then he noticed the logbook in Pilgrim's hand. An Official Logbook, issued by the United States Hang Gliding Association, it was adequate only to log the initial flights of a beginner to maybe intermediate pilot, and Walter was surprised to see that Pilgrim had shown up one of these in hand.

But there he stood, self consciously fingering the worn corners of his logbook.

"So…" started Walter. He tossed Pilgrim's luggage into the Ford-From-Hell. "I see you brought your logbook." Pilgrim nodded and grinned. "Where you from anyway?"

"Toronto," stated Pilgrim simply. By way of explanation, it was enough. Pilgrim might have said "Timbuktu" and solicited a happier response from Walter. The gringo had yet to meet a solid pilot from that neck of the woods. Certainly they existed. Just that Walter had never encountered them in all his travels. It was flatland of course, not exactly the breeding grounds of mountain thermal pilots.

Pilgrim shuffled his feet and said, "Your travel agent told me that if I was a Hang 2 pilot and owned a Vision Mark 4, then I can fly your tour." This was true. The Vision is a forgiving wing and Walter had one in his stack of gliders on the Ford-From-Hell. "I've got lots of take offs and landings," he continued, "but not much airtime." He handed Walter the logbook.

Walter thumbed through the log. It was full of entries and dog-eared at the corners. Coffee or some such liquid was spilled across the cover and it was torn and tattered in places. Maybe chewed on by that same dog. He turned to the last page and looked at the last entry. Pilgrim did indeed have lots of flights, two hundred eighty seven to be precise. But all from a place called Farmer's Hill, a hundred thirty two feet from top to bottom, and the longest duration was thirty two seconds of flight. Pilgrim's total airtime came to one hour thirty-seven minutes and included not one soaring flight- not one!

Walter was faced with a tough decision. He could just give Pilgrim his logbook back and say something like: 'Sorry Pilgrim, but you're way over your head here in Valle de Bravo. Take the seven hundred bucks you brought me and get back on the bus. Spend a week snorkeling in Zihuatanejo and suffer tremendous sunburn. You gotta make circles to fly this place Pilgrim, and emergency medical care is non-existent. Come on back when you're a soaring pilot.' But this would mean another week of beans and tortillas and Walter yearned for the good life. Spend some time and money in the bars and cafes of Valle de Bravo and maybe score on a lovely señorita, this was Walter's agenda. He had his eye on the sweet young thing who worked in the flower shop and always looked so bored. If he was to make any sort of impression on her, he needed Pilgrim's Canadian dollars.

His alternative was to take the money and become an instructor for a week and try to keep Pilgrim out of trouble. Stick him in the Vision and put a radio on him and radio-control him around the Mexican sky. And... hope there was enough tubing back at headquarters to keep the glider flying.

Alternative number two was not really Walter's style, but it did cross his mind. That would be to take Pilgrim to some dark road in the middle of the night, far from civilization, and roll him for his cash. Just dump him out somewhere and wish him luck. Head straight to Disco Paraíso for some fun.

What kind of name was Pilgrim, anyway?

He could probably talk Luigi into helping out for a cut of the take. Here comes Luigi now, decked out like some hipster from Telluride, which is what he is. "You must be Pilgrim," observed Luigi from under his sombrero. The Canuck nodded, and they shook hands. Luigi was pleased to see that payday was upon them too, to purchase fuel for the Ford, and finance another week of flying.

With Pilgrim's luggage in the Ford they set sail for Doña Maria's Hospedaje. "So where ya from Pilgrim my boy?" inquired Luigi. Pilgrim did have a boyish look about him, myopic and studious too, as he peered out through thick glasses. A large pimple dominated his nose.

"Toronto," answered Pilgrim. Luigi gave a quick glance at Walter. As an experienced instructor and demo dude, Luigi knew exactly what Walter had on his hands: a raw beginner, a thermal newbie.

"Oh yeah? You ever flown big air?" This was in reference to the thermal conditions in evidence daily at El Peñon del Diablo where the flying took place. Launch yourself at El Peñon around one o'clock on any given afternoon in January and you were usually headed for the clouds overhead. But you had to know how to circle in the lift.

"Uh... no," admitted Pilgrim.

"Oh ho ho my boy," said Luigi. "But we have a treat for you!" Luigi could afford to be jovial. It wasn't his glider Pilgrim would be flying. Nor would it be his responsibility to ship home Pilgrim's carcass in the worst-case scenario. Nor would his ass languish in a Mexican jail while the authorities took their sweet time deciding what to do with the gringo.

"I'm good at take offs and landings though," reiterated Pilgrim in his own defense.

Luigi grinned at Pilgrim. Then he grinned at Walter. Then back at Pilgrim. "We'll get you out there mañana," he offered. "Let the Peñon kick your butt up to the clouds. You ever been into the clouds Pilgrim?"

"Well... we get umm... fog back home and sometimes..."

But Luigi cut him off with a laugh: "Baahaaaa, fog? No Pilgrim. I mean fluffy, high-cloudbase cumulus top-of-a-thermal clouds. Cold and damp. Scary! Or maybe a big black cumulous, all anviled-out and dropping verga. Huh Pilgrim? You ever been there?"

Pilgrim only squirmed a little and tried feebly to match Luigi's demented grin. Of course he hadn't. A fact established only moments earlier when he admitted never having flown big air.

"Knock it off Louie," said Walter. "No sense frightening him needlessly. I'll take good care of you Pilgrim. And we got nice soarable conditions here. No reason to worry. Yer gonna love it."

Luigi laughed and grinned some more but kept his mouth shut as they arrived at Pilgrim's accommodations. Walter helped Pilgrim down the eighty-three steps cut into the hillside, past the chickens and rooster. Past two very territorial hen turkeys, about whom he cautioned Pilgrim from approaching. "I recommend you're wearing eye protection around these beasts," he said. "If they decide to attack you they always go straight for your eyes." They stepped over an enormous pregnant sow hog sleeping undisturbed on the bougainvillea-shrouded walkway and finally into Doña Maria's humble abode, whih was so covered in rose bushes that it was hard to find the door- roses of every hue. Despite the sow pig, the place smelled delicious.

"This is it Pilgrim. The rooster starts about first light around six, so don't expect to sleep late. He also crows each time he rips off a piece from one of his many hens so you can keep track of his love-life. There's drinking water in that bottle, and you'll wanna knock on Doña Maria's door before you shower. Just point at this here water heater and she'll understand and light the flame. I don't recommend you do that yourself as they are fussy contraptions and you might loose your facial hair." Henry looked about his accommodations and nodded his consent. "Oh... yeah," continued Walter. "One other thing. You owe me six ninety five dollars too. I prefer small-unmarked bills. And if anyone makes any pointed inquires about our business here in México, you tell 'em you paid back home. Right?"

Pilgrim looked around and reached nervously for his wallet. Walter marveled that Pilgrim had made it this far with the obvious bulge from small bills in his pocket. Must have been a holiday for the pickpockets in the México City bus terminal. "You... you want that now?" he asked.

"Well, Pilgrim, I actually wanted it some weeks ago, when I was in Austin, Texas and met that Longhorn cheerleader, but that's not how I operate," said Walter. "So now will do fine."

Pilgrim pulled out seven crisp smilin' Bens from his pocket and counted them out. "You got change?" he asked. Pilgrim was worried about his five dollars change. Walter snatched the bills from Pilgrim's grasp and they disappeared into his pocket.

"That's a start on your tubing bill Pilgrim. You'll remember the warning on my brochure, just like your own glider, you break it, you buy a new one. I got a big stack of tubing back at HQ and I can sell you anything." Walter planned, HOPED, to sell some tubing this week.

Pilgrim looked around again to check his accommodations. They were Spartan but comfortable. An intense aroma from the rose garden floated in the open window and the whole place was draped in colorful bougainvillea. "Are there locks on the doors Walter?" he asked.

"You're safer here than back home," pointed out Walter. "These people want my pesos more than they want yours Pilgrim. I'm the goose that lays the golden huevo. These're honest working folk who would be shocked if you had any bad experiences here. Don't worry about anything. And if you have any problems, consult me. They don't speak much English here so don't expect conversation. Doña Maria has three daughters though, one cuter than the next. Maybe you'll find your future bride right here in Valle de Bravo." Walter said his farewell, and dashed back up the eighty-three steps to the Ford-From-Hell waiting above.

He found Luigi listening to tunes and smoking a joint, sweet smoke quaffed down the walkway and the stereo blaring Elvin Bishop:

> If I had the wings
> Oh, of a bird
> I'd fly so high
> Over this bitter Earth
> I'd fly away...
> Where Trouble couldn't reach me"

Walter jumped into the cockpit and rolled away from the curb, leaving the cloud of pot smoke behind. Luigi looked back with a stoned countenance and grinned some more at Walter. He handed Walter the joint. "Oh boy Bwana," cracked Luigi. "Got yer work cut out for you this time."

"Gonna need your help," said Walter between clenched teeth as he toked the joint.

"MY help?" questioned Luigi. "What can I do?"

"We gonna RC him."

"RC him?"

"Yeah... RC."

Luigi took back the joint. He fingered it for a better toke and said, "You mean we'll Radio Control him around the sky and hope to get him topped out in the thermal?"

"Exactly," said Walter with a rush of smoke from his lungs.

"Totally experimental, Walter. Unlikely too. Maybe we should just roll him instead."

"Don't think I haven't considered it," returned Walter. It was amazing how they were both on similar wavelengths.

"Consider it again," insisted Luigi. "That way, he may be stranded and broke in México for a week, but he won't be busted-up and hospitalized. You'd actually be doing him a big favor. Know what I mean?"

Walter took another toke and looked at Luigi, but said nothing. The pot settled into Walter's brain and relieved some of the stress. They rode back to HQ saying nothing more.

Elvin played on:

> "Fly so high, way up over it all
> 'Cause I know,
> That my wings
> Wouldn't let meeeeee fall!

Luigi steadied the Magic Kiss and hollered a brisk 'CLEAR!' He took three solid steps and pushed off from the forth. The glider sailed into the blue sky in front of launch, was battered and knocked around by turbulence, and then floated upwards. He stepped into his harness and turned left towards the resident thermal. Like a good house wine that you could always count on, the lift was there too, and Luigi began to circle out. Pilgrim and Walter stood together at the cliff and watched him soar overhead. A buzzard joined him, and the electronic song of his variometer indicating rate-of-climb, drifted through the afternoon air.

"That's all there is to it Pilgrim. Take off and clear the trees. Turn left and count to ten. When you feel the glider lift, and the vario start to sing, turn away from the hill and keep circling. You got that?" Pilgrim just nodded his helmeted head. "I'll jump in underneath you and we'll all circle out together. It'll be a piece of cake." Walter didn't know who was the more nervous- he or Pilgrim. It certainly wasn't Luigi, as a whoop of joy came floating down from far above.

"WAHOOOO!"

Pilgrim stood on the launch and made an imaginary glider with his hand. He went through his flight plan like a mantra. "Take off, turn left, count ten, circle away..." Walter busied himself with an extra pre-flight on Pilgrim's Vision Mark IV. Suited up and ready to fly, he would bring up the rear while Luigi offered advise from above. Together, they carried Pilgrim's glider to the cliff edge.

"Take off, turn left..." muttered Pilgrim again. "Do I push out?" he asked with concern.

"Just like in the directions, Pilgrim. When you hear that vario start to scream, shove your nose up and crank those circles. Now let's git while the gittin's good."

Pilgrim clipped his harness into the suspension loop and did a hang check. He picked up the Vision, steadied it for a moment against the breeze at launch, and yelled "CLEAR!" He followed the three steps like Luigi had minutes before and 77was yanked skyward. Walter stood there for a moment as Pilgrim cleared the trees in the launch slot. He raised the radio to his lips and commanded, "Turn left, parallel to the ridge," and watched the wing respond. He held his breath and watched as Pilgrim blundered into the house thermal. His outside wing lifted in the thermal and pointed him briefly towards the mountain. But even as Walter commanded, Pilgrim brought the wing down and cranked a turn to starboard. "That's right Pilgrim," Walter spoke into the mic. He heard his own words now, emitted from Pilgrim's radio overhead. "Luigi!" he commanded, "Take over while I launch!"

"Gottcha, Bwana," responded Louie over the air. "It's totally happening out here Pilgrim. Surf's up. Just stay away from the hill and crank those turns!"

Walter sprinted back into the trees and grabbed his Magic Kiss. He hooked in and carried the glider to launch. He was moving towards the cliff when a glider shadow slid rapidly over launch, going the wrong way. The shadow was very distinct, as though cast from near the ridge-top, and traveling very fast over the ground. He dropped the glider and lunged for the radio but even as he did he heard Pilgrim's radio spark to life overhead and Luigi's voice came calmly through the air: "Turn back Pilgrim. Don't get caught back behind the ridge where you can't penetrate out. Move out in front and make circles!"

Walter couldn't stand the suspense anymore. He carried the Magic Kiss to launch and just continued moving. Walking first, then jogging, finally sprinting and then running hard, he punched out from between the trees.

Banking into the house thermal he craned his neck and saw Pilgrim above, circling serenely into the firmament, with Luigi above that. A fair-weather cumulus cloud was forming overhead. With any luck they would all arrive at cloudbase soon, and the fun would really begin. "Crank those turns and push out Pilgrim," he spoke into the radio. Glancing up again he saw Pilgrim, glider banked, arms extended, thermalling out like a seasoned vet.

Heavenward climbed the gringos over the Rock of the Devil, intent on the Heavens Above.

Quickly climbing up to join his charge, Walter dove into the thermal and held a position opposite Pilgrim, turning the same direction and matching him turn for turn. Together they quickly climbed from the seven thousand foot level of launch through eight thousand feet, and the lift congealed and grew stronger.

"Keep that bank and push out when you hear that vario really scream," came Luigi's voice.

"The lift gets tight here Pilgrim, tighten up that circle," said Walter. "Don't worry about me, I'll clear out before we get too close." He had eye contact with Pilgrim across the thermal now, and began to relax. His heart was pumping adrenaline from a dizzy blend of apprehension, exhilaration and outright fear.

"You're really slippin' those Surly Bonds now Pilgrim!" came Luigi, paraphrasing Magee. From a hundred feet of separation Walter saw Pilgrim's hand reach and grasp the microphone dangling on the flying wire. His glider was buffeted and he dropped the mic. It dangled in the wind while Pilgrim re-gripped the control bar with both hands. As Walter watched, Pilgrim was knocked into a hundred-eighty degree roll reversal and the glider pitched nose down. Pilgrim then performed his first maneuver of what thermal pilots everywhere call 'going off the falls'; an inadvertent and frequent event in rowdy thermals, during which the glider stops flying for a moment, due to a stall, and then recovers airspeed and control after falling to gain airspeed. This occurs occasionally during most long thermal flights and requires that the pilot simply turn back to reenter the lift.

Pilgrim did the recovering all right, but then continued heading straight away from the lift. Walter spoke clearly through the radio: "Turn back Pilgrim and come back towards us." he willed. He let off the mic key and heard a static squelch and then Pilgrim's voice:

"CCCCCCHHHHH urly what? Am I slipping?" he squawked with urgent voice, apparently not familiar with Magee's poem.

Immediately after that Louie's radio squawked too: "GHGHGHGHCCCCHHHHHH go back Pilgrim!"

Walter gritted his teeth. They were all trying to broadcast on the radio at once, stepping on each other. Walter had carefully explained to his little fledgling that he would be doing the talking during the flight, he and Luigi, but mostly himself, and all Pilgrim would need was to do was to listen and follow directions. Now here he was, having apparently recovered the dangling microphone and yakking when he should've been flying. Suddenly, his voice came clear and strong.

"What am I slipping?" he asked.

"Forget it man, yer not slipping anything! Just fly, and turn back here NOW!" cried Walter. "Hang that mic back where you got it or... or just let it dangle. And Luigi, let me do the talking!" He dove out of the lift too, and glided out behind Pilgrim, who made a gradual turn back the way he had come. Together they headed back towards the house thermal and their varios again screamed in delight. "Crank on that lifting wing Pilgrim."

"Slow down!"

"Push out!"

"Climbing again!" Looking up, Walter saw Luigi climbing more efficiently and at around ten thousand feet, he was approaching cloudbase. The clouds looked low, maybe eleven-five with some higher bases behind the mountain. Walter and Pilgrim had the thermal core again and climbed back through nine grand, maintaining eye contact. Walter noticed that Pilgrim's helmet was apparently too big and kept falling down over his face. Pilgrim kept pushing the helmet back up periodically, just to see where he was going. "You're doing great," soothed Walter. "Just maintain that climb a little more, and this lift will start to smooth out!"

Together they climbed through ten thousand and on towards eleven grand, where the lift began to lose strength and smooth out, but still they continued their climb. "Back off on that bank angle a little Pilgrim and we'll climb better—flatten it out a bit. Fly with just a little bank and push out when you feel a core amigo." Walter was pleased to see his command followed promptly and watch Pilgrim's Vision surge upward. "Just sorta drive around in the lift Pilgrim, and we'll be to cloudbase in no time." A red-tail hawk, also on winter vacation from Toronto, jumped in and mixed it up with the gringos. Walter could clearly see Pilgrim's face, grinning from ear to ear.

"Move back behind launch now," crackled Luigi, who had been exploring the air above. "Clouds are higher back here."

Together they extended their turns over the back and climbed through eleven-five. Up the side of a cloud they flew, navigating through a dark cloud canyon. The air was much colder here. The lift was growing weak now as the thermal energy dissipated. Soon everyone ceased to climb.

Topped out, they drove in lazy circles and enjoyed the view while drifting over the back. Zipping up his collar and pulling on insulated gloves, Walter watched the red-tail dive once on Pilgrim and then disappear under the clouds. Looking further over the back, Walter could plainly see the generous large fields where he hoped to drag Pilgrim for a landing approach. The fields were still out of glide but they had a good start, and anything looked possible now.

Walter relaxed a little more and remembered to enjoy himself. This was what he lived for after all, and was obsessed with, and for which he would neglect family and friends, sacrifice ambition and responsibility, to practice on a daily basis.

Soon he decided that the drift was offering diminishing returns, and that they should glide over the back of launch towards the distant fields. They had already gained considerable distance, just from circling and drifting.

"Let's start floating over the back now Pilgrim, and see if we can float on some lift." radioed Walter. He saw Luigi disappearing over the back already, turning tail to dive towards the next house thermal on the 'Zacamacáte', another enormous volcanic lava dome jutting up behind the ridge. Soon all they could see of their amigo were his tailfeathers.

With Pilgrim in tow, Walter drifted, glided and floated towards Valle de Bravo. He didn't want to take Pilgrim all the way to Valle, because the landing field in town was restricted by the lake and tall trees and required a reasonably precise approach, with which Pilgrim was unfamiliar.

Pilgrim might have been good at landing, but he'd never made a serious approach in his life. So Walter drifted to an intersection on the road into Valle, and another popular and ample landing area called 'tanke de gas' for its propane service located there.

"How's it goin' Pilgrim?" he inquired over the radio.

After a moments hesitation Pilgrim's voice faded in and out over the radio. "...s is fant... ish I'd brought my camer...till I tell my girlfr..." Unaccustomed to talking to a radio, Pilgrim was almost inarticulate. Walter laughed to himself, but remembered that the landing, perhaps the most difficult part, certainly the most dangerous, was still to come.

"You see the giant tank of propane down below us Pilgrim?"

"Uhhhh, I think so..."

"An enormous field, half green and half brown, just south of the intersection of those two roads."

"Uh, yeah I see it now," came Pilgrim's reassuring voice. He was getting the hang of the radio, so to speak.

"Well, that's where we're headed. I'm going on down and assist with your landing as we discussed. Stay over the intersection and watch my approach. You'll be landing the same direction." Walter put his Kiss on edge and sunk towards the earth below. He wasted no time getting down and was soon standing under a generous shade tree and stripping off his harness.

"Okay Pilgrim," he radioed. "You can come on in now. Gentle breezes from the lake. Just keep up your airspeed."

"Uhhh..." said Pilgrim. "I sure do like it up here... How about if I do some wingovers?" he asked, naming a mildly aerobatic maneuver best left for more experienced pilots.

"Wingovers!" said Walter pointedly. "Are you gone nuts Pilgrim? Your brain deprived of O2 from the Windswept Heights? You've had a personal-best kind of day already. Let's just finish it off with a safe and gentle landing."

"Go for it Pilgrim!" interrupted Luigi's voice from somewhere high above. "No guts no glory!"

"Forget it Pilgrim. Restraint is the better part of valor." Walter spoke as the voice of reason. "Let's not, and say we did Pilgrim. And shut up Louie. I'll confiscate your glider if you don't behave!"

"Neya na na na naaaa na, Walter's gonna cry-eye," he heard from Luigi. "Just wring it out Pilgrim! You might never be this high again in your whole life! Don't listen to him! He's a control freak, Pilgrim!"

Walter was surprised to hear his ol' buddy Luigi speak so harshly of him. He realized that Louie was a loose canon, rolling around the poopdeck on the good ship Sky Tours, a free spirit... But, 'control freak? He decided he would have to do something to bring him back to Earth. And Louie was flying one of Walter's gliders, too...

As the Mexicans would say; ¡Que cabron!

But back in the sky, "Here goes..." he heard Pilgrim's voice trail off. Looking up, Walter cringed as Pilgrim threw the glider into some pitiful turns that resembled in no way a wingover, or any other aerobatic maneuver known to man or bird. Nonetheless, his little birdling was obviously enthused, as Walter heard a distant 'WHOOP' emerge from the sky above.

"WAHOOO!"

Soon Pilgrim's glider began to fly straight again, his aerobatic routine exhausted. It was time for more serious matters- like a gentle reunion with Mother Earth.

Positioning himself in the center of the field, Walter stood with arms raised straight up over his head as he'd discussed with Pilgrim, to indicate that he was too high to turn final, and that he should remain in his holding pattern and fly figure-eights to lose altitude. As Pilgrim's glider descended lower and lower, the time soon came to turn final. Walter then held his arms straight out like a bird to indicate that now he was on course and he should turn straight at him to land. As Pilgrim made final, Walter turned profile for one more signal: and pretended as though to pull in the bar to gather airspeed. Pilgrim responded to the signal and the glider nosed down, gathering speed. He came in on target and flew over Walter's head, settling into ground-effect flight. His wings remained level and he was aiming for the center of the landing field.

Running beneath him Walter realized that there was one missing ingredient to a perfect landing. "Put your feet down,

Pilgrim," he yelled. "Put your feet down and get ready to..." But by now Pilgrim's airspeed had been bled off to near stall and his landing gear dangled readily below him, storklike.

Remembering Pilgrim's confidence in his landings, Walter refrained from yelling the final word. Instead he watched as Pilgrim slowed the glider... slowed the glider... and then with a well timed and executed FLARE, he stopped in mid-air and settled the last two feet to the ground. It was a textbook-perfect landing, Pilgrim had survived in style.

"WWWAAAAAAAAHHHHHHOOOOOOOOO!" hollered Pilgrim. "WAHOO!" he cheered again.

Walter ran over and saw the glow in Pilgrim's face. He wanted to kiss him right on the pimple for not destroying his glider, but practiced restraint instead. Walter's reputation amongst the locals would suffer, he was sure, if he were seen hugging and kissing his gringo pilots.

Pilgrim's eyes were bulging from his head with excitement and fulfillment. "I did it!" he exclaimed.

"You did it!" came Loose Louie's refrain from the firmaments.

"You did it," said Walter with relief.

Perhaps he could make a pilot of Pilgrim yet. Pilgrim had just flown his first three-sixties, his first thermal, his first big altitude gain, his first over-the-back XC flight, and his first out landing. Not to mention his first 'aerobatics'. Not bad for a skinny white boy from the Great White North.

"Tomorrow we fly to town!" said Pilgrim, growing warm to this notion of get-real-high-and-travel-someplace type of hang gliding. Walter suddenly felt quite spent and turned from Pilgrim towards his glider to start bagging it.

"Let's go Pilgrim," he offered. "There's cervesa and señoritas awaiting your victory fiesta."

"Better to be on ground wishing you were in sky than to be in sky wishing you were on ground."
--Confucius

Hand Gliding With Dangle Dale or, Sure Looks Like He's Holding On To Me

It was blowing a gale atop Sheba Crater in the Painted Desert east of Flagstaff, Arizona. The wind was howling straight up the southwest face, at least forty miles-per-hour. Above the cindercone, giant lenticular wave clouds stacked up in the sky like enormous plates of hotcakes, and they were turning colors in anticipation of sunset. Several hang glider pilots were clustered atop the crater, as it was a popular place to practice their passion. They remaining sheltered in their trucks however, hoping for a little respite, hoping for the wind to back down slightly; any opportunity to get some badly-needed airtime before darkness killed the day. The sun, setting on the distant horizon, seemed like an inexhaustible blast furnace that generated an unstoppable force.

A cloud of dust spouted up the face for a moment or two, and then a 4 X 4 pickup bounced up the steep road to the top. Dale had arrived. He jumped from his truck and started to untie his wing, a measure of urgency in his step. He may have yelled something like "Wahoo!" but it was impossible to be sure. His lips moved in excitement, but his words were shredded and carried off by the buffeting wind.

The other pilots atop Sheba Crater were a bit surprised to see Dale's big hurry to get set up. In a flurry of hurry he assembled the control triangle of a rather beat up Seedwing Sensor 510 that had seen much hard use. It was Dale's new pride and joy though, and he was determined to give it a test flight. To prevent the wind from grabbing his new baby and turning it into complete trash, Dale tethered the glider's nose to the bumper of his truck, and then began stuffing battens. The sail flapped wildly, protesting the wind. It sounded like a fitted bedsheet hanging on the laundry line in a hurricane. Soon, Dale had the sail tensioned and was pulling on his harness. The wing danced at the end of its tether like a giant demented butterfly.

Mellow Mike pushed his door open and stepped from the shelter of his wagon into the maelstrom. A blast of Jimi Hendrix slid out the door along with Mellow, but it too was quickly extinguished as the wind slammed the door closed. As Mike strode over to Dale's wing his hat blew off in a ferocious gust. "You nuts or what man?" he hollered.

"What?" grinned Dale dementedly. He was fastening a helmet atop his noggin, a sort or Red Baron beanie affair made of old leather.

"It's frikin' blown out, man!" declared Mellow.

Dale, pointed at the wing. "Sensor 510!" he yelled as if in explanation. But Mellow just didn't get it.

"So?" he asked.

"Fast!" was what Dale replied, "It's really really FAST!" Then he continued: "Grab the nose, will ya?"

Reluctantly, Mellow Mike did as he was bid and together they headed for launch. On the way to the sloping edge of the crater Mike was thinking, *this should be exciting...* Half way there Mike made another observation: "Hey dude what's with them hang loops?" he asked. Hang loops, for those who don't know, are essential for flight in a hang glider, in fact they are the 'hang' part in hang gliding. They are very strong fabric loops which support fifteen hundred pounds or so, and from which the pilot hangs. Also, there are two hang loops, in case the main loop fails the flyer would fall but an inch or so, and continue flying on the backup loop. These particular hang loops of Dale's were swathed in a big gob of duct tape, and seemed to be hanging un-naturally off to one side of the keel, rather than in the center as they should. Some of the silvery tape was torn and hung in tatters, flapping in the wind.

"I had to change the length," hollered Dale. "They were just a little short."

"Did you do a hang check?" asked Mike.

"Yeah, sure," said the pilot with a scowl. "Of course!" Hang checks are another integral element of hang gliding: just before you launch your hang glider you lay down in the hang suspension and check your hang... It's wonderfully simple.

"What's the tape for?" asked Mellow, who thought this a reasonable question. But Dale just scowled again and looked through Mike who stood holding the nose wires to judge the wind out front, ducking his head this way and that. There was little doubt about the wind however- it was strong and it was straight up. Dale whistled at two other glideheads who were hunkered down in their trucks and motioned them for an assist. In such ferocious conditions as these, the more hands the better. Together, the glideheads carried the wing bucking and flapping to launch with Dale hooked in and tip toeing along.

"Okay," said Dale. "On three, everybody let go, okay?" He looked to his wire crew for confirmation- they were all experienced with what was soon to happen. They had all been there themselves, it was always tense.

It would be critical that everyone involved should release their grip on Dale's glider at once. They each nodded their understanding, so Dale gave the order: "...a One, a Two, a THREE!" he counted. In the vertical blast of wind up the crater, released from its human bonds, the emancipated Sensor screamed straight up from launch with little to no forward movement even though Dale had the bar stuffed to his knees. It continued to climb as the pilot pushed out and flung himself into the sky. The wing surged upwards some more, and actually backed up a bit, traveling in reverse over the ground as aircraft rarely do. From the lofty heights Dale let out a happy, "Waaaa HOOP!" He pulled in and parked the glider over the crater- nose into the wind. The sky may have been moving at forty-miles-an-hour, but Dale was going nowhere fast. Happy now, Dale waved at the other glideheads- mere Earthlings too lame to follow him into the angry sky. Soon, Dale pulled in on the bar and began a painfully slow progression forward. He let out another howl of joy."

"WAAAAHHHHHOOOOO!" he hollered.

The other pilots gazed up and watched his progress carefully, everyone holding onto their hats. "Ahhh, I think I'll let it mellow some," observed Mike, characteristically mellow. "I ain't quite that air horny." But the sun was already very low on the horizon. In a few moments the fiery orb would touch the far mountains and slide into tomorrow. It was doubtful that there would be any mellowing of the wind at all this evening. They must be content to watch Dale do his thing- a vicarious thrill.

For his part Dale could see that he was center-stage, so he obliged the groundlings with an air show. He flew out front slowly at first, then faster and faster. He dove steeply, and gave the Sensor a few steep-banked turns, the sail rippling and flapping like a torn bird. His maneuvers became progressively steeper and faster with each try. Soon, Dale was doing wild wingovers in the strong ridge lift just atop the cone. He stopped long enough to crab back to launch and park there at three hundred feet for some showboating. He let go with one hand and waved with the other. Next, he let go with both hands and held them out to his side like wings. He flapped them a bit and then grinning, waved to his audience. He swung around backwards in the control frame and let his feet do the driving.

He was... really sumpin'!

Dale swung back to the control bar and then came out of the prone position. He stuck his feet in the corners of the triangle and drove the Sensor like, "Look ma, NO HANDS!" Dale, and Dale alone, was having himself a ball. He penetrated slowly out from the crater and wanged it some more. The turns were getting dangerously steep now, and they were low. Dale was actually scaring the other glideheads with his wild antics. He roared in on launch with the bar stuffed, and then let out suddenly, sending the Sensor screaming, flapping, and whistling back into the evening sky. Dale laughed with unbridled joy and whistled, beckoning the others to join him in his wild, carefree dance.

"C'mon up!" he implored.

"Maybe if we stop looking at him, he'll stop frikin' around," shouted Mellow Mike to the other pilots. Mellow was looking strangely agitated; perhaps he was not enjoying the show. Finally the other flyers nodded and turned as one for the shelter of their trucks. It would be quite a relief just to get out of the wind. Turning back for their trucks, all were surprised to notice that a Wuffo had shown up atop Sheba Crater in yet another vehicle- an SUV. The window rolled down and a woman beckoned them. "What is he doing?" she shouted. A peculiar question, Mike surmized. How to answer... Having fun? Having a blast? Going wild? Losing his mind? Entertaining a death wish? Certainly, that he was flying was plain enough for anyone to see. Even a Wuffo could see that. Mellow heard Dale's shouts drift down from on high, again.

"WAAAAAHAA!"

"He's flying," shouted Mellow feeling a bit foolish. The woman peered up again and shaded her eyes against the setting sun.

"Doesn't he get tired of holding on?" she asked.

Now, this is the atypical Stupid Question that a Wuffo Might Ask. That one and this one: 'What happens when the wind stops?'

Mike stuck his head in the window and explained; "He's not holding on see... he's hanging in a harness."

"Uhh... oh," said Lady Wuffo. "Really?" She was quite an attractive female, a true rarity up here atop a windswept desert cinder crater in the middle of nowhere, the private eerie of ugly locusts, buzzards and a few dusty glideheads. Mike was happily leering down her shirt at a hint of lacy brassiere and delightful cleavage when she next continued.

"Sure looks like he's holding on, to me," she said.

Mellow Mike glanced wryly over his shoulder with a laugh, but before any more words came to his lips, he was struck speechless by what he saw. He spun around for a better look.

Dale was, indeed, holding on! Somehow, and against all planning, Dale's hang loops had failed, and he now dangled from the base tube with both hands- gripped, as it were, for Dear Life. The remains of his hang loops flapped in the wind behind him and all his weight hanging so far forward had the glider plunging out of the sky.

"WAAAAHAA!" It was a modern-day, high-tech, Call of the Wild.

With Dale now dangling from the base tube the wing's center-of-gravity was very far forward and that Sensor MUST have been doing sixty-plus miles an hour, almost straight down.

Mellow Mike dashed to the edge of the crater for a better look, and was soon joined by the other flyers. As they watched in amazement, Dale's glider screamed down the side of Sheba crater. His airspeed of sixty, minus the wind of thirty, yielded about a thirty mile per hour descent from the heights of the crater. Dale would soon be on the ground one way or another. The only question remained: Could he hold on?

Lady Wuffo had stepped from the shelter of her truck and arrived at the edge to peer down with the others. Once again she made an astute observation... "Sure looks like he's holding on to me," she repeated. The pilots answered in unison now;

"He is!" they cried. "HE IS!"

Lady Wuffo was really confused then. "He is?" she asked. "He IS?"

"Yes!" came the answer from everyone. "Yes! Holy shit!" Dale soon arrived at the alluvial of the crater's bottom flanks. The glider was about two seconds from impact, and at maybe ten feet off the ground, when Dale bailed. He had just flown down the side of Sheba crater about a thousand feet in an out-of-control hang glider, and it was something of a miracle, but Dale bailed and hit the ground a runnin': Gumby goes hang gliding. Having shed its excess baggage, the Sensor's sink rate suddenly improved dramatically. Lighter now by far, it pitched nose-up and soared wildly back into the sky. Although the release speed was too much for Gumby, he was a scrappy sort. He tumbled and performed a quick shoulder roll in the cinders and was back on his feet, running full speed under his wing, looking up. As the wing pitched back down to crash, Dale grabbed at it and slowed its fall. From the vantage perch above, the pilots all heaved a breath of relief, not believing what they'd witnessed.

"Blessed Jesus!" said one. "Holy shit!" exclaimed another.

Lady Wuffo turned to Mellow Mike. "What happened?" she asked, still a bit confused...

"Somehow his suspension failed," explained Mellow. "He crashed."

She looked at Mike and the others as though they were all quite nuts. "You guys are nuts!" she said, and ran back to the safety, the comfort, the... sanity, of her Sport Utility Vehicle.

Dust Devils for Desayuna or,
Breakfast of Champions

Walter and JJ strode through the streets of Valle de Bravo with liquados in hand. Walter had learned to stop at the liquado stand every morning to purchase one of the delicious beverages which would get him through another day of flying just fine. His was always made the same with apple, banana mamey, leche, granola, wheat germ, chocolate, vanilla, bee pollen and a raw egg. The old señora who mixed the concoction had looked Walter over and explained that he needed the bee pollen: "Para la sangre," she had said. *For the blood.* Walter didn't argue.

JJ had ordered the same tasty fortifying beverage, and now with liquados in hand they headed for the square to relax.

The two gringos pushed through the chaotic ad hoc market the local indigenous types erect each Thursday in the street in front of the hotel. Here you could purchase all sorts of familiar items, and many strange things that Walter had never seen anywhere else. They walked past taco stands selling eye, lip and brain tacos at 9AM on a sunny morning. There was already a crowd formed, and the tacos were selling briskly. Walter ducked his head so as to not bean himself on the awnings slung in ambush over the street.

They passed the pulquería where drunks and dogs alike were passed out in the gutter. One of the dogs raised his head in lazy appraisal of the gringos, but the drunks didn't move at all.

They kept stride as they passed the Municipal Jailhouse buildings, where uniformed guards held their weapons with nonchalant ease, and finally they broke out of the narrow alleys at the lovely zocalo.

"Did you hear what happened to Bobo last night?" inquired JJ with a grin.

"No," said Walter through slurps of his liquado, hoping nothing serious had become of one of his pilots. "What happened to Bobo?"

JJ laughed and slapped his thigh as they settled onto an antique park bench, coated in many layers of ancient paint. "Last night we were all sound asleep about midnight when suddenly there was a commotion outside and the door burst open," he recounted with a chuckle. "Next thing we know, some guy was standing there by Bobo's bed and yelling something in Spanish. He was motioning Bobo out of bed, and when Bobo didn't respond, the guy pulled the covers off and tossed them on the floor."

"Me llevo la chingada," cursed Walter in Spanish. He was sure he'd resolved this situation with Doña Tede, the diminutive señora who owned the tiny boarding house, but apparently not. "What happened then?" he asked, holding his breath.

"I guess Bobo decided the couch in the living room looked more comfortable than sharing the bed and he left the room," laughed JJ. Walter knew what was coming next: "Then the Mexican stripped to his skivvies and just crashed into bed and started snoring and farting."

"Oh shit!" said Walter. "Damn! This happens every Wednesday night. Apparently that guy comes along but one night a week and thinks he owns that particular bed. Damn it anyway, but I thought I'd settled that with Doña Tede. Christ!"

"He's still there I imagine," said JJ. "He was sound asleep when we left this morning. Somehow, in the middle of the night he got my pillow too..." Walter could only shake his head and wonder. He paid Doña Tede good pesos and filled up her tiny hotel for weeks on end. But expect some service? Uh uhh. Walter would have to sermonize before he paid her again- she'll just have to tell the guy to find other digs.

The church bells in the old catedrál on the square tolled nine o'clock as Walter and JJ slurped the last of the liquados and considered the situation. The square was already bustling with activity under a warm morning sun. Nearby, an old callejero checked out the trash in a can that was bolted to the flagstone walkway of the zocalo. Birds in the nearby trees created a deafening cacophony and coated the street with their pale droppings. A pile of dog shit, dried hard enough that it no longer attracted flies, and squished flat by at least one unfortunate passerby, lay in the sidewalk near their feet. Walter tried to ignore it. JJ still chuckled about Bobo's unfortunate experience.

Suddenly, the dust from the square began a miniature swirl and leaped, in slow motion, towards the clear blue sky. As Walter and JJ watched, a perfect little dust devil, the size of a bushel basket and tall as the nearby church tower, swept the dirt and dust from the square and rose straight as a plumb-bob in front of their eyes. Together they jumped up from the park bench and moved next to the whirling dervish.

Walter stuck his hand into the vortex, creating a ripple effect that lasted for several meters up, where the dust again formed a perfect column to continue its ascent. The twister moved slowly along and swept the dust from the square where it was lifted to the top of the column and then spit out again, to fall earthward like water from a fountain. As they stood transfixed the devil moved over the pile of dried dog shit and lifted a small stream of dog shit dust from it, which rose into the sky and then, from all appearance, settled as fine powder atop the two gringos.

Several passers-by glanced at Walter and JJ as they stood dumbfounded and spellbound. JJ checked his watch, as though unwilling to believe the church bells, which were still chiming 9AM. He turned to Walter, "Gonna be a good day, Bwana!" he predicted.

"What say we go load gliders?" suggested Walter. They watched the dust devil subside, a temporary phenomenon, a chimera, an enigma, a premonition of great things to come.

Eagerly they left the square to meet the day's thermals, the monsters of lift over the Rock of the Devil, and maybe the Granddaddy of all the dust devils, somewhere in the wild skies over Valle de Bravo.

Boy, you cross that border,
you're in a whole different world!
--Bogey

Mexican Ambush In The Night or, Two Gringos, Too Stoned...

Heading south, Walter and Wayne turned the last curve on the highway between Tamaulipas state and the state of Nuevo Leon, in Ol' México. They had a dozen new hang gliders on the roof rack of the Ford-From-Hell and were embarked on a winter-long flying trip.

Around this curve they were accustomed to encountering the Federáles and their shakedown roadblocks- it was typical of the law to lie in wait at the state lines. But peering through the high beams they were surprised to see no evidence of the Federáles at all. Here were the yellow warning lines painted on the road, and there a couple of crushed smudge-pots left behind on the side of the road, but no arrogant Feds, no army snipers in sandbag bunkers, no spotlights and no menacing dogs. They had been there, only one week earlier when the two gringos had headed north they had been stopped and searched quickly, interrogated as to what role they might play in drug trafficking, and then been allowed to continue.

Rolling through the danger zone the two gringos pulled off the side of the road to take a piss and grab the bag of tasty buds that were secreted in one of the gliders on the roof. Wayne moaned in relief as he relaxed his bladder along the road in the Mexican darkness. "Guess they musta took the night off," he speculated.

"Probably got a roadblock at the cantina tonight," offered Walter.

"Whatever," said Wayne. "That's a load off my mind, in more ways than one."

"Them guys musta scored something good," said Walter. "I bet they're taking it out on the local putas right about now."

"Just so they leave us alone," said Wayne. "I find I drive much better in Mexico if I can take the edge off with a good reefer."

"The way you drive, I feel more relaxed wearing a helmet. Or a blindfold. Must we go so damn fast? What's your hurry anyway?"

"You ain't in no hurry, you're welcome to walk," said Wayne. It was his van and he liked to lord it over Walter at every opportunity. Even now he zipped up his fly and jumped back in the van impatiently. He waited for Walter to unzip the bag on a glider and fish around inside until he found the dope, but that was about all... As Walter jumped in the van, Wayne popped the clutch and spun onto the dark Mexican highway.

Walter cranked some Warren Zevon and started to roll a joint. They'd managed to score some sweet sinsemilla buds in Austin and had stashed them for the trip. Now that the Federáles had disappeared here at the state border and abandoned their usual lair, it was safe to believe there would be clear sailing for a couple of potheads from here all the way to Bahia Tenacatíta, on the Pacific coast of Jalisco.

At least until the next state border anyway.

Walter fired up the doobie and took a big hit. "I wonder how's the flying in Valle?" he managed through clenched lips and over the rock 'n roll.

> *I hear mariachi static on my radio...*
> *And the tubes they glow in the dark...*

Wayne took the joint and sucked hard. "I hear the summer rains have stopped anyway," he said with relief as a cloud of pot smoke escaped his lungs. "We'll have to get on up there for some serious flying."

"If the air's as awesome as last season I'll be a happy gringo."

> *And I'm here with her in Ensenada...*
> *And I'm there in Echo Park.*

"I just hope that little chica Carlita is still workin' the disco."

"I hope Carlita's little sister has kept a tight grip on her panties."

> *Carmelita! Hold me tighter!*
> *I think I'm sinkin' down...*

A haze of blue smoke filled the van as it roared through the Mexican darkness. The gringos rocked out and relaxed, secure in the knowledge that they had left the Federáles far behind, or at least until the next state line at Potosí.

The song ended and another began. Zevon sang of trouble for an innocent bystander. The joint was down to a roach now but Walter and Wayne still toked on it, good to the last drop.

The van sped around a blind curve and suddenly... there they were, the missing Federáles! They had moved their smudge pots and barricades ten miles down the road, and set a new trap for the gringos.

It was an AMBUSH!

Between a rock and a hard spot...

"Bwwwaaahhh!" The smoke rushed from Walter's lungs in a thick gray cloud. "Oh fer Chrissake!"

Wayne slammed on the brakes. In frenzied unison they rolled down the windows and let the smoke exit on the cool evening air. The Ford had been traveling at a high rate of speed, in moments they were atop the shakedown.

And I'm down on my luck. HEY!

"Throw that thing out!" demanded Wayne. "And that bag too!" But it was too late for that. Walter flicked the roach out the window, but the bag was in the pocket of his shorts. If he fished it out and disposed of it now, it would be obvious lying in the road. The jig would be up. He would have to stay cool and pray they wouldn't search his person.

An hombre in civilian clothes, with a Federále hat on his head and an automatic weapon slung over his shoulder, approached the van with an insolent swagger. Nearby stood a sandbag bunker on each side of the road, machine guns mounted on tripods and soldiers languished in the semi-darkness, smoking cigarettes and waiting for some unfortunate *chingada* gringos to arrive with the bag of forbidden herb.

Send lawyers, guns and money...

The Fed arrived at the van and stuck his head inside, where he found Walter paralyzed with fear. He immediately got a whiff of the sweet pungent smell of the Evil Weed.

"¡Marijuana!" he barked with a growl. He swung his weapon around and pointed the business end at the startled gringos.

And get me out of here, HEY!

"¡Sale!" he barked. *Get out!*

Wayne, at least, kept his head about him; as he opened the door and stepped out he casually reached a hand under his seat. He kept a stash of old Penthouse and Ouí magazines there for just this sort of eventuality and with a flick of his wrist he swiped them out the door and onto the crumbling blacktop at the soldier's feet. Startled, the soldier shone a flashlight on the glossy publications and a glistening blonde beaver grinned invitingly back at him- the vertical smile.

Now I'm hiding in Honduras
I'm a desperate man...

"Oh hooo...!" he snarled, disregarding the gringos now. He stooped and scooped at the magazines. Pornography like this, beautiful women in startling poses, photographed under well-lit circumstances and published under strict quality control, while not exactly unknown in México, was hard to come by so to speak. Also quite expensive... A teasing treasure had been deposited on the dirty asphalt at the Federále's feet.

"Oh ho hoo!" he exclaimed again. It was part snarl, part grunt. "Capitáno! CAPITÁNO!"

Send lawyers, guns and money
the shit has hit the fan!

Another soldier approached through the headlamps of the van. This one wore an actual uniform and an official bearing. He reached the door where Wayne stood under guard, apparently oblivious to the sweet smoke still pouring from the gringo van into the night and admired the glossy spread of smut. A gorgeous young woman, a princess really, spread her labia with slender fingers, revealing the whole of her virtue and that mysterious place where the sun don't normally shine. Out of the glossy pages, her pink and brown rectum winked at them all.

Both gringos and both Federáles groaned in appreciation, "UUMMUUUAAHHH!" Wayne offered the Feds a weak smile.

Capitáno flipped the pages to see what lay ahead, so to speak. Next, their girl stroked a well-shaped breast, pinching a tasty nipple between slender fingers. She lay sprawled invitingly on her back, wearing nothing more than a desperate expression of pain, ecstasy or extreme need depending only on your imagination, and one lucky Nike sneaker.

The soldier gleefully passed the magazine to his superior and bent down to scoop up more of the porno. As he did so, the Uzi swung down off his shoulder and pointed at the photos as though eager too, for an eyeful. The Capitáno whistled softly through his teeth and exclaimed: "¡Caramba!" He flipped through some more pages and caught the señorita in other provocative poses. In one she galloped through the viewfinder atop a white stallion clad only in her birthday suit. In another she splashed water across her gorgeous upturned ass in a provocative manner with a standard half-inch garden hose. In still another she rubbed her glistening self with one hand and sucked on two fingers of the other with scarlet lips.

Suddenly, the Capitáno had seen quite enough. He slapped the magazine shut and turned to Wayne. Eyebrows arched he inquired politely now, "¿Hay mas de estos?" he said.

Are there any more of these?

Wayne was unsure of exactly what he had been asked but he usually just shook his head 'no' out of habit when talking to any Mexican authority anywhere on any subject whatsoever, hoping thusly to absolve himself of any trouble, blame, incrimination or sorrow, it was just plain habit. He was too scared now to form any more elaborate plan.

"No!" he said, and shook his head.

Capitano spun on his heel and barked a series of commands to his subordinates. "¡Vamanos hombres!" he ordered. "¡Hacia la cantina!" All Walter recognized for sure was that one word: *cantina!* He knew from experience what happened there.

His knees still trembled as he watched the soldiers all rush for the squadron of sinister vehicles parked in the flickering gloom of the smoky smudge pots alongside the road and fire up the engines with a roar. Apparently they knew a direct order when they heard one and they were aeger to comply. Capitáno strode past Walter without a word, a pile of porn in his grasp, and entered a pickup truck riding shotgun. He gave Wayne nothing more than a glance and a stern look of admonishment as his driver pulled recklessly onto the road and gunned the engine into the night. The other vehicles roared into the procession and the squeal of rubber and growl of four-barrel carburetors droned into the darkness, leaving the two gringos standing amidst the barricades and smudge pots, stoned and amped with a fading rush of adrenaline. The whole encounter had lasted about dos minutos.

"Holy shit!" exclaimed a gringo. Otherwise blessed silence engulfed them.

Walter looked across the darkness to where another gringo traveler and a Mexican family stood along side the road in the northbound lane. They too, had been stopped for the impromptu shakedown. They peered back at Walter with bewildered expressions:

What had become of the Federáles?

What had become of their ambush?

Where were all the soldiers and their Uzis?

Did they really just vanish into the night?

Why? ¿Por que?

More importantly: would they return to cause more trouble or was it... safe to continue now?

As if on cue, they jumped back in their vehicles and sped off without a glance, leaving only Walter and Wayne to ponder the recent events.

"Can you think of a more safe place in all of Mexico to smoke a joint?" asked Wayne. Walter pulled out the bag while Wayne took another leak. With trembling fingers he twisted up a fat joint. They stood along side the highway and smoked it under the starry sky, trying to settle down. A few other vehicles slowed for the *parada*, but seeing no one there to stop them they continued on their way. They might have wondered at the sight of a fancy van idling alongside the road and two gringos puffing on a fattie.

"Another Mexican welcome," hicced Walter through puffed-out cheeks.

"Looks like it could be a long hard night for the local cantina talent," speculated Wayne between tokes.

Lorenzo's Lesson or,
Who's Lesson Is This Anyway?

Lorenzo Lester sat moping in a lawn chair in the hangar, a chair looked as though it was about to suffer a structural failure under his considerable bulk. Everything about Lorenzo was bulky. From his out-sized feet to his big black lips, this was a big man. He reminded Walter of Kunta Kinte from the ROOTS television novel. Sprawled as he was in the lawn chair, Walter thought about slipping up behind him and giving one of the legs a swift kick. If he could just get a leg out of column a bit, it would surely surrender its duty and collapse. That would have been a terrible dirty trick however. Besides, the big man might just pick himself up off the hangar floor and clobber the honky.

"Lorenzo," he suggested instead. "Let's get on out there." The black man jumped to his feet, suddenly animated.

"I can do it!" he exclaimed. "Jus lemme go, I can do it! Jus lemme go!"

"You can do it all right, I have no doubt. You just need some more dual."

"But you said we don't have another trainer," complained the giant man. It was true... Walter had explained that he was going to sit on the ground with Lorenzo instead of flying, because the two-place trainer aircraft was already signed out. They were left with only a Phase II with no instructor steering bar for the nose wheel.

"I know. I've consulted with the boss and we've decided you can handle the fork. You're gonna have to steer." Walter pointed at a Cosmos Phase II trike with a Chronos 14 meter wing. The trike had no dual controls set up for the front fork. The instructor could not steer the fork from the back seat. Also, the switches were hidden under the front of the seat frame, where they would be difficult or impossible to reach from the back seat. This could lead to problems, but there was little choice if Lorenzo was to continue his training this morning. The real trainers were all busy.

"Ahh..." decried Lorenzo. "Them guys are soloed. Just lemme go!" He pointed at the sky over Valle Gusto at the other flight students who were cutting up the pattern. Walter grabbed two helmets and shoved the Cosmos out from the hangar.

"Show me what you got," he said. "Maybe then I'll cut you loose."

Walter and Lorenzo turned final and Walter leaned into Lorenzo's ear. "Switches OFF!" he demanded. The big man's big hand left the base tube and reached under his big leg, and with a fumbled flick the fan behind them shut down, and stopped pushing. "Keep up your airspeed now," demanded Walter. "Fly her to the ground... now round out... level off... slower... slower... push, push... SLOWEST!" Walter shoved on the big man's elbows and the trike kissed the earth, rolling down the runway completely straight and under control.

"SEE?" cried Lorenzo. "Just lemme go! I can DO it!" It was his mantra. Lorenzo had come all the way from Guam to learn to fly trikes. This was the last day of his trip, and none of the instructors were very confident of the outcome.

"Patience," counseled Walter. "Take me around the patch again. You nearly flew us into the ground that time. I had to coach you to round out. Didn't you feel the pressure when I pushed on your elbows?" The massive head in front of Walter's nose nodded slightly up and down. "I can't let you solo until your landings are consistent, and you're doing them completely by yourself." Walter was feeling smart which is never a good idea in flight instruction. Cautiously stupid is best... Since he couldn't control the fork, he was having his student shut off the motor. That way, there could be few problems after the trike was stuck to the runway.

Together they reached overhead and pulled the recoil starter rope as the trike continued to roll along. "Let's try 'er again," insisted Walter. "Gimme full throttle. Bar out... lift off... pull in for airspeed," the trike shot upward toward the departure leg of the pattern. Walter relaxed. The big man had handled the fork just fine. This time Walter would not bother having him turning off the motor.

They flew the downwind leg of the pattern, the base leg, and turned final. The Phase II glided down under an idle throttle and Lorenzo flew the machine towards the ground. This time I'll teach him a lesson, thought Walter. I'll let him drop the plane that last two feet or so. Let him realize his inadequacy.

Rounding out, Lorenzo slowed the big trike too suddenly and ballooned upward. Walter remained silent but coached him with his hands on Lorenzo's big elbows. The trike reached the point of stall while still two feet above the dirt. It dropped those last two feet, and when the front wheel plunked the runway, Lorenzo's left foot came off the fork. In a flash, Walter was in trouble. With Lorenzo's left foot off the peg, the big man applied pressure with his right foot only. The trike veered wildly off to the left and aimed for some tall bushes that separated parallel runways. The throttle was under Lorenzo's big right foot too, and Walter felt his student tense just at the worst possible moment. The propeller began to spin up as Lorenzo inadvertently added throttle, pushing them both towards the bushes. The big man didn't realize what he was doing!

Walter pushed hard to roll the wing away from danger, but with no control of the front fork, it was too little, too late. He futilely tried to get at the switches, but they were out of reach. If he could just get the prop stopped in the next few seconds, he would minimize the damage. But Lorenzo was too big, too tense, and the switches too far...

"GET OFF THE GAS!" hollered Walter. "SWITCHES OFF! SWITCHES OFF! OFF OFF OFF SHIT!"

The trike hit the bushes while accelerating at near full throttle. The front wheel attacked the bushes and climbed over them. The propeller blades caught the bushes as they appeared behind the plane and spun themselves to pieces-chunks of fiberglass flying everywhere. The engine continued to sputter and burn as the trike toppled over into the bushes. "SWITCHES OFF, SWITCHES OFF!" repeated Walter. But it was far too late; the trike toppled over onto one leading edge with a crash, the other wing pointing skyward like some high-tech monument to failure

Suddenly, Walter wasn't feeling smart anymore.

"SHIT!" sputtered Lorenzo. "What happened?"

"You all right?" asked Walter. Lorenzo's head nodded a 'yes'.

"My fault, my fault," said Walter. The dust was settling but they still hung in the seat. "Pop that lap belt, will you?" he grunted. Lorenzo fumbled for the button and fell away into the bushes. Walter fumbled with his own lap belt and eased himself out of the wreckage.

"What happened?" repeated Lorenzo.

"Let's get this wagon back in the hangar," said Walter. "We screwed up. It was my fault, don't worry."

Lorenzo had no problem with that. He lifted the trike until it plunked back on its feet single-handed with hardly an effort. "Does this mean I won't be solo?" he asked. His huge back muscles hardly flexed as he tugged it back home pulling it along as Walter pushed and wondered to himself...

Who's lesson was it anyway?

Leche Anyone? or,
Just Like National Geographic in the Guatemala Highlands

Delvin was a glidehead from the beach, kind of a nerdy type. He was determined to make the most of his vacation in Guatemala, and was keen on experiencing every aspect of local culture.   Shortly after his arrival in Panajachel Maria appeared in his life.

Maria was a small Guatemala woman with big breasts. Her breasts were big because they were ripe with motherhood and full of milk. A nursing child had laid claim to each of them. They would reach through the nursing slots in Maria's guipil (blouse), grab one of those shapely jugs with both grubby hands, and have a happy lip-smacking feast. Delvin was astonished, delighted, astounded, and fixated too, and Maria full well knew so. She had seen the gringos go crazy to watch her children nurse before. She knew opportunity, when she saw it.

Maria would stop by Walter's house every day after the flying when the gringos were in a festive mood, to peddle her wares. She was willing to give the gringos an eyeful if that's what marketing took. Walter had to admit, it was something to see. Maria's breasts were kind of dirty as was the rest of her, she looked as though she had not bathed in a week. She was covered in layers of indigenous costumes and had a coating of dust. So did her poor small children of course, although they certainly seemed to make the most of their situation. Maria's hair somehow always looked shiny and satiny clean, but the family had an odor of unwashed bodies.

Maria's breasts were quite pleasing otherwise as well, in a fulsome sort of way. They were full and outward pointing, and ended in a substantial black nipple, punctuated by the rich white milk that regularly dribbled or squirted down her chest; *chocoláte con léche*. Their skin was the color of fancy grade bee honey, one of them with a provocative birthmark at center stage. Her children had complete unabashed reign over them, kneading and massaging them, suckling and burping with pleasure.

Delvin went wild. He too, wanted a taste, it was written all over him.

Maria, for her part, was willing to showcase her "charms" in an effort to spark sales, but for many bystanders there was just nothing sexy about them at all. They were more like a buffet than a formal affair. But she was not at all ashamed to exhibit them, bending and stooping in whatever this-and-that direction would reveal them in the best light, now and then arching her aching back, thrusting them hopefully through the nursing slots. Occasionally during her negotiations she would scoop her hand over them, drying a little spilt milk, and wipe it on her skirt. Her titty would stretch for a moment under pressure from her grip, then spring back in a most evocative manner.

Walter himself found it a tantalizing display, if not for erotica then in an educational *National Geographic* sort of way...

Maria would appear at their doorstep, deposit her children to the Earth and drop the bundle of goods from atop her head. She would unroll the bundle in one practiced motion and suddenly her wares would be spread at your feet like an offering from some Mayan god of textiles; shirts, pants, Bermuda shorts, bracelets and baubles. It was a time-tested sales method.

Meanwhile, her tits were splendid as they poked their eyeballs through the blouse.

Delvin just stood with his jaws agape. He looked wide-eyed from Walter to Maria back to Walter and the others with an expression that shouted: 'Do you see what I see?' We all saw of course. But Delvin never tired of looking. He bought so much stuff from Maria, that he was soon decked out head-to-toe in colorful Guatemalan garb like some kind of Brooks Brothers' worst nightmare. He probably wore Guatemalan underwear for all Walter knew. He bought so much Guatemalan stuff from Maria that he had to buy a large duffle bag too, just to tote it all around. He claimed to anyone who would listen that he was buying gifts for the folks back home, who were just gonna love it.

Each day, Maria would appear after the flying, intent on selling more stuff to the gawking gringos. Each day, Delvin bought. And each day he himself became a little more familiar, a little more brazen. Soon she was calling him by his name in a strange Mayan way, and he was standing so close to her that Walter figured soon they would become as one. He kept expecting Delvin's hand to become unstuck from his sides, to drop the duffle, to reach out and caress and cradle one of those tantalizing titties, and his lips begin to suckle. Turning to leave them alone, Walter heard Delvin's observation:

"Just wait 'till I tell the guys in the office," he said. "They'll be sooo jealous!"

The Fuel Stop From Hell or,
Busted Down, in Old México

Flying over Cerro Zorrillo Walter went high and skirted the Federále checkpoint more than necessary. Having once tangled with the Feds down there, and recalling what a close call that had been, the gringo had no desire to test his luck yet again. Better to just cruise high and quiet around the hills east of town, and be as invisible as possible, a tiny gnat in the enormous sky.

Out this way was nothing but low mountain peaks and dry valleys anyway, some of them so arid they were just saline waste lands and dry lakes. Hardly any cattle, even. Plenty of snakes and scorpions, maybe. Even the few buzzards he encountered were skyed-out, drifting downwind for greener pastures.

Fuel was becoming an issue though, another reason why Walter didn't want to land near what passed for civilization out here in the midst of the Sonoran Desert, or near any humankind for that matter. Remembering the last fuel transfer in these parts, when he had encountered the Mexican dope chasers, he scanned the horizon for a suitable safe place to land- far from the maddening eye, so to speak. A nervous glance at his burn jugs suggested he back off throttle and set a descending cruise for the next valley- they were getting low all right. Certainly, down there somewhere, would be a wide-open piece of flatland to set down a TrikeZilla, siphon fuel from the spare jugs, have a drink of water, and take a leak. Maybe even a spell of silence with only the wind for company.

A bit of an intermission on Terra Firma.

The spare jugs were a salvation; they carried enough spare go-juice for the entire flight from Nogales, Arizona down to Hermosillo, Sonora and on to the ranch at Alma Perdido. Having rigged the jugs himself, Walter was feeling pleased with the results. The two five-gallon jugs sat in an aluminum rack that was suspended on a stainless cable that hung off the Jesus bolt. Three Velcro straps held the rack firmly on the mast just above the engine. It was a dirty arrangement in terms of airflow and drag, but the TrikeZilla was so loaded with baggage, there just was no other place for extra fuel. The list of necessities Walter felt compelled to heap on his trike included clothes, groundcloth, bedding, myriad tools, a case of two-stroke oil, various spare parts including a spare tire, an extra helmet for passengers, lunch, two gallon jugs of H2O and a fresh un-opened bottle of Jack Daniels for the Mexicans. A torque wrench was lashed to one landing strut, and a machete to the other.

But the fuel was his most precious cargo- the gringo needed enough to carry him over hostile terrain where he was just an illegal alien in an illegal flying machine, and on to the safety of his amigos at the remote rancho known as Almas Perdidas, *Lost Souls*.

In the near distance a dry lake beckoned to the flyer. Feeling something akin to Slim Pickens astride his bomb, the gringo chopped throttle and hit the kill switches. As the prop quickly spun down to a stop he rode the 'Zilla down, for better or worse.

Next stop? Fuel.

¡Ándale!

Walter lined up on a narrow two-track that wandered across the salt flats. He was a good five miles from the highway, in the middle of nowhere, about three hours flying south of the border in Nogales, and about four hours away from the safety of Lost Souls. If he could just get there, everything would be fine. The warm spring day and the light winds equated to a bumpy ride down, one that got bumpier as usual with the descent. Dust devils danced across the lake, so he circled some over his chosen runway, hoping to ride any lift out. It was tough to tell if there was a thermal building or busting off over the runway, simply because his wagon was so heavily loaded- it had a Hell of a sink rate. Gathering the last few inches of bar to his chest, the gringo pointed the nose down for the final hundred feet, and then rounded out above the dirt. TrikeZilla blazed in, leveled off, and reached its rear wheels for México.

The mains began to drag as the gringo slowed to trim. Pushing now, the nose wheel bare inches from touchdown, Walter slowed to the front strut. The runway sure looked sandy here. Keeping the nose as light a possible, Walter hoped for the best- but got the worst. The nose wheel turned sharply in soft sand, the mast leaning right, the trike going left. The left rear wheel rose off the sand and Trikezilla sped along for a flashing eternity on two wheels. It leaned a little more and then flipped suddenly onto the right leading edge.

KablOOM, the wing hit the ground!

The hapless driver reached out a hand towards the ground in self-defense and the controlbar corner bracket nearly amputated his pinky at the nail as it beat into the ground. An instant later a sudden blow fetched him upside the head and glanced off his helmet with a sickening crunch. Something large and heavy flashed past Walter's right ear and smashed into the undersurface sail with a resounding thump like a timpani drum. The trike bounced a little in the soft earth, then settled to a stop in a cloud of alkali dust. Happily, there were no snakes.

Shit!

Walter struggled for a moment with the harness, using only his left hand because his right pinky was stuck between his lips. He noticed the blood right about the same moment the harness released and he was deposited in the sandy soil of México.

Shit again!

He sucked his pinky to stem the flow of blood, and scrambled out from under the wing, doing a dance of pain and swinging his pinky in agony. He struggled left-handed with the catch on his helmet, and finally dropped it to the sand, too.

AARGG!

Though his heart was pounding from the flash of adrenaline, and his finger felt as though it had just been slammed in a car door, Walter was engulfed in a sudden intense silence. He had gotten his wish- only the wind to keep him company now.

Disregarding the pain and discomfort in his finger and some other areas as best he could, Walter grabbed the trike by its downed leading edge and heaved, to little effect. Redoubling his efforts, the gringo heaved with all his might. TrikeZilla arose from the desert, a bit less dramatic than the Phoenix, and plunked back on three wheels with a groan and another cloud of dust. Walter stood back to survey the damage and realized what it was that had fetched him such a horrible blow in the head and flashed past his view on its way to smashing into the sail- the twin five gallon fuel jugs were still hanging from the Jesus bolt, and still in their rack that he was so proud of, but they had broken the Velcro straps that held them to the mast and performed a pendulum-like maneuver with Walter's head in the way. OUCH! It had been a demonstration of the law of physics that states: matter, once set in motion, wants to stay in motion.

SHIT!

Walter sat still for a while, just to let his heart settle somewhat. It was too early to tell if he was downed permanently, or could carry on. He reflected that his decision to land 'out' had good points and bad. For the good- it appeared unlikely the Federáles would notice him here. There was nothing, no sign of man or beast at all except this one-lane *brecha*, wandering through badlands, and a few buzzards circling overhead. Gazing into the distance Walter noticed a vulture had settled atop a scrawny tree nearby and was giving him the hairy-eyeball. On the down side: he might be walking out of here. Heck, he might be buzzard bait. He would necessarily have to mark his route in the desert, or just leave his wagon behind forever.

I can't do THAT, thought the gringo. But I might have to. I can walk out to the highway. Crawl part of the way. Bum a ride to Hermosillo. Rent a truck. Get Guillermo. Get back here somehow. I'll never be able to show my face in the hangar back home, if I abandon my wagon to buzzards, snakes and thieves.

Walter decided it was nice here, in the desert, a beautiful spring day. The clouds had taken the day off, and vanished. A gentle breeze from the north had caught the gringo by surprise and may have contributed to the Landing From Hell; he had landed tailwind.

It was nice here, but it wouldn't last long; the sun was traveling west, and Walter was busted.

Shit!

He stood up rather shakily and began an inspection. Working his way down the leading edge that had hit the ground, Walter inspected the tubing for dings. There did not seem to be any- a miracle, but the wing had hit in soft sand. At the wing tip, he peered into the sail, looking for bent tubing or hardware. Amazingly enough, there was only the natural reflex of the tubing in the sail cut.

He inspected the other wing and the wing keel, as well as the trike mast and keel. Incredibly, the only damage seemed to be to the hang bracket, which was tweaked to one side, but not broken anywhere. The trike and wing now sat crooked, the wing pointing one way, the trike quite another. The engine and prop were shut down during the landing, so they had not suffered during the groundloop- they would operate just fine.

The gringo gathered up a few items he had scattered around, found some more straps to re-secure the fuel rack again, and began siphoning fuel. A bead of nervous sweat dripped inside his sunglasses as he worked and he felt light-headed, he decided he might be experiencing mild shock.

With the fuel transferred and his jugs now filled for travel, he flicked the switches and spun the prop. Incredibly, the 'Zilla started on the second pull, it sat at idle, nothing apparently the matter. He brought the throttle up and tried the sparks. They both worked fine. He sat down in the driver's seat and surveyed the situation; quite obviously the hang connection was badly bent. He shut down the fan and got out of the trike to make an adjustment. Slowly, he began to shift the wing into alignment.

Grabbing the right wingtip Walter gave it a shove and twisted the wing around, re-bending the hang bracket. TrikeZilla creaked and groaned under the pressure, but each attempt, each shove, brought things a little more in line. It was not a very scientific or precise manner to get the bracket straightened out, but what else could he do? Another shove, another twist, then he sat down in the driver's seat again. It seemed to Walter that he had made a bit of an improvement. He climbed out of the seat and walked around to the rear of TrikeZilla and stepped back for an appraisal when suddenly...

What was that?

Did you hear something?

A motor? A motor vehicle?

My ears must be playing tricks on me!

More tweaking, an urgency now, each shove made it a little better... twisting... tweaking... Step back for a quick inspection.

There's that noise again,

Sure sounds like a vehicle,

The Federáles?

Come to bag a downed airman?

A Mexican posse?

SHIT! Now I can hear it stronger!

Definitely a motor vehicle!

Engine racing clattering wheels pounding!

Headed this way!

Irrationally- maybe it was help after all, a rescue party?- Walter jumped into the 'Zilla, buckled up, and spun the fan. He let the 503 warm up as much as he dared, then stepped on the gas and began to roll. Up ahead, the brecha wandered past a low hill of scrub and scrawny cactus until it disappeared from view. The vehicle; whoever, whatever, must come from that direction. Freaked-out but determined, Walter poured on the throttle and shoved up the nose. After what seemed like forever, his wagon popped off the ground. He held the 'Zilla there for a moment, gathering speed and waiting for disaster. The connection held as he let up the nose. TrikeZilla soared into the sky, just as the approaching vehicle came into view.

A crowd of men stood in the back of a gatebed pickup truck.

They held guns in their hands.

Or were they guns?

Shovels?

Picks?

Brooms?

Machetes?

Whatever they were, they waved them at Walter as he blazed overhead, the tiny motor at full cry. He flashed overhead and cranked a turn that followed the hill, seeking the quickest way out of sight and holding the bar to his gut. Gaining the other side of the hill, he set the hammer down and shoved the nose up. His pinkey finger still squealed in protest as he pointed her south, for rancho Almas Perdidas.

Close Encounter Over Donner Summit or, HAND gliding with... a LEAR!

Walter's fingers were frozen numb, his aching back was killing him, his bladder was beginning a protest and he was overall delighted with himself. Life just didn't get much better than this he realized, as he wiped a dribble of frozen drool off his chin. Gazing still further west Walter gave it one last shot, one last effort to locate Blue Canyon Airport (KBLU) out there in the distance- he knew it was out there far below him somewhere, about two miles below him. He'd seen it on the chart a few days ago, just didn't recall the details, should have calculated the mileage, should have been more aware.

But what were the chances?

It was indeed a rare day in the High Sierra when the lift was so good over the back of Glide Mountain as to draw a glidehead all the way out over Donner Summit, some thirty miles distant. Yet, there he was, about as far west over the forested mountains as he dared go without some viable plan of action, without somewhere definite to go even if it was a stretch... Blue Canyon runway would be the logical place to go, would be very spacious in fact, if Walter could just get there.

Leveling the wing and pointing west, Walter glided for another half-minute or so, concentrating on the distant forest. Interstate Highway 80 wound over Donner Summit below, and there were myriad other man-made scars upon the Earth, but nowhere Walter could be sure of landing safely. Nothing stood out and called to the flyer, beckoning him with refuge...

Dropping his head and gazing back under his toes Walter could just see his last real option for a good landing area- the parking lot at Boreal Ridge Ski Area, just on the west side of the summit. It was quite vast as out-landings go, and it would be fairly easy to turn around now and scurry back there- back to safety. But safety out front- that was another story. In front of Walter's nose, as far as he could see, was nothing but High Sierra forest, mostly Ponderosa pine trees, a few burn scars, a few road scars, the highway. Was Walter prepared to land on Highway 80 if... if all else failed?

Nope. This flyer was just not that gung-ho.

Even disregarding the dangers of vehicular collision, there would probably be a fine to pay for landing on the interstate, maybe points on the driver's license for creating a traffic hazard. Who could say, maybe even a court appearance? *"Only licensed and registered motor vehicles are permitted on public streets and highways... How do you plead?"*

"Desperation, Your Honor... I was desperate!"

There would be Hell to pay somehow.

Walter glanced at his altimeter and it sent a shiver through his already frigid frame. The numbers jumped out at him: seventeen thousand, eight hundred, thirty-two feet... YIKES! Comin' up on eighteen kay? Above sea-level!

WahOOO! Walter was SKYED-OUT! Any higher, and he just might blow a valve.

But... was he high enough to jump the gap? Somewhere out there lay Blue Canyon airfield, safety and safe refuge, he need only follow Highway 80, because the field lay just a few hundred yards from the road. But Walter was just too chicken to go for it. He must turn his wagon around, head back for Boreal Ridge. Heck, the way things were going he could probably fly all the way back to the Truckee airport and the comfort and convenience of his motor home parked there. The lift had been just fantastic since leaving Mt. Rose at sixteen grand, a beautiful late-summer day for soaring...

Walter had taken off at Glide Mountain in his Wills Wing FUSION one-fifty and immediately hooked into a booming thermal. Shortly, he'd topped-out around twelve grand, and pointed his nose at Mt. Rose. He'd arrived just above the peak at Rose and gave a wave to a few hardy hikers who had summited the peak, and then hooked another boomer, this time to above sixteen thousand feet where he'd started whiting-out in the clouds. By the time he stopped circling and pointed her for Truckee he must have truly been just a speck to those grounded Earthlings below, just a vague notion circling under the clouds.

Leaving Mt. Rose Walter had copped a fabulous glide to Truckee. By simply flying fast in the sink and then slowing in the lift Walter had glided and soared along about ten miles with a net loss of only a thousand feet or so. With a carefree attitude, he'd just kept the nose pointed west and held the wings level, was soon over Donner Lake, and then Donner Summit, where he'd finally stopped to work a bitchin' thermal. He was directly over Mt. Judah at Sugar Bowl Ski Area at about twelve thou, when he hooked into that rascal and climbed above seventeen grand.

This thermal had taken Walter right up to the floor of forbidden Class "A" airspace. At seventeen thousand nine hundred ninety nine feet he'd stuffed the bar and dove down a few hundred or so, to keep from busting Federal Airspace Regulations.

Ha! The stinkin' Feds!

It seemed so ridiculous now; the sky was so big and so empty- what was their issue? Those pathetic office rats, where are they NOW? Sitting in their Ivory Towers and counting the days to Retirement...

Fuck 'em! Walter pushed out in another core and let her climb. He reached over and turned off the altimeter. That was one way to avoid Class 'A' controlled airspace.

The day had truly been awesome and Walter felt blessed to be a part of it. Now here he was, at the Edge of No-Man's Land, or maybe No-Man's Sky, peering across an enormous space, but scared to go there... He would have to turn back.

Diving the glider for a moment, Walter ripped off a wing-over for the pure joy of flight, and then settled back into wings-level, now pointed east, back towards Boreal Ridge, Sugar Bowl, Donner Lake and Truckee, back towards life itself. Gliding, gliding... Walter was but a happy participant in a spectacular movie. Effortlessly, he soared along the High Sierra, half frozen, but now that he'd given up on the foolish "Cross the High Sierra" plan, quite relieved.

Approaching the west end of Donner Lake Walter reached up in front of his nose and turned on his aircraft radio, a hand-held ICOM A-22, and began to monitor the Truckee airport traffic UNICOMM channel 122.9. Immediately, he was pleased that he had. Over the airwaves came the following announcement:

"Truckee-Tahoe traffic, this is Lear three-five Bravo back-taxiing for takeoff on runway two-seven Truckee-Tahoe."

Walter focused his attention on the distant runways, peered over the top of his sunglasses and... sure enough! About fifteen miles distant and more than two miles below, a tiny white dot was slowly moving along the taxiway, headed for the numbers on runway two-seven. *Must be Lear three-five Bravo!* Staring as he was straight down the gunbarrel of this same runway, the Lear suddenly commanded all of Walter's attention and set his soul to tingling. He squinted and watched, waiting for the next announcement. He found he needed to keep blinking his eyes to keep them free of teardrops, which tended to freeze on his eyelids, blurring his vision. The business jet reached the end of the taxiway and swung its tail about for a run up. Walter had a better view now that the jet had turned profile. He kept his cool as best he could, and listened expectantly. The radio keyed back to life...

"Truckee-Tahoe traffic, Lear three-five Bravo taking runway two-seven, departing straight out over Donner Summit, Truckee-Tahoe traffic."

Hmmm...

Walter thought it over for a moment and decided this called for an announcement of his own. He keyed the microphone to speak but only produced a frozen mumble. Determined to speak up, he had to stop for a moment and rub his mouth, wipe the drool off, get some circulation back to his frozen lips. Finally, "Truckee-Tahoe traffic and especially Lear three-five Bravo, I am in a hang glider directly over Donner Lake at seventeen nine-ninety-nine and I've got a visual on you, Truckee-Tahoe traffic." There was an expectant pause and the Lear remained stationary on the run-up pad for two-seven. Then:

"Truckee-Tahoe traffic this is Lear three-five Bravo, about to roll for take off two-seven. Do I understand... there is a... a hand glider... at flight level one-eight over Donner Lake, Truckee-Tahoe?"

"That's a HANG GLIDER captain," clarified Walter. There was no time to elaborate however, so he just continued, "and I am indeed hanging out at seventeen nine-ninety-nine over Donner Lake. In fact, I am right smack over the center of the lake, Truckee-Tahoe traffic."

Walter winced at his own choice of words, "smack" just didn't seem appropriate somehow, but too late now. Now the Whole World would know where he was, well, anyone within about a hundred-mile radius of Donner, and who happened to be monitoring the same UNICOMM channel would know of his lofty location.

WahOOO!

He watched with intense excitement as the Lear sat there for a few more moments, and then began to move. It rolled up on the tarmac and turned for the centerline, then quickly began to accelerate. Walter kept his wing level, aimed at Truckee, and studied the jet. He saw it lift off and turn slightly for the noise-abatement departure pattern around downtown Truckee.

And then it pointed directly at him.

"Truckee-Tahoe traffic Lear three-five Bravo has just cleared the interstate and we're heading west on a Gateway departure... We'll be looking for that...ahh... haa haa... hand glider..."

"It's a HANG GLIDER captain, from below it's bright orange, and I have you on visual. What is your planned altitude over Donner Lake?"

"We'll climb to about thirteen thousand feet over Donner Lake hand glider."

"No problem, I should be at least three thousand feet above you."

Walter's grip stiffened-up a bit as he watched that Lear lift its nose and begin a climb. The skipper pointed her straight over Donner Lake, if he held this course he would go right under Walter. Maybe that's what he wanted, to try and find the tiny orange dot in the otherwise empty blue sky.

Walter watched her come, and then slide right underneath him, marveled at her sleek lines and her wonderfully fast track through the sky. She whizzed silently under Walter, maybe he heard or perhaps felt her throaty rumble, on top of his own airspeed he couldn't be sure. As she slid past underneath him Walter was mesmerized by her presence; he swung the FUSION about too, his eyes glued to that Lear until she was but a hurried little speck on the western horizon. Then he made one last call, "Lear Three-five Bravo, I'm admiring your tailfeathers now... Happy landing!"

There was no reply, but it had been a fabulous encounter, on a fabulous flight. Content with life for yet another day, Walter flew a long final glide to the Truckee airport, to land with the big boys.

A Gringo Goes to Guatemala or, Getting There is Half the Fun

When Taca Airlines flight 321 from San Francisco finally touched down in Guatemala City, a big gringo nearly went over the top of the rest of the passengers in an effort to disembark. This would not have been extremely difficult, since most of the Guatemalans standing in front of him were about half Walter's size. Instead he waited patiently for those in front of him to exit the aircraft and then he stepped out into the tropical morning sun.

Walter's plane had been unable to land in 'Guate', as the seasoned Central American traveler called Guatemala City, on schedule the night before due to thick surface fog, and had been rerouted to Tegucigalpa, Honduras for the night. There, Walter had wrapped the handles of his gearbag through his arms as a precaution against thieves, and fallen asleep on the hard tile floor.

But now as he finally stepped from the plane his aches and pains disappeared with his newfound enthusiasm; Walter was here for ten days of flying, another busman's holiday so to speak, and headed happily for the baggage claim. There was a baggage carousel in the terminal, of course, but Walter knew his bag was too long to be sent through there. At least he hoped no *pendejo* would try to shove his wing through the carousel.

Walter spotted a service door, which obviously led to the loading area from the plane he'd just left. Boldly throwing open the door, he looked out and spotted two baggage handlers leaning against the building about ten feet away. They looked more surprised than Walter to see a gringo suddenly standing there, peering about. One of them had his cheeks puffed with smoke and an obvious lung-full. As Walter watched, the other lowered a large reefer from his lips and tried to hide it behind his back. No use though, as just then his compadre exhaled a gush of smoke. The sweet smell of pot was everywhere.

Spotting his glider being dragged by one end across the greasy tarmac under the plane, Walter made a dash out the door. Another handler had Walter's glider by the nose and showed little regard for the aircraft as he made a roundabout route towards the carousel. Hearing running feet approaching, he turned just as Walter spoke:

"Parate amigo!" he insisted. *Stop friend!* No sense riling up the help, especially when you're out numbered, thought Walter.

The man showed surprise to see a big gringo towering over him and as Walter gripped the handles of the glider and quickly shouldered it, he thought for a moment that the guy might call out in alarm. "Calmate amigo," he ordered, "es mio." *Calm down friend, it's mine.*

The baggage handlers all stood aside as Walter easily shouldered the glider and headed back through the door to the terminal. Then, with the Magic Kiss on his shoulder and his gear bag on his back, Walter headed for Guatemala customs.

The officials there looked skeptical when Walter replied to their questions. "What's in the long bag?" they inquired. "¡Papalote!" Said Walter: *Kite!* He pulled a photo of John Heiney ripping off a loop from his pocket and suddenly they understood. "¡Aye, porsupuesto! ¿Porque no la dijiste?" said the Federále. *Oh, a kite, why didn't you say so?*

And just that easy Walter was allowed to enter Guatemala, papalote and all.

This next part would be a little trickier, he guessed. He spotted a shoeshine stand near the terminal exit. Beyond the doors he could see taxis waiting, mostly aging Chevys and Dodges from the States. They would do nicely as transport, but Walter was not keen on paying extra baggage fees for his Magic Kiss.

He dropped the glider next to the shoeshine boy, a disfigured old man who slid around the floor on a rickety dolly. The old man readily agreed to 'guardar' the item for 'un ratito' while Walter negotiated with the cabbies.

Stepping through the terminal gate Walter was immediately set upon by several drivers, all vying for his dólares. He quickly swung a deal with the nearest cabby for transportation to the bus terminal of Transportes Flor de Mi Tierra, some two miles distant. The fare would be fifteen Quetzales, about three US dollars. Handing his bag to the driver Walter said: "Espera me Señor." *Wait just a second sir.* "Voy por mi papalote." *I'm going for my kite.*

Walter left the cabby standing there with a puzzled look on his face. *The gringo was going for his kite?* He dashed into the terminal where his Magic Kiss lay on the floor, and paid the old shoeshine boy a Quetzal for his trouble. Quickly unzipping the bag, Walter grabbed two miniature glider racks he had stashed there. Made from twelve inches of airfoil downtube each, with K-Mart rubber suction cups, they were very portable and effective. He tucked them into his belt and shouldered his glider. Balancing the weight, he strode from the terminal back out to the waiting cab.

The driver had turned his back on the terminal and Walter, to watch the hectic pace of the street in front of the airport. He turned back to see the gringo with his 'papalote' in the giant bag atop his shoulder. Surprised and alarmed, he made as if to protect his ancient taxi and shouted "¡No se puede Señor, no se puede!" *You can't do this sir!*

"¿Por que no?" inquired Walter. *Why not?*

The cabby shook his head adamantly. He brushed the top of the ancient Dodge Dart as though the paint job was still fresh from the factory. "¡Por la pintura!" he said. *For the paint!*

But Walter had anticipated this too; this was what the mini-racks were for. He reached behind his back and pulled the miniature car-top racks from his belt. He put one in front and one in back on the roof and began to off-load his Kiss from his shoulder. The glider spanned the car from bumper to bumper.

"¡Cobro doble por esto!" declared the cabby. *I charge double for this!*

In response to that statement Walter quickly re-shouldered the glider and popped the suction cups from the roof. Without a word he headed down the long line of cabbies to negotiate another deal. He was pursued by the same cabby however, who asked: "¿Donde vas Señor, donde vas?" *Where are you going sir?"*

"¡Buscar algien que no me chingan!" answered the gringo. *Looking for someone who won't screw me!* The cabby hustled along in front of Walter as though to slow his progress. Here was one gringo who would not be so easy to take for his 'dólares'.

"¡Pero señor, el papalote es demaciado de larga. Las policias me dan un infracción!" *But your kite is so long sir; the police will surely give me a ticket!* "Falta una banera rojo para ser carga legal," he added, backpedaling in front of the gringo. *It lacks a red flag to be legal.*

"No hay problema señor," assured Walter. *No problem sir.* He reached into his back pocket with one hand and pulled out his bandanna. It was red, with a large safety pin to fasten it to the glider. "Vengo preparado Señor," *I come prepared.*

"¿Y sogas?" he asked. *And rope?*

When Walter produced two twenty-foot lengths of rope from inside the wing bag, the cabby just shrugged his shoulders. Resigned and deflated now, the cabby pointed to his Dodge Dart, leaking, smoking and wheezing at idle by the curb. As Walter set down the glider he said, "Le doy vente Quetzal señor, no te preocupes." *I'll give you twenty Quetzals sir, don't you worry.*

At that news Walter's cabby became downright cooperative. "Me llamo Manuel, señor. A sus ordenes." *They call me Manuel, sir. At your service.* Walter tossed him a length of rope and quickly tied the rear of the glider to the Dart's rear bumper. Turning his attention to the front of the car Walter discovered Manuel tying the glider to the hood ornament, as though that would do. Manuel had wrapped the line several times around the glider and was opening a pocketknife to cut off the surplus when Walter stepped in.

"Con su permisso," he said. *With your permission.* He untied the mess from the hood and re-tied the glider securely at the front bumper. So far so good... "¡Vamanos!" he ordered then. *Let's go!*

Manuel eased the cab from the curb and departed the airport. He swung into the chaotic traffic of Guatemala City with no regard for the drivers around him. Everyone honked their horns incessantly and paid slight attention to traffic signals.

The most dangerous part of flying is the ride getting there.

Manuel talked constantly as they rode towards the bus depot. He asked about the giant 'papalote' and when Walter told him it was a 'papatole tripulado', *piloted kite*, and not just some giant thing you hang from a string Manuel seemed duly impressed. He put his arm out the window and made swooping motions with his hand. He grinned at Walter now and Walter could see that his status had elevated somewhat, as though Manuel could appreciate an honest-to-God daredevil in his cab. He talked longingly of Lake Atitlán, Walter's destination, and informed the gringo that Atitlán is a natural wonder, something Walter already knew, from photos.

Soon they arrived at the bus station for Transportes Flor de Mi Tierra, and Walter could see why the bus line had such a beatific name. Old Blue Bird school busses were lined up in the terminal, and painted with a remarkable scheme of wild jungle flowers in the Mayan motif, with Quetzal birds and pyramids and Mayan princesses. Transports Flower of My Land was certainly a beautiful means of transport, if somewhat dated. Decrepit was a better word. But drab? Certainly not!

Walter and Manuel swung into the depot and pulled up next to a colorful old bus wearing shiny new paint. Walter noticed that one of the dual tires in the rear, the only one he could easily inspect at a glance, was worn to the point of threads showing through the rubber, and he went forward to inspect the front tires. As Manuel could be heard excitedly bargaining for a ride on the gringo's behalf, Walter confirmed his suspicions: this particular set of rubber would not withstand many more trips over the Guatemalan volcanoes to Atitlán.

When he returned to the cab, Manuel was proudly explaining the 'papalote' atop his cab to the men working the terminal, spreading his arms and whistling and saying "Verdad señor, verdad?" There was a custom rack atop ships the length of the old Blue Bird, with rails that stood about a foot high, and which could easily accommodate about a hundred gliders like Walter's Magic Kiss. A ladder ran up the stern of the bus to facilitate loading.

Walter untied the glider fore and aft, and when he shouldered it solo, everyone appeared quite impressed with the gringo. Offering help, Walter indicated in Spanish that the biggest of them all should stand behind the bus exactly by the ladder and prepare to hold the nose of the glider pressed on the ground with a toe, while Walter stood the wing on end, next to the ladder, like a big pole. The operation went smoothly enough and from that position the glider was easily hoisted atop the bus. Then Walter hoisted himself above to inspect the proceedings and to inquire as to whom would be responsible for loading subsequent freight. Shaking the worker's hand he was introduced to Rojelio, a scrawny man who was all smiles, and appeared very pleased to meet the gringo. He explained to Rojelio that his 'papalote' was somewhat fragile, and that no one was allowed to sit, stand, lie on or otherwise abuse the parcel, or be subject to Walter's wrath.

Rojelio agreed and assured Walter that no harm would come to the bundle, and that he should enjoy the ride to Atitlán, as it would be truly spectacular.

"Muy hermosa la vista," he promised. *Very beautiful scenery.*

The driver revved the engine and Walter climbed down from atop the bus. He slid into the first seat behind the door, and was pleasantly surprised to discover the bus was totally empty, except for himself and the driver. In compound low gear they rumbled from the terminal and back out into the streets of Guatemala City.

PROPERTY OF INDIANAPOLIS SCHOOL DISTRICT was still printed inside Transportes Flor de Mi Tierra, bus number 113, which sputtered out of the terminal and into the hectic traffic. Walter was surprised to see that he, alone, was a passenger. Certainly they were not planning a trip to Atitlán with only one gringo aboard? But the plan soon became obvious; the driver geared down into compound low and let the machine rumble along at idle. Guatemalans of all types met the bus along side the road and, with no attempt to slow down or facilitate their entry except for the aged and infirm, the driver allowed them to board.

Rojelio then sold them tickets to their destinations.

Occasionally, the driver would stop, but only when a passenger had too much freight to carry on, or was too feeble to jump aboard. Chickens, eggs, fruit, bundles of fabric, a case of Bibles, several dogs, all went up the ladder with Rojelio and were lashed in place. Little by little the bus filled with passengers and their commerce. By the time the bus arrived at the outskirts of the city, all seats were occupied.

The bus was a cacophony of sounds, human and barnyard, as

well as a serious squawling from cheap stereo speakers in the front and rear of the Blue Bird. The volume was turned up to the point of such distortion that Walter couldn't understand anything, only that it had once been music. Just when Walter was sure that the bus had been loaded to capacity, another Mayan family would appear standing in the road and gesturing to the driver who, in turn, would apply squeaky air brakes and lurch to a halt in the middle of the highway.

Soon all the seats and the aisle were full.

With standing room only, Walter yielded his seat to a very weathered-looking woman with a child sucking at each breast. He would stand all the way to Atitlán, if necessary. How far could it be...?

Very far, as it turned out. Twice, soldiers at military checkpoints stopped the bus, searched suspiciously up and down the aisles for something or someone, and then let the travelers pass. More families and animals were loaded at every opportunity. Finally the transport was so laden that it would only reluctantly climb the steep, pot-holed path that passed for the highway. Just when Walter thought that surely now, there was no more room, the driver would ply the brakes, stop in the middle of the road, and eight more tiny Mayan types would climb aboard. Rojelio would exhort the occupants to make more room, actually shoving those first in the aisle when necessary. In that fashion Flor de Mi Tierra #113 wheezed up to the summit above their destination and Walter got his first glimpse of Lake Atitlán, spread out blue and beautiful below.

The three volcanoes that dominated the far shore stood out in majestic relief. Cumulus clouds reflected off the still waters and a buzzard soared over the vista. Walter was reminded of the high alpine waters of Lake Tahoe and suddenly felt right at home. Overhead, circling in an azure sky, the buzzards were a reassuring sight.

The bus rambled down the treacherous highway, jammed into low gear and Walter prayed to the Gods that the tranny and the brakes held. The road was a sinuous snake, dropping at a steep grade, a mountain on one side, a precipice on the other. Finally and abruptly, it emptied out at Walter's destination, the end of the line- Panahachel.

He quickly exited the door. By now there was a patina of dust over the bus and all its colorful occupants. He helped Rojelio unload the glider from the roof, and helped also with some of the other freight. Standing head and shoulders above your average Maya, Walter was good help. Ultimately, the driver re-entered the bus and roared off with a belch of smoke. Rojelio ran to jump on the rear bumper and waved the gringo a hasty farewell.

When again the dust settled, Walter stood among a pile of goods. Not just his glider and gearbag actually, but other luggage and crude packages were also piled at his feet. One by one they disappeared as the other passengers fetched them. He noticed that across the street was a bicycle shop. AQUILA BICIS read the sign- *RENT BIKES*. This seemed like a good omen to Walter, and a good idea too; at least he wouldn't have to walk far. He threw the gearbag across his back and shouldered the glider. He took the six or eight strides that separated him from the bike shop and dropped the gear and glider again. He ducked through the tiny door, designed for Mayans not gringos, and met the owner. He introduced himself and announced he would rent a bike.

Mauricio told him he had just the thing, and pointed at the largest bike in the rack. Still a little small for such an overgrown gringo, if it could support his weight complete with glider it would have to do. He paid the man for a week's rental and they both walked outside. When Mauricio spotted Walter's strange luggage, he offered to give him a ride to his hotel in a most incredibly beat-up Datsun pickup. But Walter had had enough of rattletrap vehicles and declined. He could use the exercise, and was quite willing to pedal somewhere. Besides, he would make more of an impression pedaling through 'Pana' toting a wing on his shoulder.

The streets were crowded with a very international bunch of people. Walter heard English and Spanish of course, but also French and German. Plus, some tongue he could not distinguish, which he later learned was probably one of the many Mayan dialects spoken hereabouts. He had agreed with Mauricio to return once he had found lodgings and arrange for a lift tomorrow to a launch- Mauricio insisted he knew where the 'papalotes' flew. Again he loaded the gear bag on his back and shouldered the wing. He straddled the bike and shoved off in the direction of the lake. He had been informed that the landing area for flying Atitlán was on the shoreline. He wanted to rent as close as possible; every glidehead dreams of landing in his own front yard.

Pedaling through the streets with the glider on his shoulder elicited quite a response from the villagers. While the tourists and expatriates more or less ignored him, a cadre of children began to follow the gringo on their bikes. Some ran along side for a while and then dropped off. A couple of mangy dogs ran howling at Walter, interested in the strange apparition, and received kicks from the kids.

One child was particularly bold and spoke right up: "Ju fly doze Meester?" he asked.

"¡Porsupuesto!" said Walter. *Of course!*

"Tambien vuela mi tio," said the child, picking up more easily on Español. *My uncle flies too.*

"¿Sabes donde aterrísan?" asked Walter. *Do you know where they land?"*

"¡Claro que sí!" exclaimed the chavo. *Sure!*

"Vamos por alli," ordered Walter. *Let's go there.*

"Vamanos," agreed the child, and sped off ahead. The streets of 'Pana' were a souvenir shopper's dream. Along each side, covering the facades of all the buildings, hung from make-shift displays or piled in heaps on the dusty ground, hung multitudes of Guatemalan crafts. Sombreros, serapes, guipiles, cachuchas, huaraches, vestidas, chamaras, chanklas... Everything from tiny bracelets to complete suits. Jewelry and local art, pottery and tools. It looked as though the merchants had all brought out their goods for an enormous sidewalk sale, and indeed they had. Glimpsing inside the doors, Walter could see workers busily sewing more garments for display or inventory. And they were all very colorful. Strolling the streets were hundreds of hipster types, looking like refugees from a Grateful Dead concert. *I think I'm going to like it here,* thought the gringo.

He followed his young guide down the gentle slope of the street until the shimmering waters of Atitlán hove into view. Together they rode the last few feet and out from under the trees and flowers that overhung the street. Walter braked at the water's edge. The lake looked as inviting as any he had ever seen.

"Gracias amigo," he said to the boy. "Como te llamas?" *What's your name?*

"Mi nombre es Carlos de Beltran Francisco Ignacio Hernandez Cruz del Rodrigo y Cortez a sus ordenes señor," said the child. "Pero todos me llaman Nacho." *Everyone calls me Nacho.*

"Nacho," said Walter much relieved. "Mucho gusto." *A pleasure to meet you.* "A mi me llaman Walter." *They call me Walter.* Nacho and Walter shook hands. Nacho grinned and offered to take Walter's wing. It was a nobel offer, just not very realistic, weighing as he did, less than the wing. The child's spirit was willing, but the flesh was not up to the task...

"Quiero rentar una recamara cerca de aqui," he said instead. *I want to rent a room near here.*

"Vamanos," said Nacho, and sped off towards a tiny hotel, palm trees sprouting from the courtyard within. Walter pedaled after him. The glider was getting heavier as he pulled up to the entryway where a sigh announced POSADA DEL LAGO ATITLÁN. Appropriate, thought Walter; *REST OF LAKE ATITLÁN.* Nacho dropped his bike and dashed inside hollering for the manager. Walter heard a low whistle and then someone whispered:

"¡Señor!"

He looked around and noticed a young woman, child in arms, gesturing from under an enormous bougainvillea. The woman gestured with a finger that Walter should come to her.

Curious, he set down the glider and gearbag. He took three steps in her direction. She was not dressed like the local Mayans. She wore a simple cotton dress and make-up. When Walter approached she set down the child at her feet and gestured again. Then, in a move that surprised the gringo, she quickly unbuttoned her blouse to the waist and flashed her breasts at him,

"Ju likey?" she demurred. She licked her lips lasciviously and stuck her chest out. Under other circumstances, Walter would have indeed 'likeyed'. Her breasts were smooth and nicely shaped, probably nourishing too. Her nipples were the size and color of a small blackberry. The child at her feet waved his arms and began to fuss. Apparently he too, likyed them. But under these circumstances, Walter just felt foolish, and a bit alarmed. Reluctant to stare, Walter turned, embarrassed.

"Ju likey dis?" he heard. Glancing now over his shoulder, the woman had turned around and hoisted up her skirt, revealing a firm and shapely butt, just barely concealed in a scarlet G-string.

OH GOD! thought Walter. *The woman is desperate!*

He reached into his pocket and brought out the small wad of Quetzales he had left from the trip. He walked up to the woman and stuck out his hand. "Un regalito." he declared. *A little gift.*

The woman saw this as her chance. Instead of simply taking the money, she grabbed Walter's hand too, and pulled it to her left breast. A small squirt of milk exited the breast and dribbled down Walter's hand. He pulled away then, shocked at such behavior. Only in his wildest dreams did stuff like this happen. He turned again, determined now to separate from the woman. Not that she was ugly by any means, or even unattractive. Quite the opposite, she was a Latin Lovely.

She was just... BRAZEN,

He turned and there was Nacho; he had apparently seen this last act. He didn't look surprised at all, or embarrassed, but Walter was. He strode over to Nacho and asked foolishly, "Que pasa?" *What's happening?* It was all that came to mind. Nacho looked back and forth from Walter to the woman, who had not bothered to button her blouse. From under her flowery lair, she grinned back luridly. "Hay vacancia?" he asked of Nacho, as though to clarify the situation. *Is there any vacancy?*

"¡Sí!" said Nacho.

"Vamos, entonces," said Walter, feeling ever more stupid. *Let's go then.*

"JU COME," implored the woman. "I wait ju!"

Walter ducked into the gate, leaving the glider there while Nacho grabbed the gearbag. He had seen some wild things traveling in México, but never anything like that.

The Euro Rally Southwest or, Culture Clash with Wings

In May of 1996 I began working with Cosmos ULM, the ultralight trike manufacturer from Dijon, France. The owner, Renaud Guy informed me that I would be getting a call from another Frenchman named Thierry Caroni, notorious in sailing circles for having wind-surfed from New York to London. That's right- windsurfed!

Caroni, it seems, had an adventure travel company named Veloce 21, Paris based, that specialized in far-flung and exotic vacations. He wanted to organize a rally in the North America, in which his wealthy clients would fly trikes on a long route around the States, and travel in style. They would have all the logistics worked out, and plenty of ground support. Renaud, himself would participate.

I agreed to be the right-hand gringo, and visited Mr. Caroni on a rally he held in Tunisia, North Africa, called Le Chott, to experience how he works. Then, in March of this year, Caroni and I piled into a small plane owned by Ivo Zdarsky, noted designer and manufacturer of propellers, and pre-flew the US route, making contacts and arrangements across California, Nevada, Utah, Arizona, Sonora, Mexico, and back to California.

It is a spectacular route. The trikers would over-fly the Sierra Nevada, the Great Basin, the Canyonlands, the Sonora desert, the Sea of Cortez, and finally the Coachella Valley, to finish near Palm Springs.

I spent the summer making final hotel arrangements. Caroni and his crew worked the other side of the pond, lining up the clients. On September 26, the group arrived in San Francisco, where the planes had all been shipped in wooden crates and tubes. The following chronicle is the result.

There are other players involved here. Often, we were separated all day, in contact by radio or cellular phone, and only getting together at night for an organizational briefing. I imagine that their take on these events may differ greatly from mine. I began this as an e-mail post to Ultralight Flying! magazine who, at this stage of my career, are my only publishers. That's why it begins:

I see from the story you published last issue that I will be reporting on the Rally. This will be kinda difficult since

Ultralight Flying! is a family-oriented magazine and the words I have to describe these pilots are not all 'G' rated. Arrogant and rude will be putting it lightly.

This, happily, does not apply to the leader of the bunch, Thierry Caroni. He is a very outgoing, friendly and level-headed Frenchman, the gracious host, the kind of guy who brings his mother on his adventures, and accommodates her in luxury. So far, everybody likes Thierry.

There were some incidents with the other Euros that we had not counted on, of course. There are two elderly women along, who stepped out of the shuttle van in San Francisco for a tourist moment, and promptly disappeared. Our associate Jeff Goldsberg spent much of one day looking for them, and finally left them to their own means and they somehow made it to the small airstrip in Lodi themselves. These are the same two women who got themselves lost out on Le Chott, a dry lake in Tunisia, raising the possibility that this is how they vacation; If you ain't lost, it ain't vacation.

We had a pilot who reported a lost bolt, without which, his Clipper wouldn't fly. It was a weird-looking eyebolt, nothing you can readily find here, so he asked me if I could make a bracket, which would substitute. I swung into action and found a welding shop in Woodbridge, California, some fifteen miles away. When I arrived there the old guy who owned the place was closing up shop for the day. I convinced him to re-open for as long as it would take to fashion a bracket. Within an hour I was back with a bracket that would have worked fine. I say would have, because the pilot had found his bolt after all. No problem... But I had spent $50 (shop minimum) for this bracket, which the Euro did not want to pay.

"Zees must be some kind of joke," he says.

"No joke, les ami," sez I. "You owe me fifty bucks." He finally responded to certain threats, but I look forward to leaving him to the carrion-eaters somewhere in the Great Basin.

September 30, 1997 Day 1, Ultralight Rally Southwest Lodi, California to Auburn, California

We embarked on the first short leg today. We have been the past two days guests of my old friend Steve Smith in Lodi, CA. I suspect he is glad to see us depart, as some of these guys have been quite rude to him, disregarding his advice and being very rude. We are six trikes; four Cosmos Phase II and two Air Creation Clippers. That's it. A disappointing turnout, but one we can work easily with, for our first effort. The pilots are French, Belgian and Taiwanese. There are also two Cessna 182s that we use, one as an air taxi for the paying guests and one is exclusively for Thierry, so he can travel in advance of the group, or behind it, however he sees fit.

The group arrived safely and without incident in Auburn, CA. I am ground support. I can fly Renaud's trike, between legs, and I may even fly a leg or two. For that matter, I may poison one of this bunch, so I can commandeer a wagon. Let the buzzards rip their flesh!

October 1, 1997 Day 2- UL Rally Southwest
Auburn, California to Fallon, Nevada

This is a Big Day for the Rally. We will cross the Sierra Nevada at Donner Summit, an infamous place in American history. Here, in the 1860s, a group of pioneers were stranded by deep snow, also in October. Starving, the strong ate the weak in one of the West's most notorious episodes of cannibalism. The weatherman calls for a fast moving front to drop down from Alaska and the winds to kick in to 50 mph by this afternoon, but no snow, so we plan to leave early. As road crew, I leave the hotel at 5:30 AM and drive hard over the pass for Truckee. The French ground crew follows with a pickup full of fuel. We get a quick breakfast in Truckee, hit the supermarket, and then drive straight for the Truckee airport. We are surprised when the first UL enters the pattern just as we arrive; they have had a very fast trip over the Sierra. One of the Cessnas is there, too, with three Veloce 21 clients. They are being piloted by a kid who looks as though he was just weaned; he is trying to grow a mustache. But he can, apparently, fly. More on him as the week progresses, I hoped. But this kid was soon cut loose and replaced by Blair 'Stick' McDonald, a friend of Ray O'Neal, the other Cessna pilot, both of whom are old leather.

I leave with the wind in a Ford Club Wagon V10. The thing really flies. I head straight for Fallon where I am now waiting their arrival. I hear a broadcast from Renaud, and soon they arrive in Fallon. Renaud reports high winds from Truckee, and big turbulence. There are wave clouds capping the Sierra behind us and they all got first big lift, and then big sink, while crossing the mountains. The Euros are smiling now, which seems to lighten up the atmosphere. One of them even goes to the lengths of hugging me there on the tarmac in Fallon! I'm thinking maybe he's queer.

Having flown that section of the Sierra for years in a hang glider, I have never crossed the whole range, canyons, forests, etc. I can only imagine the experience. I ask Renaud if this is the most awesome flight he has ever made. He grinned and thought a second then sez, "No. Zee Goobie Dessert." You must say it like Inspector Clooseau with his mouth full of snails: Zee Goobie Dessert.

Suddenly it dawns on me: the Gobi Desert. "You flew the Gobi Desert?" I ask. "How high are those mountains?"

"Ummm..." says my Frenchman. "Six souzand meterz. But zee turbulenze today? It iz umm, 'ow you say...? Rrrrrrrrrock and rrrrrrrroll!"

The flyers all arrive with stories to tell, even the ground crew. I was not in Truckee when they launched. When I left Truckee there were still fairly light winds and just the first signs of lenticulars. I hear that by the time these guys fueled, had a bite, and took off again, the airport manager had shown up to look over the show, and a big wind had set in from the southwest. He stood on the runway and gaped as the trikes powered up to full throttle, popped quickly off the runway, climbed straight up and exited his pattern from above. One of the Belgians insisted on having a ground crew escort him to the end of the runway, holding his wires. By all accounts, he was trembling with fear. The trikes were lighter, now, because most of the passengers elected to travel by surface transportation instead of suffering more of the turbulence they experienced over Donner Summit. It must have been awesome.

One of the Euros traveling in one of the Cessna 182s reported that he banged his head on the ceiling of the plane as it bounced across the mountains. I suggested that tomorrow he bring his helmet.

The trikes, by the way, are all Euro registered, French or Belgian, and the pilots all have European licenses. The Euros all look very XC ready, very prepared. They have nice, lightweight and modular flight suits, digital cameras, sectionals, radios, GPS and ELTs. Caroni has prepared a Flight Log, with the whole route on sectionals with GPS waypoints. Each turnpoint or change of altitude is neatly logged. You need only follow from waypoint to waypoint and adjust your altitude as indicated. You don't need to know how to read the sectional, only fly the flight log.

This, as it turns out, is what Caroni is really interested in: navigation. He has explained that the real reason he windsurfed across the Atlantic was the navigation, not so much the sailing, which can be tedious, I'm sure. No... this guy likes to get very lost, yet know exactly where he is. Back when he was sailing, he navigated with a sextant, a compass and a watch like Ponce de Leon. Now that he has GPS he is totally located and a happy traveler.

Jim's truck breaks down in Fallon. Won't start actually. He spends about a half hour cursing his luck and trying to call me on the cell phones Caroni has assigned us. With no success, he begins to walk east. Behold: the Comfort Inn, Fallon, but a block away. What Luck!

October 2, 1997 Day three UL Rally Southwest Fallon to Ely, Nevada

Strong winds and thunderstorms are forecast, and unseasonably cold temperatures. I leave the hotel well before dawn at 5:15 in the Clubwagon. Behind me come the two

French ground crew in a Ford Crew Cab pickup, with all the fuel. The other Clubwagon shuttles pilots and passengers to the waiting trikes and the Cessnas, then travels east, too. It is being piloted by Jeff Goldsberg, of New York and California. Jim Telshaw has the tools and supplies and leaves the Fallon airport last. He will get the full blast of a thunderstorm, but everyone else escapes.

Caroni flys on ahead to Austin in a Cessna being piloted by Ray O'Niel, of California and New York, and awaits the ULs. Caroni is always playing leapfrog with the Rally pilots. Ray O'Neal is a retired Jumbo pilot, who is experiencing a learning curve getting back into 'the light stuff'. So far, he has kept the 182 on the centerline, but just barely. Again, Jim Telshaw brings up the rear. After leaving Austin airfield, he is pelted with rain, then hail, and finally zero visibility.

Austin, Nevada is The Weirdest Town in America. We make the mistake of stopping for breakfast at the Wild West Saloon. We have a disgusting meal, covered in grease and buzzing with flies. The airport in Austin is just a patch of tarmac and a few lonely shacks, stuck in the middle of the Great Basin.

The pilots cover the ground FAST with a tailwind. They are waiting at Austin, Nevada, for a refuel and a rest, even before I can get there having stopped for breakfast. The French ground crew stays in Austin only long enough to drop off the fuel jugs. The pilots fuel, jump back into the sky, and Jim hauls the empty jugs. Caroni mops up, as he and Ray leave last. The UL Rally Southwest has come and gone, from Austin, Nevada, in what seems like the blink of an eye.

I race for Ely and deposit the bags at the Hotel Nevada, home of the Jailhouse Casino. On the way to Ely the skies looked threatening, but we travel with a blue hole. I am hit by two suicidal jackrabbits. I see two coyotes, numerous crows and a buzzard or two, all of whom are eating roadkill bunnies. Apparently, we are in the midst of a bunny proliferation, they are everywhere. Otherwise, nothing moves across the Great Basin, except the Rally and the sky. By the time I can reach the Ely airfield, all the trikes and the Cessnas are there, being greeted by Jack Vanderkamp and the White Pine Ultralight Flyers. The trikes are easily moved into their rather cavernous hangar and we are all safe and accounted for once again.

The Ely flyers fire up a grill and whip up hot dogs and hamburgers. Caroni contributes wine of course, and a good time is had by all.

Jack Vanderkamp is so excited to have us here that he insists on hauling each and every one of us (including the women, one of whom is Caroni's mom) directly to the local whorehouses. There are three of them here in Ely, the only town in Nevada, or the entire Land of the Free for that matter, that offers these services right in town. Gentleman's Social Clubs ostensibly, but the menu, posted on the wall, leaves

nothing to the imagination. Or everything, depending on your imagination.

When Caroni points out that the whole group is rather spent and would like a siesta, Jack looks stricken with disappointment. "But...but..." he stammers, pointing. "I just went and fetched my limo." He does succeed in getting the limo full after all, and disappears happily with a crowd of horny Euros, down the back streets of Ely.

Just in time, as the shit hits the proverbial fan. A tremendous gust front blows through and I sing the Euros a few bars of 'Driftin' along with the Tumblin' Tumbleweeds'. We pull into the Jailhouse Hotel and go to our cells for a badly needed rest. I have to talk the restaurant manager into creating a Rally menu with three or four cheap dinner items and a beverage included, alcohol separate. If we're not creative, the Euros will all order Turf 'N Surf and blow our dinner budget. We may spend the rest of our days in the Jailhouse. He is reluctant at first, but then I take a dinner menu, calculate three dinners, three drinks, add tax and divide by three. Bingo! Dinner will cost us $15.62 per head, plus tip. I even generate a menu in WORD and COREL and fax it to the front desk. The guy is so impressed that he capitulates. We will have ribeye steak, or chicken teriyaki or lemon baked chicken or filet of sole. Seating begins at eight, after the pilots briefing. As the French would say: "Vuallah!"

Caroni is forced to economize unlike he is accustomed. There are just not enough paying customers to make this event a moneymaker. He seems to have had enough success on his other far-flung adventures to take a wash with this one. He says this is how things began in France, too, and I can imagine, my own small tour business took some years to get rolling. I think the average gringo pilot hears of this or that crazy scheme and figures he'll pay his entry fee and never see us or a hotel room again; Fly By Nighters.

But the money flows off Caroni. He is always doling it out on one expense or another. Wine is a favorite. I have yet to see him pass up a liquor store. Economize, yes, but with style.

The Euros do not seem to be a drunken bunch however. They can hold their liquor. There is a couple here, Marcel, who appears to be around sixty-five or seventy years old, and his wife Marie, looks about thirty. They brought their three-year-old son, who is still living on Paris time. He gets up at 1AM each morning, ready to start the day. Wine is prescribed by Dominique, the Flying Doctor, in hopes of jolting the little terror's system with some sleep.

In Ely, I manage to piss off Crusty Jack Vanderkamp. Crusty Jack is the crustiest of the Crusty Weedhopper Pilots. We all know the type. They sit around and wrench on their machines and occasionally spin the prop to make some racket. When the winds don't blow, they may actually go ahead and fly.

Well... for two years now, I have been telling Jack that we will be passing through Ely. Jack was very excited, and he had big plans. When I first arrived at the hangar for the White Pine Flyers, Jack is pleased to announce that the Ely Chamber of Commerce has pitched in $650 for him to "show you guys a good time." Well... we had the barbecue at the hangar, sponsored by the White Pines Flyers. While this was a nice gesture, the food was marginal considering the budget. I didn't complain, of course, but when the chef points out that

their club takes donations, would I tell my pilots?, I reply that there are about $650 in donations to finance our stay, and take it up with Jack.

Also- we are passing out Veloce 21 t-shirts and hats. But the Ely club is selling theirs. Some of our clients buy them, even though they feature an embroidered Weedhopper on the brim... I wouldn't be caught dead in them, so to speak.

So later we have arranged dinner reservations for a party of thirty. We hope that a few White Pine Flyers may join us. I call Jack, so I don't appear ungrateful. Jack answers on his cell phone from the hangar. He asks if we are coming out to visit. I point out that a) it's dark out and b) it looks like snow. I explain that we will just eat and hit the sack for an early departure tomorrow. Jack says, "So are you guys going to make a donation to our club? Or what?"

I say, "Well, Jack, about that $650 from the Chamber..." There is a long silence. Then Jack sez, "Well, gosh... we spent $140 on that barbecue." Another pregnant silence... "And we spent the rest on hats and tee-shirts." These are the ones he's trying to sell us. So I suggest:

"Golly gee, Jack, I thought that money was for showing us a good time."

"That's right," sez Crusty Jack.

"Well... maybe the club can just pick up our dinner tab. You can join us." This brings another long silence then...

Then Jack bursts out, " YOU KNOW? THAT'S THE LOUSIEST THING I HAVE EVER HEARD! You have ruined my whole day! I don't even want to talk to you!" and he hangs up.

I feel really bad and call again. Jack's even more agitated. He just hangs up. I feel even worse until I go tell Thierry what I have done, and he laughs. "Good job." he says.

"Huh?" sez I.

"But of course you are right," laughs Thierry. "Zees man get zee money from zee sky. Eee does not want to share eet. I bet you can find him at zee... how you say? Een zee cathouse!" Thierry thinks this is hilarious, and he continues to laugh at our predicament. Whatever Crusty Jack and the White Pine Flyers may think of me, they must realize that their club is somewhat richer as a result of my passage through Ely. While I appreciate their hospitality and their shelter from the storm, I feel I've been took by Crusty Jack. I don't know why I'm the bad guy.

October 3, 1997 Day 5, UL Rally Southwest
Ely, Nevada to St. George, Utah

I hope Jack doesn't miss me too much at the hangar this morning, but I am always out of town first. I hit the road at 5AM. Jack is probably still back at the whorehouse with the Chamber's money. We were there too, last night... just window shopping. I am surprised to see two young girls with spectacularly sexy bodies. Voluptuous yet skinny, one of them very tan- almost black, and the other so white she looks albino. They give us a 'tour' and show us their merchandise as it were. Promises of delights to come, so to speak. My Euros go wild. Ray O'Neal is the happiest man. He sits between them grinning and looking down their skimpy bras. When I left him there, he looked like a kid in a candy store. That's appropriate, since the tan chick's name is Candy. I don't think Ray actually availed himself of the house services, but he sure had a fun drink or two.

This morning I drive out of Ely and there is a spectacular fog bank gathered in a basin. The fog has flowed across the highway and surged against the mountain foothills. It slowly splashes the foothills and makes waves, just like in the ocean, really cool. Then, leaving Lincoln, Utah, another fog bank becomes obvious in the distance, very dense and about five hundred feet thick. I drive parallel to it for an hour wondering if it's just left over from the storm, or is this a local phenomenon that happens frequently? Maybe there's water out there. The fog just looks so strange here in the desert.

Finally, the highway heads into the fog. But the fog has begun to rise and break up. As I enter the fog bank, I am reminded of nothing so much as cloudbase. But this cloudbase is only ten feet high. Then twenty, then fifty. Finally, there are flat-bottomed cumulus clouds at about two hundred feet. Very cool.

The day is near perfect for flying. There is no wind and temps are not too hot or too cold. The trikers arrive without incident in St.George, Utah. This evening they depart for a photo session over Zion National Park. Tomorrow we don't travel- a day off.

An interesting situation develops tonight, one that I would rather hadn't. Rolando Cogens, one of the Belgian pilots who happens to fly an Air Creation Clipper, comes to me and asks if I can post an e-mail on his behalf. "Sure." I say.

He comes to my room and types up a post to a client of mine, who saw his Clipper in Lodi. This client, who owns a Cosmos, expressed interest in the Clipper I guess. Now, I know that this guy will not buy the Clipper. He already owns a trike, he has a new baby, and his wife has put her foot down. Hell... she wishes he would get rid of the trike he has and just stand around on the ground like the rest of humanity, not buy another.

Anyway, Cogens is writing this e-mail post, about which I know nothing. Cogens and my associate Renaud Guy, who is Captain Cosmos himself, seem to hate each other. Next thing I know, Renaud is standing in my room, looking over this guy's shoulder at my computer, and an e-mail post in which he is trying to sell his Clipper to my client.

Renaud flips out. The two Frenchmen have at each other. If not for the fact that my trust is at stake here, I would think it's funny. But it ain't.

Renaud leaves, angry at me it seems. The Clipper pilot is full of remorse for my predicament. He leaves, too. I am forced to go to Renaud's room and explain that I am not trying to sell Air Creation trikes, I am the Cosmos distributor for the USA after all. Renaud just nods and goes about his business. End of story.

The Belgian who didn't want to buy the bracket back in Lodi had a birthday, today. In a show of magnanimity, I present the cake. I resist the urge to shove it in his face. I am the host, after all. Besides, he is an orthopedic surgeon. You never know when you'll need one of those.

October 4, 1997 Day 6, UL Rally Southwest
St. George, Utah

I awake late this morning because we have a day off. I stumble into the hotel lobby and the manager confronts me. The manager is a very nice guy, a young Mormon type, upwardly mobile. He tells me that Jean Claude, a young strong Frenchman, attacked his squad of waitresses in the parking lot last night. Jean Claude actually cornered the sixteen-year-old hostess, who also happens to be this manager's daughter, and had her in tears. The young hostess jumped in her car and sped away, without finishing her work. The manager went outside to see what was the matter. By this time, Jean Claude has hidden himself in the back of a pickup truck, stalking more prey. The pickup also belongs to the manager. As the manager exited the doors of the restaurant, Jean Claude leaped from the truck in attack mode. The manager, who is quite muscle-bound, nearly counter attacked, but he realized that this was one of his (my) guests, so he didn't. It would have been a good match-up.

So I explain to Thierry what is the problem. I explain that if you must spend a night in jail anywhere in good old America, St. George, Utah may be your best choice. But that when we get to Las Vegas, there is much less tolerance of this type of behavior, and that the characters in jail in Vegas are certainly a tougher bunch. "Mother rapers and father stabbers," as said Arlo Guthrie.

Frankly, I can't stand this Frenchman. He was rude to me the first time I met him and he continues to get worse and worse. I hope he is incarcerated in Vegas, or better yet when we get to Mexico, and he gets what he deserves.

Thierry says he will explain the problem.

There was that issue. Then... the manager explained that in Utah, the penalty for smoking in a public place is a $3,500 fine. Furthermore, if the management is caught allowing his clients to smoke in his public place, the Tobacco Police fine him $3,500 as well. There will be no more attacks and no more smoking in the Hotel Rococco, or the police will be called.

I hope so.

11:00 AM and Renaud just walked in like I'm his long-lost amigo. He has been flying. He has whacked his plane. He destroyed a complete leading edge landing on a desert trail, when the wing tip hit a fence post. He managed to fly it back to the field, a decision that seems pretty marginal, considering the damage we find. The front section leading edge is only slightly bent. But the aft section has a considerable dimple where it plugs into the front section, and it looks about ready to fail. Renaud says it has a hard right turn and I believe him.

I am gleeful at the news in my own selfish way. I discover that a) I am not the only one who whacks planes, even the boss man does too, and b) I seem to be back in Renaud's favor, at least as long as it takes to fix his plane.

We call down to Phoenix and talk to Greg Silva at the Ultralight Flight Center of the Universe, at Pleasant Valley Airport, one of our planned stops. Yes, he has the spars we need to fix the wing. Ray O'Neal is filing a flight plan right now for Pleasant Valley in a Cessna. That front section LE is not going to fit inside the plane. I wonder what they will do?

Caroni has been flying this morning, the first flying I've ever seen him do. I don't inquire about whether or not he has a license. I think I'd rather not know. He flies a couple of bystanders and then he loads Jeff and they take off. When they come back to the field I happen to be out on the runway, watching. Caroni blows off the pattern and turns final in front of a Mooney. They both land together on the only runway, the Mooney overtaking the trike at about thirty feet. I can't believe what I've seen. The Mooney pilot parks and fuels up, then leaves without a confrontation. Caroni does not offer an apology.

Renaud and Ray manage to get the damaged front section LE in the Cessna after all, by removing the rear of the luggage compartment and sliding it in through the window. They depart for Pleasant Valley. I'm sitting here expecting the law, what branch I don't know, to come investigate this crowd.

Today is a day off and I hoped to fly. But there is so much traffic on this strip that I don't want to. Besides, these trikes are not trainers, they are registered aircraft. They have no instructional sticker, and no ultralight registration numbers, so I will be totally illegal. I think I'll pass, under the circumstances. Maybe I'll fly in Mexico. I'll be illegal there, too, but there is even less enforcement there than here.

It's approaching sunset and we have no leader. Thierry has gone off to Las Vegas to pick up some new arrivals. There was a marathon run here today, and this hotel restaurant will have its busiest day of the year tonight, full of spent runners looking for steak. We must drag our Euros elsewhere for dinner. But where? To complicate the formula, when I awaken from a badly needed siesta, the blue Clubwagon has disappeared, and we have no transportation. If or when we locate it, we can shuttle our Frenchies down to the Taco Bell or some such. Looks as though this dinner is going on my credit card. They will taste American fast food, tonight.

We go to Chili's instead. Somehow, Jeff calls ahead and makes reservations. He must have done some kind of sweet-talking the hostess because we slide right in before a big crowd and avoid an hour's wait. I dine with the old gals who like to get lost. I find they are easier to converse with in Spanish and we get along fine. They share a stern facade, but are quite pleasant.

I ask them how long they have traveled with Caroni. "Ahhh!" they say: "Uhh... Greece three times... and zee Sahara twice." Caroni, they explain, is always looking for the different.

"Zhere iz no one who do zee ULM in zee States, but Thierry!" Well... I might agree, I know of no other tour operated quite like this. But this market is more the EXPERIMENTAL rather than the ultralight. Let's face it, you just can't do this in the UL category, here in the States.

As a footnote: I have no problem with the UL regs here. I think FAR Part 103 is beautiful. There are few places you can fly anything without some paper. I like the UL trainer exemption too- a cheap commercial ticket. But there needs to be something that permits recreation (nothing commercial) and travel in these microlights. They are fantastic flying machines.

I have lost track of this journal due to all the crazy shit that has happened. There have been few dull moments. Yesterday we crossed the Mexican border against all odds. We had to forge a letter of authorization to bring the vehicles, which we did. It was easier than I had imagined, I always imagine the worst, but between the ULs and the trucks it takes about twelve hours to pass through the border. In fact, the ULs almost don't make it. They only get permission to pass at sunset, postponing their flight until this morning. I think I might have closed under the pressure, but Caroni never wavers. More on this later but now back to our story...

October 6, 1997 Day 6, UL Rally Southwest
St. George, Utah to Monument Valley, Utah

Departing the next day for Monument Valley, the air is just about perfect for flying and is crystal clear. The Euros have a fast voyage to Marble Canyon where they are so taken with the bridges over the Colorado river there, that they begin multiple flights under the twin spans. Soon everyone wants to do this and they are loading their friends, flying under, over and around Marble Canyon bridge with abandon and then landing back at the strip and loading for another flight.

It doesn't take long for a ranger to appear and shut down the show. He explains there is a Federal law forbidding the flying of aircraft under bridges without permission and that they could have gotten permission for a photo shoot if they had inquired in advance. Ben Nappey, one of the Euros who is stinking rich, sticks his nose up at Ranger Rick and puts on a bad attitude. Ranger Rick writes him up for $250. Ben thinks this is a joke. He begins to tear up the ticket, and the ranger points out that this type of behavior can only lead to more trouble. The ranger hangs around until the Euros depart.

Ben thinks this is funny, or something. I believe he has no intention of paying, but I can't be sure. If he neglects this ticket, and US Customs ever runs his passport at some border somewhere, he will be sorry. This is a ticket issued by a Federal Ranger and there will be a felony bench warrant for his arrest. They will certainly incarcerate him and it could be a week or two of languishing in jail before he gets to apologize to a judge and pay the fine and interest and other penalties.

I race to Monument Valley and find my sister parked at the strip there, for a quick visit with me. She has lived on the Navajo Reservation and worked with the Navajos as a schoolteacher for some years. She only visits for a couple of hours, and then departs before the true culture-clash takes shape.

The Navajos at Monument Valley get some measure of revenge on the white man during our stay, and they run with it, straight to the bank.

There is of course, no drinking of any alcoholic beverages allowed on the Navajo Reservation, sacred turf for these indigenous peoples. This is largely because the Native Americans cannot handle alcohol. Booze is one reason for such great incidence of diabetes throughout the native cultures. The Euros have been warned about this, but take a typically cavalier attitude towards native customs and decrees, as they do to all others. As we arrive out at the monument they uncork the bottles with the satisfying 'POP' that can be heard around the camp.

But first, a little background: When Caroni and I scouted this area for room reservations last March with Ivo, there were none available, except to wait for cancellations at Goulding's Trading Post, the only hotel actually within Monument Valley. Since the chance of a cancellation that would accommodate thirty people was zilch, we were at a loss for what to do. Then, someone suggested that we speak with Virgil, of Totem Pole Tours. So we did.

There are no totem poles, by the way, for many miles. There are not even any poles in Monument Valley whatsoever, or trees to make them with. Also, totem poles are the invention of some other tribe. He might as well have called his outfit Igloo Tours.

But Virgil assured us, back in March, that we could be supplied with a more-or-less luxury camp for our group at $90 a head. We assumed that for such a price, we would indeed have some measure of luxury. There should be cots with clean sheets and pillows? There should be plenty of grub? "Oh yes," agreed Virgil. "You bet!" The clincher was the promise that the Euros would camp out in the monuments, where otherwise the white man is forbidden to tread. Food, bedding and entertainment were all to be included.

There was another catch- the airstrip at Goulding's Trading Post is half dirt and half tarmac. The tarmac, it seems, belongs to Goulding's – a beligani white man named Wayland LaFontane. He has paved the strip to the edge of his property, to accommodate the Scenic Airlines planes that provide him with the majority of his tourist dollars. The Navajos, for some reason which in retrospect may be pure lassitude, have left their half of the strip unimproved dirt. Well, Wayland LaFontane insists that any air traffic arriving at the strip and USING THE PAVEMENT, will be obliged to line his pockets with gold by taking a Jeep tour of the area, or staying at his hotel, or by some other means...

Since there was no vacancy in his hotel, we did not want to spend the extra cash. Besides, if you can tour Monument Valley from the air, why take a tour on the ground? Furthermore, we would have little time to spend on such a trip. When I told Virgil what Wayland had in mind for us, Virgil exploded. He explained how half the runway was owned by the Navajos, and that Wayland had no control over the dirt. We could land there and stay on the dirt and never incur any costs from Goulding's.

Monument Valley Airport... Half Navajo, half beligani

So that was the plan. Virgil also pointed out that Monument Valley is sacred turf of the Navajos, that the air space is restricted, and that recreational overflights are prohibited without special permission.

But now that we have arrived the Euros, of course, disregarded all these parameters. They land at Goulding's and taxi up on the pavement. They refueled and took off on flights that strafed the desert and circled the monuments with total abandon and disregard. Virgil points out that the people who live in the tiny hogans sprinkled around the valley, were not happy about the Euros blazing their turf. Would we please STOP.

Caroni thinks only of his clients, however. He points out that we are making a video, which will be taken back to Europe as advertising, so that we can bring back even more Euros with more flying machines. But this doesn't fly with Virgil. He replies that special permission must be made with the Tribal Council to video in Monument Valley. He says the cameras will be confiscated under Navajo law. Happily, the sun sets, and the crisis is averted, but only through Divine Intervention.

Meanwhile, the Navajo bus has arrived to take us to camp. The driver says we must go now, because it is a two-hour trip to camp. This at about 5PM, while the Euros are still blazing the desert.

Two hours?

Yes, two hours.

We discover why when we finally do depart. The bus is capable of only agonizingly slow progress over the bumpy dirt trail. Our vans are very fast, but we are forced to follow. Into the darkness we caravan, miles out into the monuments. We navigate one of the worst roads, considering that it is mostly flat, that I have ever encountered, even worse that the worst roads in Mexico. But we finally end up at a truly spectacular location as promised, under an overhanging monument, which towers above us. But by the time we arrive Virgil is pissed. The white man has shown incredible contempt for Navajo ways, and there is no end in sight. For our part, we are very disappointed by the Spartan accommodations.

The food, described as 'traditional Navajo fare', is quite humble. This may indeed be what the Navajos have always eaten: theirs is not a land of plenty. But I wonder where the Navajos got fresh lettuce and tomatoes for the Navajo tacos, in bygone days? And for $90 a head, we had expected more, to say the least. How about some buffalo steaks?

We look around for our accommodations and discover a van full of sleeping bags and Thinsulite rubber pads. Spartan, indeed.

By now, the corks are popping and Virgil puts on an indignant act. Yet, it seems as though Virgil himself may be intoxicated, although I cannot substantiate this. He gets up on his soapbox and gives a harangue about the evils of alcohol for the Native Americans, and I could swear he wobbles and his words are slurred. This goes on for a good half hour, but to no avail. Soon, there are empty wine bottles scattered around camp.

Finally, the entertainment begins. This consists of a bunch of Navajos in gaudy and (who knows?) authentic garb, banging snare drums and dancing in circles, raising a cloud of dust over camp. The songs are Navajo chants, I guess, but sprinkled with trite English phrases and song snippets. I think I hear some Stevie Wonder and I wonder about the authenticity. I wonder about sleep. No wonder- I am exhausted.

I go for bedding. I am given one thin pad and one bag from a stern-faced Navajo. I point out that I live in pain, and that I need more comfort that this. I will need many bags and pads, and pillows for my head and for my legs. I explain that I cannot hope to sleep soundly unless I have one pillow clenched between my knees. I am told that there are only enough bags and pads for the guests and the guides, one each. I point out that there are NOT enough, that for this kind of money we should certainly have whatever we want and need, regardless. Would it have been too much to throw in TWO bags and pads for everyone? THREE? Sheesh!

But the Navajos are resolute. They disregard my suggestion, taking I suppose some well earned revenge upon the beligani. Certainly, we whiteys are guilty of far worse disregard.

I take my humble digs and sack out on the ground. The ground is hard and rocky. The Thinsulite is thin. The sleeping bag smells. There are no pillows, which makes it hard for me to sleep. The sky is awesome, though. I hope that a large slice of monument decides to peel away from the cliff and smash mercifully down upon me. They won't even have to bury my bones. Under the Milky Way, my exhaustion rules, and I drift off into fitful sleep.

Next morning Caroni awakens me with a question: How much deposit we have on this camp? I check my bankbook and find we have a $750 deposit. "I sink zees iz enuff," he announces. But Virgil will have none of it. He launches into a diatribe about how the white man continues to disregard Native customs (about which I must agree) and that he will call in the Navajo Tribal Police, if need be. The camp will be $2,700, leaving a balance of $1,950 payable immediately.

Caroni asks what I think. I tell him I agree we have been scalped, but also that the Navajos have us over a barrel. They might as well stake us out in the sun, urinate all over us, and cover us with molasses. Caroni tells Virgil that he will pay only after he has been escorted and transported from the camp to the runway at Goulding's, thus prolonging the standoff.

Breakfast, such as it is, is served very late. The Navajos should have had coffee when we awoke. Would that have been too much? You'd think that they would be in a hurry to get us off their sacred land. Instead, they have not even a fire going. Finally, they put two large coffee pots in the fire and slowly commence to make cowboy coffee. They sit around and watch the fire as the crowd grows. One of the Navajos is very

interested in one of the Euro women, who is shapely and quite scantily clad. He, too, appears drunk, and thrusts his pelvis at her in an unmistakable gesture.

Breakfast consists of more humble fare, washed down by bitter coffee.

We all depart, Navajos, Euros and gringos. Virgil has apparently radioed ahead for reinforcements, because when we arrive the planes all have a Navajo guard, armed with small weapons. For a while I feel as though I am part of a John Ford movie- John Ford who made Monument Valley famous in western films.

But Caroni finally capitulates and pays for our scalps. It's anticlimactic, then, as the Euros spin their blades and blaze off towards Grand Canyon Valley airport.

As for Wayland LaFontane- he never showed his face. Perhaps he just figured we would have to learn our lesson the hard way. A wise man, he.

October 7, Day 7, Les Ailes de'l Aventure
Monument Valley, Utah to Grand Canyon Valley, Arizona

The Grand Canyon leg must have been a spectacular flight. The trikes fly around restricted airspace and follow the Little Colorado river. This is a precipitous canyon, dropping very narrow and deep from a flat plateau. For me it is uneventful. But our host at Grand Canyon Valley Airport Bob Reed puts on a welcome bar-b-barbecue, about which we are very grateful. At least I am. The bill is quite reasonable too, at $90, which must be about what he spent. The food is adequate and plentiful.

This night is uneventful too, spent at the Best Western Squire Inn. But the next morning I crawl out of bed and see a flash of lightning illuminate the darkness. A quick weather check with Flight Service reveals that this is more than just an isolated thunderstorm. In fact widespread rain, and strong winds are forecast. We are forced to fall back on Plan B.

October 8, 1997 Day 8
Grand Canyon Valley, Arizona to Las Vegas, Nevada.

All the guests are loaded into the vans and we speed for Las Vegas, where our rooms are already paid in full. The Cessnas manage to get out under the storm and haul all the trike pilots to Vegas as well. We spend two nights in Vegas, with the trikes back at Grand Canyon Valley airport. This gives us a day off, and the Euros disperse over Sin City. Some go to see Siegfried and Roy. Some go looking for a brothel. Jim Telshaw finds an amateur lurking around the bar. He appears at the room we share and asks, "Are you leaving?" When I say no, he says, "Well... could you? Just for a while?" I go sit in the bar while he has his way with the hooker. This doesn't take long, fortunately. I just want to hide in my room, have room service, and make a few phone calls, in preparation for the next few legs.

October 10, 1997 Day 11
Las Vegas (GCV) to Phoenix, AZ

When our Vegas stay is over, the pilots are ferried back to GCV in the Cessnas. We all dash for Sedona, Arizona for lunch at some fancy French place, totally overpriced, where we eat quiche. If not for my hunger and concern for my diet, I would have declined. It's a very nice place, though, and Caroni pays the bill. Money falls off him like water from the duck's back. We finish the day at John Kemmeries' hangar, the Ultralight Flight Center, outside Phoenix. We stay at The Windmill Inn, another luxurious place. Tomorrow is another Big Day, as we plan to cross the border, and take Mexico by storm.

Here's how Veloce 21 travels on a typical day: I leave early with the bulk of the luggage. I drive straight to the next hotel and prepare for the arrival. Then I dash to whatever field and provide support for the trikes when they arrive.

Jacques and Nichola, the two Veloce employees driving the CrewCab, leave early also and go to the first PPO with fuel. (PPO is some kind of French for Obligatory Passage Point) Jeff Goldsberg, in another van, shuttles the pilots and passengers to the field, where we can lift a total of twenty people in the trikes and Cessnas. Then he heads out to the various PPOs where the passengers have an opportunity to swap means of transport.

Ray O'Neal is Caroni's personal taxi driver in the Cessna 182. Caroni is last to leave the hotel each morning, after settling the bill. As the trip progresses, he has more and more trouble with his credit cards. He and Ray arrive at the field in time to catch up to the trikes and race them to the destinations.

Jim Telshaw's job is to mop up in his pickup and carry the tools, spare parts and camera equipment.

Blair McDonald is piloting his own Cessna 210, which he has owned since 1971. He provides taxi service for those who cannot fit in the trikes, because there are too many Euros, or not enough trikes.

The whole show moves rapidly, I find myself driving at break-neck speed just to keep up, and yet often I don't. It's really wild. We have cell phones and radios for communication and we have organizational briefings each day at 6:30 PM and the client's briefing follows at 7 PM. Still, there is so much going on, and there are so many variables, it's hard to grasp the whole thing. But move we do. So far, and against the odds, we are on schedule.

October 11, 1997 Day 12
Phoenix, AZ to Magdalena de Kino, Mexico

Mexico could really be a cluster-fuck. We have three rental vehicles that were not supposed to leave the state of California, let alone go to Mexico. We are informed by a Mexican source that if we are caught in Mexico with these vehicles, that they will be considered stolen vehicles and we car thieves. Caroni points out that this is ridiculous; that car thieves do not travel en-mass and announce their presence wherever they go.

So, adding fraud to the list of crimes I am about to perpetrate or participate in in Mexico, I draw up an official-looking Letter Of Authorization to operate these vehicles in Mexico, on my lap-top. I wonder if this is what the Arizona Department of Rehabilitation Services had in mind when they bought me this little wonder of hardware. I am even assisted in my fraud by the airport manager in Nogales, Arizona, who seems to think we are the wildest bunch of flight-crazed people who have ever descended on his runway. He comes up with a Notary stamp in his computer, which we edit for our purposes. We even print it slightly cock-eyed on the copier so it looks like a stamp. Now I am a counterfeit.

But we remain stalled on the runway at Nogales, AZ while Caroni, Renuad Guy and Ray O'Neal fly across the border to Nogales, Sonora, seeking permission to bring the trikes along. I would have gone on this mission too, to use my Spanish skills, but we decide this is not wise. The last time I was at that airport, I was denied permission to enter based on the fact I had no pilot's license and no 'N' number, etc. I went anyway, and we are afraid that that incident could adversely affect the success of this fiasco. My 'Zilla would have been the only trike those people have ever seen I must imagine. Wait 'till they see six more...

Though these are not technically 'ultralights', but registered aircraft with numbers and papers. That may help. So we wait and wait. The pilots are getting restless and every ten minutes they ask me if I have any news, as though perhaps I am psychic. The airport manager here in Arizona tries to keep tabs with the airport manager there in Sonora, to have any news. We hear that Caroni must call the Distrito Federal for permission, and that to do so he must first take a taxi into Nogales and buy some plastic phone cards, since the only operational phone in that facility requires pre-payment. There is a fax line there, however, so we still have hope. Remember: just because we get the trikes in does not mean success. We still have the illegal vehicles and many people with Euro passports.

Things look grim around sundown, but here comes Ray and Renaud and Caroni in the 182 for a landing. They are given a cursory search by the sole customs official first, and then announce that they have successfully convinced the Mexican authorities to allow us passage, and that we fly on the morrow. The pilots will stay behind at a hotel in Arizona tonight. Everyone else will get in the illegal vans and head for the border and, if successful, eighty kilometers south to Magdalena, Sonora, where we have hotel reservations.

A loud cheer greets this news, but I get a sinking feeling in my gut. I'm the gringo that is supposed to lead my flock through the border. I get a vision of myself languishing in a Mexican jail. But Caroni's resolve is formidable and I feed off it. If this is my fate...

Before I leave Arizona I call across the border to the Hotel Kino in Magdalena and explain to Señora Atemisa that we will hopefully be there, that we will need a few rooms less, and try to explain the next dilemma. But how to explain this? We have no deposit down on rooms there, or anywhere in Mexico, just verbal agreements. I hope they hold our rooms, but I also hope they don't loose a night's worth of rent because of us. Oh well, here we go!

Actually, I live for these moments. Mexico beckons me, and I can't say 'no'. I like the fact that everything changes the moment you cross that border. I like trying to out-fox the foxes. I only hope my behavior does not get me in too much trouble.

We get to the Nogales truck crossing just before they close. This is important, because if we are turned back here, we still have another shot at crossing in town at the all-night border. This one is usually easier, though, and sure enough, we are given a quick revision, but we tell them we are just going in to Nogales for the night. How they believe this I'll never know. Maybe it's our honest faces. But we are soon headed south for the checkpoint at 18 kilometers, where the real face-off will take place.

We arrive there in force. There are three rental vehicles, as mentioned, and Jim Telshaw, who lives in San Carlos, has Sonora plates on a Mexican truck. We are French, Belgian, Tiawanese and American. The Federále who bangs on the typewriter takes a dislike to one of the French ground crew. He had asked to see the visas for the foreign devils, but of course they don't have visas. They had all gone to the consulate in Paris to get visas and were told they were not necessary. What they should have been told, of course, is this;

"Hey! We are Mexican bureaucrats. We are too lazy to spend a few moments pushing paper on your behalf. Just go anyway and they will give you plenty of hassles at the border."

So Nichola, the Frenchman, says something indignant like: "Vee doon't need nozing." That's all the Federále needs to hear. If they don't need 'nozing' to enter this country then they can damn well go with 'nozing'. He sits back with his arms crossed over his chest and refuses to proceed.

MY papers are in order, though. I get my tourist permit. Oh... yea. This is Sonora, where it's supposed to be easier to travel. As long as you don't cross into Chihuahua or Sinaloa, you don't need a credit card to bring a vehicle. This is yet another Mexican reg that I can't fathom. But I point out to the Fed that we are coming to Sonora because of the lure of the ONLY SONORA program. Also, I say, there is an airshow scheduled for our arrival, and aren't them folks going to be disappointed if the stars of the show are held hostage at the border? This is a half-truth. There was an airshow being planned, by my friend Ruben Rios. However, as the day approached for our arrival, and it became obvious that there would be but few aircraft, Ruben dropped the ball. What kind of airshow can you have with only six trikes and two Cessnas?

Then, we begin to hear that the runway in San Carlos has been closed since the theft of numerous aircraft there. Armed gunman are overpowering the feeble old watchman and taking planes. They head south and are never seen again. We will have to go instead into Guaymas and deal with the Commandante there, a Señor Martínez, whom I know from past mis-adventures.

Somehow, we get through. But the Euros are not given visas. Instead, they are placed on Jeff's and my tourist cards as 'family members'. My permit says I am traveling with four family members and Jeff with six, or some such. This logic makes no sense at all. It is simply a result of hanging around long enough and making enough of a pest of ourselves that it is easier to throw the minimum of papers at us to get rid of us. We take what they give us and pile back into the vans.

We head south to the nearest taco stand and eat and slap ourselves on the back. We pull into Magdalena very late and go to the Hotel Kino to await the dawn and more of the same, only better. We're in Mexico, now.

October 12 Day 13
Magdalena de Kino to San Carlos, Sonora, México

Our instructions from Caroni is to be at the Magdalena/Tacicuri airfield the next morning at 11AM to regroup and refuel the planes. But they don't arrive by then. As it turns out, the authorities in the Nogales, Sonora airport, perhaps remembering the last triker who passed this way (myself), simply drag their feet and put one wall after another in front of Caroni. One by one, he scales them, not taking 'no' for an answer. I'm getting more and more nervous until finally a trike appears on final. Soon here comes Ray in the Cessna 182, with Caroni and a couple of Veloce passengers. Ray forgets he's in a 182, I guess, and attempts to land a 747, as he is accustomed.

He flares very high and bounces the Cessna on the pavement and bounces back into the air. The front wheel is the next thing to touch and Ray bottoms-out the front gear and blows the tire. The prop strikes the ground, the plane settles and rolls to a halt, dead in the water.

Soon all the trikes and Stick in his 210 are all sitting on the runway. We are late for our next arrival, which will be Guaymas, rather than the closed strip at San Carlos, and we've got a flat tire. Quickly, Caroni makes another Plan B. He will take my van and race south as soon as the trikes leave. I will flag a taxi and take Stick and Ray and the tire into town, where we hope to find someone who can fix the tire. Then Ray and Stick and I will play catch-up. Actually, it doesn't look like a plan that will work, but it's all we got. It doesn't seem that there is time for the trikes to cover the three hundred miles to Guaymas, but they will try.

We prop up the nose of the 182 and remove the tire as the trikes and everybody else get skyborne. We are left with both Cessnas, and a few Mexican soldiers who are guarding a sleek twin-engine plane that sits on the tarmac. Closer inspection reveals that our rim is bent, and so is the axle. We head into Magdalena anyway, to seek a remedy, but there is none. We turn our thoughts to the big pile of junked planes that Stick and Ray had noticed at the Nogales, Sonora airport. We jump in Stick's 210 and fly up to where we can radio back to the very helpful airport manager at Nogales, Arizona. Would he please telephone over the line and inquire as to whether that junk heap might contain a tire that will save us? He complies, and we circle Magdalena for some minutes awaiting his reply.

When it comes, it is a negative. There is no tire in the trash heap in Nogales, Sonora. But he says that he has a 'serviceable tire' that we can just have and a new tube we can buy there in Arizona. We will have to leave Mexican airspace and go back to the States. But this requires a one-hour notice to US Customs, which will reduce our chances even further. The airport manager convinces the customs officer to wave the one-hour rule, under the circumstances, and we beeline for the States, not bothering to inform the Mexicans of what we are up to.

We arrive in Nogales, Arizona, and go through a quick customs search, which is beginning to be a farce; every time we turn around some uniformed customs geek is feeling us up. The tire and wheel are quickly delivered to the aircraft maintenance man. The airport manager tells us he thinks that his airport is the only one in the state that does repairs on Saturday. But we aren't out of deep water yet. The mechanic announces that the rim is shot, it won't even hold air. Stick tries to convince him that we only need one take-off, that we can continue to Hermosillo and find the parts there. But the mechanic is adamant. He will not fix the tire. He does have an idea, though. Call Steve and Judy in Tucson. They have an aircraft junkyard, and probably have what we need.

We make the call and, taking the new/used tire and the new tube, we jump back in the 210 and race towards the junkyard. Meanwhile, The Wings of Adventure is leaving us far behind, and Ray's wounded rented 182 sits forsaken back at Magdalena, shoved off to the side of the strip.

Arriving at the Tucson junkyard, we are greeted by the owners, who have been briefed on our dilemma. They grab the broken parts and spring into action. They have a used wheel that will work and they straighten the axle. This all takes longer that we had hoped, but is probably faster than ever. We drop $250 of Caroni's cash and head south, this time just flying over the border without telling anyone. The Mexicans, after all, believe we are still headed for Guaymas, via Magdalena, as stated on our flight plan, and they are not so likely to want to cop a feel any way as their US counterparts. We fly back to Magdalena and quickly replace the wheel. Stick and Ray grab two handly rocks from the bushes lining the runway, and bang on the prop until both damaged tips sort of resemble one another. We fire up the Cessnas and clear out of Magdalena. Ray has left a 12-pack of Tecate for the soldiers.

We hurry south, Stick and I leading the way in the 210. There is not enough time to fly all the way to Guaymas before dark and we are subject to fines for flying after sunset in Mexico. But we manage to get over Hermosillo in time to hear a radio broadcast from a triker.

"This is Dominique," we hear... "I am down at an isolated ranch at the refuel point. The waypoint is wrong and there is no fuel. Repeat- the waypoint is wrong and you will have to correct." This is confusing news.

"Where is everybody?" we inquire.

"We are spread all over the route. Support has disappeared. We are all out of fuel." says Dominique.

"Where is Caroni?"

"I do not know, repeat I do not know. Can you pick me up?" I want to suggest to Stick that we leave him for the buzzards. When there's nothing left but bones, we get his trike.

Mexico is becoming a cluster-fuck. All semblance of support has evaporated as a result of losing the two Cessnas for a few hours. We finally locate Dominique, below us some two thousand feet, but there is not enough daylight to land, pick him up, and get back to an airport. Stick doesn't want to land here anyway, on what looks like a sketchy strip. We leave Dominique to fend for himself. He will be helped by the rancheros and spend an uncomfortable, but adventuresome night sleeping on what he describes later as a bench.

Stick and Ray and I all go to Hermosillo. On the way we hear one brief broadcast from Renaud, who attempts to give us his coordinates. We can't hear enough to locate him and so we go on in and land, just after legal sunset.

We pull into the terminal and I am greeted like an old amigo by the Federáles there. They all ask where is my trike? They give us no problems about our late arrival, and we are soon checking into a hotel and bellying up to the bar for Hora de Feliz.

Somehow, Jacques and Nichola appear, I don't know how they found us, and they explain that they could not find the PPO fuel stop. We tell them we know why- that the coordinates are wrong in the flight book, and that Dominique is there, but no one else. They charge off to rescue Dominique, against my advice. I tell them that a) it's an awful big desert and they won't find him and that b) there is probably fuel on such an isolated rancho anyway. Just forget it until mañana, I suggest. Nichola says they have radios and maps and GPS and is confident they will make the connection.

Turns out they do, but not until dawn, by which time Dominique has indeed found some rancho fuel. When he takes off, he sees Jacques and Nichola in the Crewcab, searching for him.

Stick and Ray and I spend a nice evening in a nice new hotel in Hermosillo. I call two trikers who are also stickheads that I know in town. They come and visit. Stick and Ray want to go to the whorehouse but I am too exhausted and leave them to their own devises. They never do get the whores, I guess. But next morning we are rolling early, to get out of town.

When we get in the sky we learn that Dominique is already airborne. Then we hear that one of the Euros had actually made goal all the way to Guaymas the night before, landing in the dark, and was being fined by the Comandante Martínez for his late arrival.

This turns out to be Rolando Cogens, who is indignant about his fine, which comes to about $25. He is rude to the point that the Mexicans come up with some other fines, which now total about $50. Rolando should be happy that they don't just impound his wagon and throw his ass in the carcel, but he remains rude. It is all our fault, he will later say.

Arriving at Guaymas, we are surprised to see that all the trikes are sitting on the runway, everybody's here! What a relief. We spend a much-needed day off in San Carlos, without the airshow, and lay plans for the next two legs, first to Puerto Peñasco and then to Palm Springs, which promise to be the most difficult yet.

October 14 Day 15
San Carlos (Guaymas) to Puerto Peñasco

The flight to Peñasco is quite complex for us ground support, but I've got it easy. I have only to make one pilot shuttle to Guaymas and then hit the wind for Peñasco. I drop the pilots and roll north. Jacques and Nichola are already driving to Bahia Kino for the first refuel. There are three stops scheduled today and it will be hard to keep up. To add to the equation, there is a stiff north wind blowing down the coast. But somehow, they do it. I have only been at the hotel in Peñasco for but a brief while when the airport manager there, also an acquaintance of mine, calls that a trike has arrived. When I get to the field I am told that, while the wind was very strong near the ground, at three grand there was none, and the trikes are able to skip the extra refueling. I am very happy as, one-by-one, the trikes arrive, and then the Cessnas.

But, I learn, one of the trikers had a problem when the engine quit after takeoff and that the pilot only just managed to get down and stopped about a meter from a barbed wire fence. Jacques and Nichola are sent back to fetch the plane and the pilot is escorted in Stick's 210, to the hotel in Peñasco. Jacques and Nichola have a very late night as a result of their efforts to retrieve the disabled trike.

The trikers have a debate about which leg has been the most spectacular thus far. Today's leg is in the running, traveling as it did up the Sea of Cortez. But Fred Wang, the pilot from Hong Kong, says that they have all been extraordinary.

October 15 Day 16
Puerto Peñasco to Palm Springs

The next morning is really a bad start for me, typically Mexican. I have a wake up call scheduled for 5AM and when the phone rings I stumble groggily out of bed and into the shower. I take a long one, trying to wake up. Then, when I step from the shower and glance at the clock, it reads 5:53, I am late. The wake up call was late.

Shit!

I grab my clothes and my luggage and hobble for the elevator. I go up to the front desk to complain and I see their clock. It reads 5:17.

Shit, again! The damn room clock was wrong, NOT the wake-up call. Now I'm early. There's no coffee until 7 o'clock, by which time I will be long gone. I bitch, but it does no good. I'm in a foul mood as I load my few passengers and head for the border at Calexico.

This drive turns out to be one of the most spectacular I have ever made. Of course, I have already seen this leg from the air, with Ivo in his 172. On that flight we had followed a southerly route that stayed over the railroad tracks where there is no road. This is what the trikes will do, too. They will overfly the Gran Desierto del Pinacate where miles and miles of wind sculpted sand dunes and volcanic features stretch away from the seashore to the mountains to the north. The

road I drive is through these mountains and it is really something. Jagged peaks form tight valleys that are thick with saguaro, ocotillo and palo verde. The whole place is bright green from resent rains and we drive through a spectacular sunrise.

The road parallels the US border. There are only heavy trucks using this road, it seems. I spot two places where it looks as though you could launch a hang glider, I must return some day. But there is one problem- there are hordes of common houseflies. Where they come from I don't know. But each time we stop, there are more in the truck. I drive about 90 mph for Calexico.

Finally, the road comes out of the mountains and crosses a stark desert into Mexicali. We stop for one more Mexican breakfast and then cross the border. I head straight for the Calexico airport- a port of entry- and steel myself for what is to come. I walk into the customs office and offer a greeting. "Hello," I say.

"Can I help you?" asks a woman in a starched US Customs uniform.

"Yes," I reply. "Perhaps you recall that I was here last March and told you we would be back on this very day with a group of ultralights." I can hardly believe it has all come to pass. "Well," I continue. "Here we are"

She looks me over for a second and then inquires, "Is that one of them that just landed?" Now I can hardly believe my eyes. I glance out the window and, sure enough, Captain Cosmos himself is parked on the tarmac. The customs lady has a tattered copy of FAR Part 103, the same one she had faxed to her when we were here last time.

Back in March, when we had inquired what would be necessary to cross into the States with ultralight aircraft, we were given the same list as any 'N' numbered aircraft which. Of course, is not correct. The list was fairly long, as I recall there was a pilot's medical certificate, pilot's license, aircraft airworthiness certificate, weights and balances certificate... the list went on. I cleared my throat and hoped for the best.

"No," I replied, "There is none of that required to fly an ultralight in the States."

"Well there is at my airport," she had stated.

"Uh... perhaps you could check the regulations. This falls under FAR Part 103."

"Sir," she had replied. "Any aircraft that comes here will need all standard documentation."

"Of course," said I. "But the regs are different for ultralights." She had stared at Caroni and I as though wishing we would just vanish.

"Just a moment," she had replied, and disappeared into her tiny office. As Caroni and I awaited the next development, Ivo snickered about our plight. I don't think he ever had any faith that we would, indeed, reach this point in our future journey six months hence. Maybe I didn't either. It all seemed so distant and so far-fetched. But... we had to be prepared. Finally the customs lady returned. She held Part 103, a fresh fax. She studied it and looked up.

"How much do they weigh?" she asked.

"I don't know," I said. This was true. I had never weighed them. I could guess, but what's the point?

"It says here they must weigh less than 254 pounds." I just nod.

"How fast do they go?" was the next question. I could guess this, too, but I simply shrug.

"How much fuel on board?"

"Five gallons, US," I state proudly. It seemed like a good time to start lying.

"Huh," she muttered. "Says here there is no license or anything required." She looked up from the fax. "You will only need proof of citizenship."

"These guys will be mostly European." I said.

"In that case they need passports and visas where necessary."

"And that's all, right?" It was agreed. We had thanked her for her trouble and said, "See you October 14." It seemed ridiculous, at the time.

But today is not ridiculous. Miraculous seems a better word. My Euros are here at the border and I've got to get them through. To make it this far and get stalled at the border would be too much. But I've announced our arrival and Renaud is out on the runway—living proof. The Customs lady is looking at Part 103, again. I am having a deja vú which, in light of the situation, seems only appropriate.

"How much do they weigh?" she asks.

"Well..." I begin. "These planes fit into the ultralight trainer category," I lie. They WOULD, anyway, with an instructional sticker, a registration number and an exemption for each pilot. We don't have these, of course.

"The what?" she asks.

"Ultralight trainer," I reiterate.

"What's that?"

"The FARs provide for two-place operations in these machines." She looks back at her fax. But then she is distracted. The passengers I have in the van have wandered onto the runway to greet Renaud and another arriving trike. This is against US Customs regulations. All aircraft must be isolated until they have cleared customs. Our lady dashes out from behind her counter and onto the runway.

"Get those people away from those planes!" she shouts. But this is easier said than done. My Euros can't figure out why I am standing in front of the terminal beckoning to them, so they don't move. And here comes two more trikes... a Cessna... the whole situation dissolves into chaos. Everyone is happy, except our customs team. Then, a radio broadcast comes into the customs office.

"You've got one down at the El Centro airport," it says.

El Centro?

"Where is that?" I ask, though I have some idea.

"That's about 10 miles thataway," points a Customs agent. "This is bad news…" he continues.

"Why's that?" I ask.

"El Centro is not a Port-of-Entry. Your pilot just violated US airspace without clearance."

Oh great…!

Amidst the chaos, the situation with the downed pilot becomes even more confusing. Seems he's not at the El Centro airport after all. This was the El Centro airport manager calling to say that there is a funny-looking aircraft in a field some miles away. A neighbor near the field has called to report the sighting. Our customs lady would like to blow off some steam, but she remains calm. "Are you in charge of this group?" she asks me.

"I'm just ground-support," I say, not wishing to assume responsibility.

"Then get over to that field with some fuel. It looks like he can't fly over here without some more fuel."

She gives me directions to where Dominique is located. I jump in the van and race to follow her directions. Of course, Dominique has taxied his plane up behind some houses, he might have shoved it into the middle of the field where it would have been easy to spot, but no, it takes me an extra five minutes to locate him. Dominique is relaxed and happy to be back in the States.

"Zee fly… spectaculáir!" he grins.

"You could be in some hot-water," I explain to him.

"Oat watair?" he asks looking around himself. He does not understand the expression.

"Trouble," I clarify.

"Why zees?" he asks.

"Because you have penetrated US airspace and not landed first at a Point-of-Entry. That's why."

"But I am too low on zee fuel."

"Dominique," I say, "the Calexico airport is ten miles behind you" Well, he is not the first lost aviator.

"Zee air, eet is FREE!" he exclaims with a flourish, "we can breeze zee air!" I'm not sure what that means, but we fuel his plane and I race back towards Calexico. I hope Dominique does not tarry at his location, because as I drive back towards the airport I see first one cop car with its lights flashing and siren blaring, and then one, two… three Border Patrol vehicles, in a great hurry, race past me the other direction. They are in a big hurry to get somewhere. I feel as though lost in a Keystone Cops episode.

When I get back to the Calexico airport, I am surprised and relieved to discover that everything seems to be OK. The Customs Lady, perhaps confused about what to do with The Wings of Adventure, has decided to just let us all pass. We have only to purchase the US Customs permit that costs $25 and is good for one calendar year. The sticker will look good on the trikes anyway, as a conversation piece. Even Dominique is processed with little trouble. I think that US Customs must just want us gone.

With the situation under control, I re-load my passengers and race for the Desert Hot Springs Resort Hotel and Spa, our final destination hotel. Along the way, I use the cell phone and contact Phil Kerr, of the Desert Ultralight Flyers, and warn him of our impending arrival. The DUF are located in Desert Hot Springs, which is itself located near Banning Pass, known for howling-strong winds. I get Phil on the phone.

"How's the weather, Phil?"

"Beautiful," he responds.

"Any wind?"

"None to speak of," he confirms, which is nothing short of a blessing.

"Here we come then." I refrain from saying any more. Something like 'Get out of the way, Phil!' while appropriate, seems too dramatic. I'll just have to hope Phil has enough character and sense of humor to sustain him over the next few days as my Euros take full advantage of his hospitality.

Happily, he does. Phil is certainly enthusiastic about our arrival. Has been ever since I suggested we conclude the Rally at his field, some months ago. When I arrive at Phil's field, the first time I've ever been there, I am delighted to see my old hang gliding buddy, Igor Vratney, standing on the strip to greet me. He had heard that the Rally would conclude there today, and that I was at the helm. Well... a half-truth.

The Euros, like a ship floundering at sea, take no direct orders from the helm. With their throttles stuck at full-speed-ahead and their rudder broken, there is just no stopping them.

The end is almost anti-climatic. There is one glitch, however. One of the Euros from Team Cosmos, having arrived over Phil's field, concludes that the GPS waypoints must wrong, or something. He was right overhead and musta been blind to not see the strip below and the trikes parked there. Whatever, he turns back and drives his plane straight to the Palm Springs International Airport, blowing through the pattern and landing with the Citations and the Lears. There is no problem, though. Lordy, these gringos are patient with my Euros.

Phil Kerr and the Desert Ultralight Flyers welcome us warmly. They admire the trikes and offer refreshments to the pilots. While I myself have still two more days to deal with this group, I am extremely happy that the end is in sight. I go to the hotel for a badly needed siesta.

Veloce 21 and The Wings of Adventure tour has concluded. I sleep for most of one day. I have neglected my business for nearly three weeks and must get back in the flow of things. This has been one of the most intense things I've ever been involved with, and I hardly flew at all. It has been fantastic, terrible, ridiculous and meaningful, sometimes all at once. The tour often resembled an out-of-control steamroller. A few people tried to stop us, and were either wise enough to get out of the way at the last moment, or were rolled flat.

Thierry Caroni is remarkable in his resolve. He never takes 'no' for an answer. When faced with an obstacle, he finds a way past. If it is so high you can't get over it, Thierry goes under. If it is so low you can't get under it, he goes over. If it is so wide, you can't get around it, Thierry just bowls it over.

Oh rock'a my soul!

Whatever more is said about Thierry and Veloce 21, if you look at this whole situation from a client's point of view, you cannot imagine a more capable skipper. When Thierry shakes my hand in the hotel lobby as he departs, he informs me that he will return in two years with a much larger group. Will I be his right-hand gringo?

"Sure!" I tell him, though I can't believe my own lips.

Amoniaco or,
A Real Mexican Road Hazard

Twenty hours drive south of the border and Walter was refreshed after a siesta in a PeMex station somewhere near San Blas. Rock 'n Roll blared from the speakers in the Ford-From-Hell, and there was cold cervesa in the ice box. It looked like clear sailing to Guadalajara. If so, he just might make it to the toll road and cruise all night in relative safety, right on through to Colima.

There were banditos, highwaymen, in the hills around Tepic he'd been warned; don't drive there at night. But Walter was too buzzed from the highway to care. He would take his chances.

Rounding a curve and descending a hill the gringo reached behind the seat and grabbed a cold Corona. He popped the lid and took a refreshing swig. It was always more relaxed driving the tense Mexican highways behind a cold beer.

The night was warm and humid and Walter had all the windows down. The smell of Mexican jungle pervaded the evening, a smell the Walter liked. Coconut shells were burning at every village to drive away the bugs, and their acrid smoky smell was not entirely unpleasant. Various citrus trees were in bloom and lent a sweet perfume to the air. Periodically, the mix was enhanced by the ripe stench of putrefying large dead animal, road kill victims. Even this had a certain appeal, thought Walter. Hell, the buzzards gotta eat, too.

Descending a steep slope Walter hit a straightaway and poured on the coal. Through the headlamps of the Ford, he suddenly noticed a cloud across the road. Thinking that it must be thick fog, he took his foot off the throttle to moderate his speed. Just then, a curious thing appeared within the fog: a cow was staggering across the road, barely visible through the mist. The fog was about five feet above the road in a distinct layer. As Walter slammed on the brakes, the cow collapsed as though struck by a sledgehammer. All four of its feet went out from under the beast and it hit the pavement hard. Then, further into the cloud, Walter noticed two men, one apparently dragging the other, they too stumbling through the fog. They covered their mouths with their shirtsleeves and wretched.

Then Walter noticed another smell. At first he couldn't identify it; it smelled strongly of laundry soap. But suddenly, horribly, he knew and slamming on the skids, he commenced a three-point turn there in the road.

The cloud that Walter was looking at was not fog at all. It was pure ammonium! A hundred feet high and who knows how thick, the fog was flowing down the mountain in a deadly stream. Walter though he'd seen everything in Mexico. But this!

He swung the Ford-From-Hell around and jumped out. One of the men had spotted Walter and waved for assistance; they were crawling now. Walter dropped the large tailgate on the Ford and dashed toward the cloud, from where the two men emerged. One man forged ahead quite strongly but he was pulling the other, who by now had ceased even to crawl. Walter reached them and helped haul the stricken man to the tailgate and load him in. The other collapsed in back of the truck and began to hack. At that moment a northbound vehicle sped out of the cloud and went careening off the road into the jungle with a horrible crash. The engine raced for a moment and then died.

Walter jumped behind the wheel and roared off the direction from whence he'd come. It was just another Mexican interlude, nothing surprised him any more.

'Tis better to have flown and barfed
Than never to have flown at all...
--Confucius

Big Air or,
Slide Mountain Payback

I met the kid at Steamers- a local Tahoe hang out on the North Shore. His fresh face didn't look old enough to be drinking designer beer in a tavern, but there he stood, fancy brew in hand. His look and demeanor reeked of rich-kid, spoiled and probably delinquent; the fancy three-phase haircut, the designer dockers, the TOMMY HILFILGER shirt and the puka shell necklace. The Rolex might be a fake, maybe just an average rich kid, maybe a full-blown trust funder. A surfer-type, not yer average Tahoe ski-bum. A gregariously social creature, the kid broke the ice.

"So you're one a them hang gliders, huh?" he asked. "I've always wanted to give that a try."

I might have set the kid straight and said something like "'Pilot'. It's 'PILOT' you sissy. A hang glider is an in-animate object that you fly when you're a pilot. I'm a PILOT not a hang glider. The wings are on the truck," but I didn't. The kid reeked of disposable riches after all.

"It's yer lucky day," I suggested instead. "Or tomorrow actually. The forecast is for dynamite soaring conditions tomorrow at Slide Mountain. Let's get you a tandem flight."

"Oh yea?" the kid beamed. He sucked on his Sierra Brewery Fat Tire Pale Ale. "So whadda I gotta do?"

"Just show up and bring yer wallet," says I. "Be at Slide by noon. Some running shoes would be good too. I've got everything else worked out."

"You gonna run me off that cliff?" he asked with a grin.

"You bet," I said. The kid was just the right size too- about five foot six, a hundred fifty pounds. I should go to work for the circus, guessing weights.

"Whoowee!" exclaims the kid. He clapped his leg with an open palm. "This is gonna be GREAT! How much you charge?" Things were looking up.

"A hunski," I reply. "I only accept cash. I'll do my best to get you an hour of flying, and if tomorrow is anything like today, that's looking like a piece of cake. We shall sky out."

"Go for it Blaney," injected another yuppie, arriving on the scene. "I heard you say it- you've always wanted to hand glide. I'll come and watch." The new arrival was a near mirror image of the Kid. There was no Rolex though. This one wore a tiny ponytail off the back of an otherwise normal 'doo.

"Let's BOTH go," offered the kid Blaney. "You first." He punched his buddy's shoulder, who laughed and walked on through the happy-hour crowd. I was not pleased with this notion. I could only fly 'em one at a time of course, and I could smell the cash. I needed some cash. I needed a commitment.

I needed a cash commitment.

Maybe I could get the other Slide Mountain Flyers here to help me out... wait for the kid to get good and beered-out and then roll him in the parking lot? Get the cash first, have him show up later?

"YOU dude!" I challenged. "Put yer money where yer mouth is and let's go FLYING!"

"Yeah sure," said the kid as he motioned the barmaid for another pricey brew, "I'll see ya tomorrow around noon."

"I'm gonna set up the tandem wing then," I pointed out. "If you tell me you're gonna be there and then you're NOT, I'll be pissed."

"Dude," he replied. "I'll be there!"

Thermal cycles were ripping up the side of Slide Mountain at noon the following morning when I showed up at launch. There were already a dozen other glideheads, locals mostly, with wings in various stages of set-up. Rooster was stuffing battens, Dougie was laying out his harness. And there goes his brother Terry, doing a handstand on a skateboard, carving graceful turns down the Slide Mt. road. Lynrd Skynrd wailed away at *FREE BIRD* from a pickup stereo, and from a more distant wagon came the Slide Mountain Rally Cry amid puffs of sweet smoke:

"Safety meeting..."

"SAFETY MEETING!"

Part of a familiar scene, I dragged my tandem wing off the Ford From Hell and began my own set-up. There were cummies popping out in the desert and drifting over launch. A couple of early birds were already circling out above the mountain. It was looking like another awesome day at Slide.

"Did you find a victim last night?" hollered Rooster over the music. This was a reference to my constant search to find some Tahoe Babe in a bar and drag her out flying the next day. Get her legs in the air, one way or another. It was the best thing for my love life, the ONLY thing really. I FLY FOR SEX. But not today.

"Paying customer," I replied as I unzipped the bag.

"Oh yea?" said El Gallo. "Who's that?"

"Just some kid I met at Steamers. A trust-funder. Swore he would see me here about now, and bring his wallet."

Rooster gazed at the sky, playing air guitar with a wing batten. "Should get his money's worth today," he observed. I hoped so. The kid getting HIS money's worth would mean me getting mine. I needed that, at least as much as the kid needed to fly. It would be fair trade.

I set up the tandem wing- a Double Vision from Pacific Airwave, laid out two harnessed, two flight suits, two helmets and four gloves. I clamped the flight deck instruments to my base tube as guys started punching off. They were turning immediately in front of launch and peeling for the blue sky, riding the thermals straight up above Slide Mountain and soon becoming tiny dots in the sky, heck- soon disappearing over the High Sierra.

One o'clock rolls around- PrimeTime and still no kid Blaney. I should have got that damn cash commitment.

"Hey dude!" yells Rooster. "You're blowing it." He was stepping over the knee-high guardrail and onto the Slide launch all clipped into his Wills Wing Talon, helmet on, gloved-up. There jus' weren't no moss growin' on Rooster. The windsock at launch was doing a demented dance straight up as Rooster steadied the wing. A vertical wall of thermal updraft awaited him about three steps out from the edge, and Rooster was about there.

"I'm waiting for my ride," I snapped, but it was too late for the Rooster. He had leaned himself through the bar, took those three giant steps and bailed. The glider dove slightly picking up speed and energy, coming alive in Rooster's grip, then shot skyward as it commenced a climb that likely wouldn't end for the next half hour or so. Rooster was climbing the Stairway to Heaven. He let out a "WHOOP" of relief and joy...

Meanwhile, it was looking more and more like the kid was a no-show wuffo. I figured him for a wuffo from the start. A no-show wuffo was the worst kind. Worse yet- I was looking like The Fool. The Slide Mountain Boys were peeling for the clouds and I was faced with the prospect of breaking down the tandem wing, setting up my other glider, and being left seriously behind by the rest of Team Tahoe. All because I put my faith in a no-show wuffo.

Shit!

Of course, I could simply stow the other harness back in the Ford From Hell and clip into the tandem glider solo. I would then be like a leaf-in-the-wind, but at least I would fly. The only 'wind' visible around Slide was of the vertical kind; Stairway to Heaven stuff. At least that way there would be no 'left behind' part. *I can be airborne in moments* I thought, as I heard Rooster's vario singing happily above me.

"Screw it!" I stomped. "I ain't wasting no more daylight." I quickly suited up and clipped into the glider.

Of course, that's when I spotted the kid again. Blaney. He was in a Toyota pickup- a shiny new one that was just pulling up to launch. I unclipped, stepped out of the glider, and went to get the hunski.

"Where ya been?" I barked over loud rock 'n roll coming from his truck.

"Aww… over slept," he said. The Wuffo.

"Noon?" I inquired. "You couldn't get out of bed before noon?"

"Well…" he replied.

"Well digger's ass!" I said. "Let's get hopping."

"Aww, I dunno," says the kid. He gets out of the Toyota with a stretch and a yawn, revealing a tee shirt with a fancy logo for Santa Cruz Surfboards. In giant block letters both front and rear it proclaimed BIG AIR!

"You don't know SQUAT!" I declared. "I'm the one who knows!" I gestured to my glider and gear, I was a little pissed after all. I was jumpy too. My buddies were getting smaller and smaller, and there were no more happy songs from singing varios.

"Hundred bucks sounds a little pricey," he whined. That stopped me; first the friggin' kid is late, now he's cheap too? He's late, he's cheap, and he's driving his daddy's graduation present.

"Oh you think so, huh? What would you say was a more commensurate fee?"

"How 'bout twenty-five," says the kid from behind a flashy pair of REVO sunglasses- three-hundred dollar sunglasses. Now THAT pissed me off, it was pure insult.

"I've got five-thousand dollars worth of equipment set up here, I've got ten years of experience, and I'm at the right place at the right time," I point out. "A smilin' Ben it is, or I'm flyin' solo. Let's rock!"

But Kid Blaney only makes things worse by remarking: "Heck, I went parasailing last week for twenty bucks." PARASAILING?

Parasailing fer Chrissake.

Dragged around by a drunk in a BOAT?

"That's not flying," I squeal, "That's trolling! How can you compare that with this?" I said and pointed overhead where a half-dozen locals were specking-out. I was mad enough to throw the kid off the Slide launch- without a wing. I was looking at bailing solo, just to spite him. Still, I could use the bucks. Maybe a compromise was in order... Plus, I would get the chance to show him what flight really is, and that was my objective all along.

We settled on half a hunski paid-in-advance and I fleece the kid's wallet right there on launch. As the First Law of Prostitution states: services, once rendered, are greatly devalued or; Get The Money First.

We bailed off Slide in what looked to be a good cycle, and started bombing into the valley below. This was NOT the plan. I had been so focused on the conditions at launch, that I hadn't noticed the rest of the tiny dots over the mountain were getting flushed; I had taken off in a down-cycle. I headed straight for the Knobs out front of launch, about halfway down. Already there were performance gliders sinking-out there too. Oh shit! What chance did I have in a tandem wing?

Suddenly, it wasn't looking so good for that hour I'd promised the kid.

We arrived over the Knobs and stopped sinking. There was a cycle building here, but it was marginal. Other gliders came and went- all of them down. But that big tandem wing had good slow-speed handling and a reasonably low sink-rate, just what a desperate glidehead needs to hang tough on a marginal thermal. We started circling and getting our sorry asses kicked this way and that. Gliders were plummeting from the sky all around, but we hung tight. I tried drifting north with each circle as we usually do, trying to drift with the lift as always here on the Knobs, but each time I would fall out the back of the thermal and loose my small altitude gain in just getting back where I'd started. A bead of sweat dripped off my brow and ran down the inside of my cheap sunglasses. It was hot and clammy inside my flight suit. I was sweating like an army mule...

Meanwhile, the kid hung silently next to me.

As I worked, a red-tail hawk drifted into my thermal from below and exited above. He thermalled right through me, putting me to shame and there was nothing unusual about this in itself. Red-tails have the best slow speed handling and sink rate of all. But his flight path was different: he'd come gliding in from the north and gone out to the south... The red-tail had drifted the wrong way! Something strange was happening today on the Knobs, it just didn't feel right. *Maybe this is a light north wind?* I wondered. So I tried drifting towards the south.

We circled and drifted and we circled and drifted, getting beyond the point-of-no-return for the normal Slide landing zone out front. We weren't exactly climbing, but we weren't sinking either, we were just drifting along, circling, circling. If we sunk out now, it would be a long glide out to a field at Bowers Mansion, instead of the normal Washoe Valley landing field. But if we drifted just a little more, there was a sunny rock face coming up below. It looked like the last chance; get up here or go down there!

Drifting in next to the cliff I felt the glider nose-up and heard first a timid chirp, then a happy singing from my variometer. I held the wing level, pointed the nose straight over the rocks, and hit paydirt.

The vario sang... I cranked.

The vario squawked... I banked.

The vario squealed with delight... I PUSHED OUT!

As if suddenly possessed by demented Angels, the wing stood on its tail at a very unlikely angle-of-attack, and we began to dig our way out of our hole, spiraling up, bound for the Heavens above.

Meanwhile, the kid hung on, not that he had much choice. He exclaimed at first, maybe yelled a little caught up in my excitement and relief, I don't recall, I was too focused. We climbed up the side of Slide, through nine thousand feet and back above launch. I could easily see the cars and people on launch and sitting on the guardrail as we corkscrewed out of there. They looked like ant people with toy ant cars. We circled up through ten thousand feet, the thermal now strong and cohesive, the vario singing a constant melody; the lift was solid all the way around the turn. We cracked eleven grand and the Tahoe Basin came into view over Slide. Still in solid lift, we burned through twelve grand... thirteen grand... fourteen thousand feet, and we had never left the same thermal!

Tahoe was a toy lake beneath our dangling toes, unreal on a beautiful summer day. Now THIS is FLYING. The kid would get his money's worth after all.

The kid? Seemed he was very quiet. "You comfortable?" I asked.

"Mmhuph," was his only reply. So I figured I might as well show him the sights; a summer-paradise of sun-splashed mountains and distant valleys, and Lake Tahoe of course- star of the show. A million-dollar view that most earthlings could never afford- even if they had the cash, a life-affirming view into Heaven, which sorta brung out the tour guide me I guess.

At the top of the thermal, just under a friendly little fair-weather cumulus cloud, I put the wing in a shallow bank and pointed a gloved finger. "There's Mount Rose down there," I said. "That's the highest peak on the North Shore." The glider swung through the compass and I pointed out more sights: "There's the East Shore there, with Marlette Lake hidden on the ridge... There's Heavenly Valley and the South Shore... and waaaay over yonder? That's Emerald Bay and Fallen Leaf Lake." The kid only mumbled again and so I continued: "There's Desolation Wilderness, there's Mt. Talac, Alpine Meadows and Squaw Valley..."I had just finished the tour when the kid erupted with a loud ralph.

"Bwwahhgh!" he said. Oops! There went his breakfast... "Nghhaaa!" he moaned. Oh no... there went his lunch.

Holy Voluminous Volumes of Vomit, Kid Blaney was really sick.

I slapped him on the back a few times to clear his windpipe, and remembered gratefully what I'd learned in an emergency medical class somewhere- that laying prone, on your chest- is the safest way to puke. I needed only be sure the victim doesn't swallow his tongue during the convulsions, be ready to shove my fist through his clenched teeth if necessary, and dig the tongue from his throat. I gave him an extra whack on the back just to be on the safe side.

"You've skied Squaw, right?" I asked, but there was no answer. The kid wasn't looking towards Squaw either. In fact his head dangled helplessly so that, if his eyes were open at all, he was apparently gazing somewhere under his Reeboks in the general direction of Reno/Sparks. I rolled the wing level and began the long glide over the mountain. "Are you all right?" I asked, genuinely concerned now.

The kid's head nodded up and down briefly now. "Yeah," he sputtered. "Urr... ahh... I'm fine! Doing fah fah fine RALPH!"

As though this were a normal occurrence, do this all the time... He sure didn't look good; he hung there exactly like a sack of potatoes might, breakfast chunks and lunch chunks smeared all over his face, blown down the chest of the harness. Worse- it was going to be a long way down even if we started now.

Then the kid commenced to dry heaving, his body shuddering and convulsing in the harness. A few minutes of that and finally he hung motionless again, wrung-out, spent. One arm was still around my shoulders as I had insisted, but the other arm dangled helplessly out in space, a wayward appendage ruled only by inertia and centrifugal force. As we glided over Slide, a tiny speck at fifteen grand, the only sign of life from Kid Blaney was an occasional twitch and moan.

Arriving over Mt. Rose Meadows I banked the wing over to spiral down for a landing. The meadow, at eighty-seven hundred feet above sea level, was still about a mile below us. At the first turn the kid sparked back to life. "No," he cried. "NO!" Startled, I wondered what I'd wrought.

"No WHAT?" I asked.

"No... no more... circles... whimper whimper whimper. Just... fly... straight.   Please...!" The whimper trailing off into a tiny sob.

That idea, of course, wouldn't do at all. The landing area was straight down below us after all, if I simply flew straight, no telling where we'd end up. From my vantage point it looked as though we had an easy glide all the way out to the icy cobalt middle of Lake Tahoe, and if we continued flying straight, we would certainly drown. We would be the objects of a gruesome dragging-of-the-lake search for our remains. We would make the Evening News in a horrible way. But I leveled off again, thinking... thinking... humm...

"You know," I chirped to my wuffo. "I kinda likes it up here myself humm? This is what I does for fun. Just look at this here glorious view will ya!" The kid's head nodded weekly, but said nothing. "I think I'll try some more circles," I offered, and banked the wing up steeply.

"NO! God NO sob, sob, sob," came the results. "Please don't... fly... circles!" I saw my opportunity now, so I went for the jugular. I stuffed the bar in a dive, cranked the wing up steeply, and shoved the nose into a big ol' wingover. "Ahh! NOOoo!" he cried again. "Please don't! PLEASE! NNOOO NNOOO gack, ack!" Having softened him up for the coup d' gras I leveled off.

"So... I suppose you want me to put you down now, huh?" I asked the kid, who gacked in the affirmative. The only way to be sure it was a gack-in-the-affirmative was the feeble nod of the head that went with it. "But I'm having FUN!" I pointed out, showing him the blade. The kid's back heaved with misery. He gagged and whined a bit more and I noticed he was drooling now, a foul strand of drool clung to the bottom of his nose and fluttered in the wind. He even had bile on his designer sunglasses. His mouth came open to regurgitate some more, but there was nothing in the cupboard. He started to cry instead; sob, sob, sob, and he looked like nothing so much as a fish out of water.

"I tell you what I'll do," I offer. "For ANOTHER fifty bucks, I'll do just that... I'll just put you down now." I stuffed the bar and aimed straight down below, to where other gliders had already landed. No doubt, the Slide Mountain Boys were knee-deep in wildflowers, and having another safety meeting even then. The kid's head started bobbing up and down again, with more conviction this time. "Yes," he sputtered as I released the bar and rolled into a wingover. "YES!"

Suddenly, one word came to me: 'epiphany'. I had an epiphany in the sky over Slide Mountain on a sunny summer afternoon. Suddenly, I saw things so clearly: *If you can't get 'em honestly, just spin 'em up until they beg for mercy, and then take what's rightfully yours. Where there's a will there's a way.* And it worked, the kid was nodding 'yes' now. "YES!"

Maybe I should be dickering for sex too?

Nah! Not my type.

I rolled level again and started zigging and zagging above the meadow, hurrying our descent. Then I remembered I had already cleaned out his wallet. How would he pay the piper?

"You got any cash left?" I asked. The kid made no move whatsoever. He might have been a sack of shit...

"You got any CASH?" I say again, louder this time, and I nudge him with an elbow. The kid's head turned and looked me in the eye. From such close proximity, this was not a pretty site, streaked as it was with the former contents of his stomach. But he simply shook his head "no" and went limp again. Hmmm...

"How 'bout plastic?" I asked.

"YES," he cried. "I've got my Dad's credit card. Please put me down now. Please put me boo hoo..." That was all the wind the wuffo had, that was all the kid could say. It was all I needed to hear too... *Charge him half-a-hunsky to take him flying, and the other half to put him down.*

I pulled on the nose and dove for Mt. Rose Meadows.

We landed uneventfully, landing on my feet only, since the kid's weren't working. Back on Terra Firma I had to lift the kid's suspension enough to get some slack in the harness to unclip him.

"We can take your Dad's plastic into the restaurant where I work," I explained meanwhile. I laid him gently back on Mother Earth, being certain that he had a clear air passage. I sure didn't want him dying now that the fun was over but before we were totally settled-up. I swung the glider around and gave him some shade too, as I bagged the wing. "I don't personally accept plastic you understand, I'm strictly a cash-and-carry type. But my employer does. We'll just head for the bar."

The kid finally rolled over on his back- the first real sign of life since we landed- but he was then at the mercy of the powerful Sierra sun blazing into his face and he moaned again. Soon, he struggled to his feet. "Watch out for those wires!" I warned, but it was too late; the kid's eyes just wouldn't focus well and his legs just didn't work well and he tripped over the wing wire. If his first step had been unsteady, his second had put him back down on the ground where he belonged.

He slowly gathered his feet under himself again and this time I was there to help. My Eagle Scout days came in handy as I steadied him with a grip on his arm and we tried a few baby steps. "We'll just stop on the way back to launch," I enthused. "Bob the bartender has already opened the bar, it's only a few minutes out of our way..." We walked about ten feet to a manzanita bush and he gestured that he wanted to kneel down there. I was unsure if he wanted to kiss the Earth, or maybe pray toward Mecca, or what exactly, when he hunkered down on all fours, opened his mouth about as far as a mouth can be opened, and tried to puke just one more time.

"Ak, Akk, AAKKK!" he said, but there was just nothing left-only more dry-heaving and a little spittle. As I walked back to my glider to finish bagging it I noticed that tee shirt again. "BIG AIR" it promised. Just not that big I guess.

Trouble At The Sheriff Bar or,
A Twisted Tale of Drunkenness And Despair

From The Peaceful Mexican Village Of Valle De Bravo
Starring Derrick Rasmatazz

I've told this story many times and yet there are those who believe I must be making it up. I wish I were. Had none of this ever happened, several lives would not be so messed up. Nobody would be dead. I have all this information second hand, yet I know it to be true, since many have told me so. My associate Derrick would probably prefer that I don't tell this story, but something compels me. At first I thought it no more than a sad and perverted story, proof, perhaps, that handguns and human nature lead to tragedy.

But many lives have been affected by the events of a sunny June morning while the village of Valle de Bravo, one of my favorite places in Mexico, awoke to meet another day. My life is one of the least affected, but has been, nonetheless.

In at least one way, this is a strange hang gliding story. If not that Valle de Bravo is the closest village to a certain hang gliding launch called El Peñon del Diablo (The Rock of the Devil), none of this would ever have happened. Derrick would not have been in Valle. I would not know Derrick. The cop would probably still be drunk- and still be alive.

The story began for me when I got a call on my answering machine from Flaco Cazar in Austin, Texas. Flaco is a fellow flyer and his message was rather cryptic: that I should call him ASAP, that there had been some sort of tragedy in Valle, and that my associate Derrick was in jail! I called Flaco but got his answering machine.

I put the phone down, and thought a moment. I decided to do the next logical thing- call Derrick directly. The phone rang twice and Derrick answered. He wasn't in jail after all.

"Derrick! Que pasa?!" I asked.

"¿Amigo?" he said.

"Yes!" said I. "When did you get out of jail?"

Derrick snickered and said something like, "Gossip travels fast."

"Tell me what happened," I demanded. I had lived some years in Valle. I like it there. I look forward to a return. I didn't want to be associated with any trouble, however remotely. So Derrick began to tell me of the events that had happened one morning a few days ago.

"Well...," he started, "I woke up the other morning before dawn and I thought I heard a party down at the Sheriff's Bar." The Sheriff's bar is called that, by the way, for unknown reasons. Why the 'Sheriff's Bar', we are not sure. A Sheriff does not own this bar and normally, there are no Sheriffs in the Sheriff's Bar. In fact, there are no sheriffs at all in Mexico that I know of. They call their lawmen something else. But... "I couldn't sleep so I got up," continued the gringo. "I put on a pair of shorts and a tee-shirt. I grabbed a cup of coffee and walked down the hill from my casa and up the stairs to the bar."

"Go on..." says I. So far there was nothing unusual. I knew the Sheriff's Bar, have quaffed a few cervesas there myself. I couldn't imagine Derrick getting in trouble there. Derrick is a peaceful gringo, not prone to brawls or violence of any type. More of a lover than a fighter, if there was ever any reason for Derrick to meet with trouble in Valle, it would probably be due to his legendary amorous conquests, which are numerous.

"When I got there, I found a bunch of drunks laughing and singing with the juke-box as usual," he said. "It was around sun-up. Fernando, the owner, was there and some other people. Also, there was a drunken uniformed Policia Fiscal slumped over the bar."

Oh oh! thought I; the Policia Fiscal are local cops, bottom-rung on the legal food chain. Not a sheriff at all, but the plot thickens. "So?" I ask.

"Well," continues Derrick, "somehow, I got into a conversation with Fernando and some others that I had a pistol, but they didn't believe me. Meanwhile, they were having fun with the cop. The cop was so drunk that he kept falling off his bar stool. They thought it was funny. They kept propping him back on his bar stool and giving him another shot of cheap mescál. He would drink it and fall on the floor again and everyone would laugh. He was part of the drunken entertainment."

"And... what?" I could sense reluctance from Derrick to continue. The part about the gun didn't sound good. Handguns are forbidden in Mexico. When you cross the border there are big signs announcing that fact. Why the chingada did my amigo have a gun?

"So I told them I had a tiny pistol on a belt buckle but they didn't believe me. They said guns are illegal and that gringos can't have them. I said 'I know that but I have one anyway'. They said 'No you don't'. So finally I said, 'Well, I'll show you.'" My heart sank when Derrick said that. I thought he was a smarter gringo than that.

"Shit," says I, "You didn't!"

"Well listen man!" said Derrick. "It's just a tiny little .22, the kind you can wear on a belt buckle. In fact that's where it was. I went back home and got the belt and put it on just to show them I wasn't lying."

"You'd been better off lying I bet," said I. "Did you shoot somebody?"

"No man I didn't shoot anyone! There were plenty of witnesses. Just shut up and listen!" I could tell he was upset.

"I'm all ears..." I said.

"Well I got back to the bar," he continued, "and everybody was still there including the cop. He was so drunk I didn't think he would stay conscious much longer. I showed them the pistól, but it's so small, really just barely long enough to hold a shell, they all thought it was a toy. They kept saying, 'That's not a pistol gringo, that's a toy.' I kept saying, 'No, this is not a toy amigos, this is a pistól!' Finally I said, 'Watch. I'll show you', and fired a round into the fireplace."

"Oh shit," says I over the phone. "You what?"

"It didn't DO anything at all," said my gringo amigo. "It made some noise but it just bounced off and everyone laughed. Everyone but the cop that is, the cop came alive! Derepente he jumped up and looked around and saw ME with the smoking pistol! Good thing they don't give them guys guns too. He'd probably have shot ME!"

"Shit!" I exclaimed. So that was it? Well, gringos have been in worse trouble. "So that's it?" I ask.

"No," said Derrick, "I wish it was..." He hesitated for a moment. "It gets worse."

"Oh Hell..."

"The cop gets all bent out of shape and we wrestle for a bit and then he takes the gun away. Really, I gave it up. He would have cuffed me and hauled me away except that he was too drunk and Fernando and the rest of the bar patrons convinced him not to. They tell him I'm a good gringo, that they've known me for years... that I've got a Mexican daughter asleep at home. The cop makes me promise to appear at headquarters before noon to stand charge of possessing an illegal weapon. He let me leave..." There was more, unsaid.

"So that's worse?" I questioned. I could hear Derrick hesitate on the other end of the line, far away in Loco Land. I could tell he didn't want to continue.

"It ain't over yet," admits my amigo. "I walked back home. I get a cup of coffee and go out on the terrace. I can still hear the laughter and the party and the juke box when all of a sudden... ANOTHER shot rings out. Then people start screaming. Then the music stops and I hear people shouting. I run down the hill again, and up the stairs to the Sheriff's Bar again. There I find a bunch of people standing around a body on the floor. I elbow my way in and see that it's... the COP! The same drunk cop! He's bleeding from a hole over his heart... and MY GUN IS ON THE FLOOR!"

"NO!" I protest, imagining the scene. "What happened?"

"Well I try to resuscitate him, of course, but what can you do for someone with a bullet in his heart? The guy just dies in my arms! I can feel him do the Death Rattle and lay still! Go limp! It was HORRIBLE!"

"Shit NO, Derrick," I exclaim. "What happened then?"

"That's what I asked. Everybody said that the cop was so drunk, he got confused. He started brandishing the gun around and telling them it was just a toy, smiling and laughing. 'No,' they said, 'It's NOT a toy, it's a gun.' 'No,' he said, 'It's not a gun, it's a toy!' This went on for a while and they tried to get the gun away from him, but finally he said, 'Watch this you fools, I'll show you.'"

"I'll show you?" I asked, though it was dawning on me what happened next...

"He shot himself man," said Derrick. "The dumb fuck put the gun to his heart and pulled the trigger!"

"No," says I. "No!"

"That's what happened, man. There are witnesses. Plenty of 'em."

"Sure, sure," I say. "I believe you. What happened then?"

"Oh fuck!" says Derrick. "Before you know it, ALL the cops show up and all Hell breaks loose. The Federáles come, too. They question everybody and they all say it was an accident, that the cop took the gun from me and shot himself!"

"And that's all?" I ask.

"They took me down to the station and fined me for having an illegal weapon."

"Yer kidding? How much?"

"Do you really care?" asks Derrick, "Nine hundred pesos." It's a sum of about $110.

"And that's the end of it?" I ask.

"Apparently."

"Holy SHIT, Derrick," I exclaim. "How long were you in jail?"

"I wasn't ever in jail. I was AT the jailhouse for a while, never actually IN jail. Those guys know me. They know I'm not about to skip town for something so... loco!" he said. "I feel bad, man, but what can I do? The dumb fuck."

It was almost laughable. Not that I laugh at someone's death. But the Mexican cops are nearly universally disliked. Perhaps this man had a family who loved him. A mother and some kids of his own. Maybe they would miss him. But the streets of Valle probably would not. Score: Gringos 1, Policia NADA!

But this did not end the gringo's tale of woe and sorrow of course; in fact the end is some time in the future. The end is not in sight yet, and the tale turns more and more bizarre. Derrick spent the following Christmas packing his stuff in anticipation of leaving Mexico, probably for good, closing a saga that began more then twelve years ago when he first visited Valle de Bravo.

You see, the cop's family, like the families of all cops in Mexico I guess, is in line to collect a life insurance policy for his death, something around $10,000; a large sum of money for a poor Mexican family. So... They contacted the insurance company, who sent out an investigator. All the witnesses said it was an accident. They say the cop put the 'toy' pistol to his heart and pulled the trigger. Well... the insurance agent hears this and he says, 'Huh. We do not pay for suicide.' 'This was no suicide' say the family. 'Yes it is.' says the insurance rep. 'No it's NOT!' says the family.

But the insurance company makes no bones about it. 'Listen,' they say, 'you put a gun to your heart... you pull the trigger... this is no accident, this is suicide. And we don't pay for suicide, case closed.'

Well, now the family is really pissed. Not only have they lost their cop, they lost their money too. They decide to get even.

Derrick had been planning to spend the summer with his three-year-old Mexican daughter in Minnesota with his family anyway. The little girl would have more opportunity there, and become even more bi-lingual than she already is. When he hears what a hornets' nest he has stirred up, he packs his stuff and departs Valle de Bravo under cover of darkness.

Enter Aracelia, the mother of Derrick's daughter.

Derrick offers to let Aracelia live in his casa while he is gone. Derrick and Aracelia are separated due to Aracelia's excesses and Derrick's mistrust of her. But... they are friends enough that Derrick feels some responsibility for her. Plus, she's his daughter's mom of course. She moves into Derrick's vacant house.

Meanwhile, Derrick hires a local attorney to negotiate with the family of the deceased cop. According to the attorney, the family does not want vengeance, only what they consider their just due- the ten grand. So Derrick agrees to begin making payments for the family. During the summer he makes these payments on time.

But, also during the summer, a couple of men break in on Aracelia and demand to know how to find the gringo. At least, so says Aracelia. But she has been caught lying before, so Derrick doesn't know whether to believe her or not. This may just be a way for Aracelia to extort money from the gringo, to continue her wayward lifestyle. Derrick decides to disregard the story as a fabrication.

Meanwhile, Derrick and I continue our plans to offer hang gliding tours, as we have for some years. Derrick rents a house in San Miguel de Allende, where we have decided to headquarter our tours and fly from Cerro del Cubilete, in nearby Guanajuato. In the fall he moves down there with his daughter to begin work. He makes several trips to Valle, and has no problem. Then he gets a phone call in the middle of the night, on December 23 of this past year. An unfamiliar voice awakens him on the phone at 4AM.

"Tenemos de tu chaba!" it shouts. *We have your woman!* He thinks maybe he can hear scuffling in the background, and what may be muted suffering from a woman.

"Como?" he asks Derrick groggily. *What?*

"Queremos de tu bebe!" he hears, *WE WANT YOUR BABY!* The connection goes dead. The conversation lasts only seconds.

Derrick gets out of bed with a panic attack, and spends a sleepless night worrying about Aracelia, the mother of his child. By this time she has moved on from his house, and he is unable to phone her, or even locate her. There is nothing he can do, but wait. Under a threat like that, he is unwilling to go to Valle to investigate.

About 24 hours later, around sunrise, a vehicle pulls into an emergency clinic in Valle de Bravo. A man walks in and says he has found an injured woman, who needs emergency medical aid. The doctor rushes out to find Aracelia, who has been beaten senseless. He carries her into the clinic and stabilizes her. He knows Aracelia and he knows Derrick and he figures this is probably the result of a domestic quarrel. That morning he calls down to the small sporting goods shop that Derrick owns in Valle, and talks with Derrick's clerk, a girl named Mariana. He explains what happened.

Mariana says that Derrick couldn't have been the culprit here, because he was not in Valle these past few weeks. She calls Derrick and tells him what has happened in Valle de Bravo. Now Derrick is freaked. He calls the clinic and talks to the doctor, who is an amigo. The doctor says that Aracelia has just become conscious and that she is hysterical. Derrick must wait until tomorrow to speak with her. The gringo begins to re-pack his stuff and make ready to depart Mexico with his daughter. Meanwhile, he gets several phone calls where the caller simply hangs up.

Apparently, somehow or another, the culprits have gotten the gringo's number. Are they closing in?

The next day he is able to speak to Aracelia over a long-distance connection. She has compressed vertebrae, a dislocated hip, and has been beaten around the face. The doctor hasn't told her yet, but there is evidence that she has suffered other indignities.

She tells him that three masked men burst in on her at a casa where she was hiding, demanded to know of Derrick's whereabouts, and that when the only information she could give them was a phone number in San Miguel de Allende, they commence to beat her. That's the last she remembered, except awakening to a painful nightmare several times. About all Derrick can do is have Mariana pay the clinic from the cash in the till at his store, and promise to find a safe house for Aracelia. Within hours he has packed up and left San Miguel, Valle de Bravo, and Mexico behind, in exile.

That's the end of the story thus far. Our tour business is no more. Aracelia is recuperating somewhere. Derrick is with family in Minnesota, where we must assume he is safe. His little girl is enrolled in pre-school. Derrick is trying to get on with his life. I can return to Valle, because the thugs have never seen, probably never heard, of me. In fact I spent Christmas week there, flying hang gliders.

Stranger stories have come out of Mexico I'm sure. But I have not heard them lately.

Flier- Miguel Gutierrez Photo- Alfredo Yazbec
Village- Valle de Bravo

XC to the Fruit Stand or,
A Short, Meaningless Adventure

www.Wallaby.com

I flew twenty-five miles in my hang glider from Wallaby Ranch in Florida, one beautiful summer day. Now, this is not a remarkable distance by any means, but it was a very pleasant flight. Soon I was getting low and it was time to land.

Conveniently enough, I was over a giant green field. But the field was surrounded by a high barbed wire fence, which was not going to be fun at all. I didn't want to try lifting the glider over such a fence, so I lined up for an approach that would allow a landing in the field across the road instead. While on my downwind landing leg I would have two choices; the giant green field on the one hand, or the much tighter field on the other. This new field would make for a more interesting and exciting landing too, because it was much smaller; barely adequate actually.

I made my decision on downwind when it looked like I had the small field perfectly dialed. I turned a quick base-to-final, pulled the nose down, and greased it on in.

It was great fun.

From here it was simple to carry the wing over in front of a little fruit stand along side the highway, just a few steps away. I was quite happy as I set the glider down between the fruit stand and the busy highway. The air was redolent of fresh citrus.

I was standing there next to the wing enjoying my accomplishment, still wearing my harness, and with my helmet in my hand. I must have looked a lot like what I was: a glidehead who had just fallen from the sky.

Now, this may indeed be a rare sighting in the flatlands of Florida, a place not known for hang gliding. But suddenly a Cadillac braked hard to a halt, squawking the rubber, and swerved off the road to stop next to me. The automatic window on the passenger side rolled down and a blue-haired little old lady stuck her head out. She looked a great deal like Aunt Freida. "How much for a bag of oranges?" she smiled. She pointed to a stack of 'em next to me.

Of course, I did not know the answer to that question, I might have inquired of the shopkeeper, but there was none in sight. Plus, it seemed like a ridiculous thing to ask me.

So I took a wild guess, waving my helmet, "Ten dollars," I said.

She consulted with her companion for a moment and then fished the money from her purse. Still in my harness, I handed the bag through the window, and they drove off with a "Thanks!"

At that moment, the owner of the fruit stand appeared. "Where did you come from?" she asked, gazing up at the sky, marveling.

"How much for a bag of oranges?" I asked.

"Seven ninety-nine," she stated.

"Hallelujah," I said, handing her the ten spot.

"It was a wonderful flight, and I am up $2.01 for the day!"

Pit Stop on the Mexican Riviera or, Just Another Mexican Road Hazard...

Tania sat in the Ford-From-Hell with her shapely legs tightly crossed. She scowled at Walter, who knew he would have to stop somewhere soon. But there was nowhere; nowhere to pull far enough off the road to provide Tania with all the privacy she needed to take a pee. It was loco, and why did women have to be that way? A little privacy sure, no problem, Walter could understand that. But Tania had to have four walls and a door to lock tight behind her. It mattered not how unsanitary the facilities may prove, only the privacy counts.

Traveling south down the Mexican Riviera about three hours out of Playa Azul they were on a long stretch of highway between towns. The country reminded Walter of a tropical Big Sur with much vertical terrain. He spotted a rare wide spot in the road, swung the Ford in and slammed on the brakes. Tania cast her gaze around and came back disapprovingly to Walter.

"¿Aquí?" she asked incredulously, "¡Aquí!" *Here?*

Walter stepped out of the truck and walked around the front and unzipped his fly. Relief was slow in coming so to speak, because Walter had a slight hard on. This often happened when he was near Tania. She was just so sexy, so golden-brown and slender and curvy, so fresh-smelling. It didn't hurt that she never denied the gringo his pleasure either... Ridiculously enough, thinking of her having to pee did not help with his symptoms. He wanted only to watch.

They had passed very little oncoming traffic in the past hour and Walter thought that yes, here was an excellent place to pee. Indeed, here was as good as any pit-stop he'd ever seen anywhere; the cliffs rose overhead until they disappeared in magnificent splendor while pelícanos and gaviótas soared on a cool sea breeze that smelled of fresh salty brine. But the chances of anyone human interrupting Tania's rest were slim to none. If she'd just agree, the gringo would cup his hands under her skinny ass, and let her pee right there...

Still, Walter could tell by her tone that it was no use. He finished pissing best he could under the circumstances, and

climbed up on the rack with the gliders to get a good look at
the land. From here he could peer over the tall grass that had
lined the road for the last fifty kilometers. The grass must be
ten feet tall he thought. It leaned over and otherwise
encroached on the highway, rendering every bend in the road
a blind turn. Peering over the grass he noticed a small and
very private opening, almost like a tiny natural ladies' room
he decided. He jumped down from the truck and pushed his
way through the grass.

"¿Donde vas?" demanded Tania. *Where are you going?* She
just wasn't happy with this pit stop.

"Aquí al baño," said Walter. *Here to the bathroom.*

"¿Como que baño?" she asked skeptically. *What bathroom?*
From her tone of voice Walter could tell she disapproved of
any 'baño' out here in the middle of ningun lugar. He just
didn't understand. How could anyone put themselves through
such agony for the sake of a little modesty. It didn't make any
sense to him at all. Just pull 'em down and let 'er loose fer
Chrissake. There's nobody to see.

"Ven te aquí," he demanded. He heard the door of the Ford
creak open and slam shut. The ten-foot grasses parted and
Tania leaned in to inspect the natural facilities. She was
dressed for travel- in shorts and tee shirt, sandals on her feet.
Her toenails were painted pink, and she smelled of coconut
butter. She held a roll of toilet paper in hand. She was just so
gorgeous, even with a scowl on her face. A long step from
where they stood the cliff dropped off to the ocean below, a
good two hundred foot drop. She could probably hang her
shapely buns right off the cliff and pee directly into the big
blue, he thought.

Tania appeared desperate indeed, and Walter thought sure
she was about to cave in. She squeezed her legs together and
held her crotch, scoping out the facilities. Walter hoped she
would let him watch- just him, and nobody else. She glanced
around the natural room, the two of them hidden from view in
the tall grass. She looked back at the Ford, barely visible just
a few feet away. Walter wished she would take the piss, she
was about to cave in... and then let him have his way with her,
right there on the spot. When it came to sex, Tania was quite
uninhibited. They had made love in some strange places. The
gringo liked nothing more than to just pull off the road, jump
in the back of the Ford-From-Hell, pull down Tania's shorts or
pull up her skirt, and let her have it. She never denied him,

never said 'no'. He could feel his erection tugging at the thought of her wriggling underneath him...

But pee? Oh NO. That was another story altogether.

Instead she turned her pretty face skyward. There, slowly traversing the Wild Blue Heavens, looking like a fragile dot in the sky, a jumbo jet left a contrail at thirty thousand feet. That did it...

"Aqui no," she stated simply. *Not here.* She spun on her pretty foot, parted the grass with a shapely ankle and climbed back into the Ford.

Walter just couldn't believe it. A jet! A jet passing overhead! Sometimes women were no fun, completely irrational. Other times... you just had to have one. He too climbed back into the Ford and they recommenced their journey south.

Walter stuck a cassette into the tape player. They were about forty minutes out from the next town he figured. Let her suffer until then, she had incredible stamina. They would find some public rest room, unsanitary, probably reeking of piss and shit, an enormous fly-covered shit cone standing in a toilet bowl that had ceased to function years ago... a trash can overflowing with used butt-wipe...

But PRIVATE!

Flies would be buzzing around inside the shitter, pulling inverted landings on her nalgas and her nethers. Unbelievable. But Tania held her bladder and pouted in the seat next to him. She gathered her knees in her arms, affording the gringo a tiny view of her silky panties, which he glanced at in hunger, it was tough to keep his eyes on the road, his hands on the wheel. She looked away from Walter and pouted out the window. Walter remembered those very same panties... he had pulled them off her body with his teeth... he had spit them onto the floor, he had dived back down on her silky muffin... he had eaten her until she begged for release...

The tunes cranked incongruously, a great Jackson Browne hit:

> *Runnin' on empty*
> *Runnin' on*
> *Runnin' wild!*
> *Runnin' into the sun*
> *While I'm runnin' behind*

Suddenly, while negotiating another blind curve, Walter caught sight of a plaid shirt walking on his side of the road. As Tania screamed, he swerved out of his lane in an evasive maneuver. A flash of leathery face flew past Tania's window, a dusky wrinkled face, a face showing dumb terror and bloodshot eyes. At the same moment a clatter of sticks broke across the windshield and went flying past, splintering in all directions. Walter swung back into his lane to avoid the possible oncoming bus. There was no traffic ahead, and maybe none behind either, but Walter could not see more than a hundred feet in either direction, due to the blind curves and tall grass.

"¡Para te!" screamed Tania. *Stop!* She was quite visibly shaken now- the old face has plowed into her side.

Walter was reluctant to stop anywhere in the near distance, there was just nowhere to safely pull off the road; no shoulder, no wide spot, only the tall grass with a mountain wall on one side and a precipice falling hundreds of feet to the Pacific on the other. Yet he knew that Tania had seen what he had seen: an old man, a peasant type, had been walking along the road carrying a stack of bamboo poles across his shoulders. Where he came from, or where he could be going, was a good question but of little concern at the moment.

"¡Para te!" screamed Tania again. "¡El viejíto!" *The old man!* She wanted to stop, but where? Disregarding common sense, Walter slammed on the brake and swung the Ford off the highway as far as he dared. He threw open his door and jumped out. Tania kneeled in the seat now looking through the back window. She wore a look of horror and Walter was surprised she had not yet peed her panties.

"¡Esperes aqui!" he ordered. *Wait here!* It was an order that did not need repeating. Walter dashed back down the road, praying for no traffic. If a vehicle approached, he would signal to slow it down. Several hundred feet down the road he came upon the old piasano who was moaning and muttering and only now getting to his feet. The old man crawled in the middle of the road and held his hands to his right ear. As Walter approached the old peasant heard his footsteps and turned. He looked at Walter and started a low howling sound and grimaced at the gringo. When he pulled his hand away from his ear it came away bloody. Walter could see that the ear had been nearly separated from his head. It was an unrecognizable tangle of skin and cartilage dangling by his lower jaw. Except for the gusher of blood and a tear in the knee of his trousers, the old peasant looked otherwise unharmed.

Bamboo poles, some as long as fifteen or twenty feet, lay scattered across the road like pick-up-sticks. The old peasant had been carrying them somewhere, lashed in a big bundle to his back. Why he had thought there was no danger in that act, especially since he was walking with his back to traffic, Walter could not explain. There simply had not been enough room for the old piasano, his bundle of sticks, and the Ford-From-Hell too, the Ford had won handily. When Walter swerved too late, some of the bamboo had caught an upright of the Ford's glider rack and ripped the whole load off the old man's shoulder, sending them scattering and spinning him around under the Ford's onslaught. The old fool had appeared for a brief instant through Tania's window and then disappeared as quickly. It was a wonder he wasn't dead.

Pendejo hijo de puta!

But he wasn't dead. Instead, he stood on shaky legs and sized up the gringo. He stuck the bloody paw back up to the missing ear and jabbed the other- palm up- at Walter.

"HUyyHUyyah!" he said. "HUyyOHH!" or something to that effect, Walter couldn't be sure. "MMMphrrugga!" It was not Spanish. It certainly was not English. It may have been some Mayan dialect, but it was probably just the pain doing the talking.

But the old guy wasn't totally out of it. With one hand on his ear, he continued to poke his other hand at Walter, in the universal sign of the beggar, *Just give me some money,* it said, *and everything will be fine.*

Walter reached reluctantly into his pocket and grabbed a wad of pesos. He wanted to kick the stupid old hijo de le chingada for causing the whole frightful mess; just kick him off the cliff into the sea. Let the crabs and the seagulls feast on his old, used-up carcass. The dumb shit! He wanted to do the whole encounter over again, and swerve into him this time. Make a blotch of road-kill out of him and leave it to the buzzards.

He handed the old guy a couple of small bills instead. The piasano grabbed them, and Walter too. He pulled himself up close to the gringo, engulfing him in an aroma of sweaty unwashed body and rotten breath. He leaned on Walter and said it again.

"MUGGAwah wha! DOEgahwah!"

This time Walter noticed that the old guy had no teeth as well, just a rotten maw. He yanked his hand away from the old man's grasp, nearly knocking him off his feet in the process. The paisano stumbled towards the gringo, tripped over some of his sticks, and went back down hard onto his knees.

"Oh shit," said Walter. He grabbed the old guy and pulled him to the roadside. The viejíto in turn, held his now empty paw out to Walter.

"TahHaw!" He declared. "Mas!"

This last sound Walter recognized. *More!*

The gringo backed away from the encounter and back-pedaled away from the old piasano. The bum came stumbling after him, forsaking the bamboo scattered across the road. He hollered again at Walter:

"MAS!" he demanded.

But he was no match for the gringo, who sprinted back to the Ford. He came around the bend in time to find Tania squatting on her shapely brown haunches, her panties pulled down around her ankles, a stream of golden pee splashing the road. She held the Ford's door handle with one hand and squatted on tiptoes in an effort to reduce the amount of pee that might splash her pretty feet.

Walter stood transfixed by the spectacle; as he watched she gave a final squirt and stood, wiggling back into her shorts up as she did. Walter couldn't believe his eyes; Tania had done it after all!

"¿Que pasó con el señor?" she asked. *What happened to the man?* Her face was etched with concern. She said nothing about her undignified pee. "¿Esta muerto?" she asked. *Is he dead?*

"¡No esta muerto nadie!" said Walter. *No one is dead!* The bus Walter feared roared into sight now, fortunately going the other way. Walter waved to the driver to slow down and heard the hiss of air brakes. As he looked back down the road he thought *maybe the old dumbass is dead now.* They jumped in and he swung the Ford back onto the road and roared ahead. Tania started to cry.

"¡Mataste el señor!" she cried. *You've killed that man!* The gringo looked at her but said nothing. If she didn't believe him the first time, she wouldn't believe him now.

There was flying to be done somewhere, best just to focus on that...

Glideheads Visit El Salvador or, No Pesos Among Thieves

I arrived back in my home turf of Lake Tahoe, Nevada after a long winter of tropical skies in Mexico and Guatemala. I headed straight for Glide Mountain and a reunion with the locals who fly there on a daily basis. After flying we all bellied up to a local beer garden for happy hour. On the way to the bar I had the opportunity to stop at the Crystal Bay post office to retrieve a winter's worth of correspondence. Now, over a cold one, I began to sort through my mail. Amid all the overdue bills and junk mail I came upon a missive postmarked from San Salvador, Central America. Intrigued, I cut it open first to find the following invitation:

Club de Vuelo Libre
Apartado Postal
San Salvador
El Salvador
America Centro

Sr. John Olson
93 Safari Sky Tours
PO Box 581
Crystal Bay, NV.
U.S.A.

Estimado Volador,
We are the hang gliding club located in San Salvador, Central America. We know you are the operator of Safari Sky Tours who brings pilots to Mexico and Guatemala each winter. We wish to invite you here to San Salvador to experience our flying sites. We have flying from mountains, ridges and volcanoes. We fly over lakes and beaches and jungles. We have hang gliders here that you are welcome to fly so you can leave yours at home. You will discover that El Salvador is at peace now and that we welcome tourists. The climate is agreeable and the flying is consistent. Also, our women are very beautiful.

Please respond soon,
Sincerely, Chito Ulloa, Presidente
Club de Vuelo Libre, San Salvador (371) 2-02-02

I passed the invitation around the bar and listened to the resultant commentary as I continued to sort my mail.
"El Salvador huh?"

"Where is that anyway?"

"You know... it's in the news. Some kinda war zone I think."

"Hey man, you ever been there?"

"Club duh Voolah Libber what?"

"You better go man, sez they got pretty women. Maybe you can find one after all."

"Baah ha ha!"

The boys in the bar had a good time at my expense as they read it over. Flying in El Salvador? Waa ha ha!

"Of course I'm going," I said. "Who better but me? When you get this kind of invite it's not polite to say 'no'. You guys got one night to get me drunk and then I'm outta here and you may never see me again." I was pleased to notice that no one at the bar was really surprised that I would dash off on such a hair-brained adventure in some far-flung land. After all, I had a reputation to maintain. "I'm going alright. Right after the last beer. And who's going with me anyway? There's new skys and new horizons out there my amigos. Who's buying this round?"

The locals had all gathered in my honor. Terry Cook was there, and Joel Craig and Gregor and Gordy, Mork and Matt and Matthew. An irregular bunch of flying disciples, one by one they poured a beer down my throat. Before long we were drinking tequila with lime and hollering about this and that. Soon the whole scene evaporated in a beer haze and the next thing I knew I was sleeping it off in the bed of my pickup.

Welcome back to Tahoe gringo!

The next day I found the invite again and read it over. I dialed the number listed therein and was connected to Chito Ulloa himself. Chito informed me that we had met briefly at launch above Lake Atitlan in the central Guatemala highlands. It was on the strength of that encounter that he'd decided to send the invitation that I now considered. By the time I hung up the phone I had assured Chito that I would catch the first available flight headed south. Chito in turn agreed to meet me at the airport on the coastal plains of El Salvador.

I found a listing for the El Salvadoran embassy and inquired about entry requirements. Then I called another old flying buddy- Bob Ortiz from the San Francisco area. Bob had accompanied me on other flying tours and had once confessed he would fly these places with nobody but me, and that, of course, had pumped up my ego. Bob was self-employed and always ready to take a flying vacation. Aside from being an accomplished pilot and old leather, Bob was a master at growing 'da kine' buds. He'd grown up in Hawaii, he explained, and learned the fine art of cultivation from his father who used the herb for "medicinal purposes". Whatever, back then Bob and I shared an appreciation for the sweet and stony effects of 'sin semilla' marijuana.

"Hey Pancho," I said now over the phone. Bob knew right away who was calling since I'm the only one who calls him "Pancho". Cross a couple of bandoleros over his chest, hand him a jug of mezcal and a machete, and Bob could easily pass for a famous Mexican revolutionary.

Except for the fact that he spoke not a word of Español that is.

But I still called him Pancho and learned that all over Mexico if I introduced him as 'El hijo de Pancho Villa', doors that had previously been locked would suddenly swing free for us. "Hey Pancho," I said. "Pack your bags amigo, we're going flying."

"Oh yeah?" Bob's voice came over the line. "Where to now Bwana?" Bob called me Bwana for my notable ability to get us lost in faraway lands. It was a quality I'd cultivated over the years. "I heard you made it home. How was the trip?" he inquired. Last I'd seen Bob was when he boarded the bus out of Valle de Bravo. Or was it Panajachel?

"There'll be time for a recap later," I explained. "I want to meet you tomorrow at the El Salvadoran embassy in San Francisco. You'll need proof of citizenship, two mug shot photos and a copy of your criminal records."

"El Salvador, huh?" came Bob's reply. "Oh boy, I hear the women are really beautiful there. But how is the flying? Aren't they havin' a war there?"

"Just get down there tomorrow at noon," I said. "We can discuss the details then," and hung up. No sense getting worked up until we had visas in hand. I jumped behind the wheel of the Ford-From-Hell and drove over Highway 80 and Donner summit. It was a lovely spring day; there was still snow on the higher peaks, and my mind wandered as I drove. Something compels me to visit and, more importantly, to fly in foreign lands. Why can't I be happy staying put in one place like so many of my friends? For that matter why can't I be happy standing around on solid ground like most of the rest of humanity? These questions and more burned briefly at my psyche and then extinguished with a whimper.

"Wahooo!" I hollered, and cranked some rock 'n roll on the stereo. "Hasta luego gringos! Looks like I'm going hang gliding in Central America!"

The next afternoon found Bob and I in the embassy making small talk with the secretary; a very attractive woman indeed, who assured us that her country was finally at peace, the Sandanistas having begun negotiations with the government, and that they were eager to have tourism return to their country. 'Maribel Zaragosa' read the nameplate on her desk, and if she was an example of your typical El Salvadoran woman, there was hope for me yet.

"Did you bring all your documents?" I asked, turning to Bob.

"Of course," said Pancho. "I had to return to the police records twice but I finally got it all," he added with a proud look on his face. Now he held up a computer-generated document that folded down like your wallet cardfile, flip flop flip flop flip...

I was shocked. Grabbing Pancho's records I started reading through them- a list that began with an entry from 1962 for marijuana cultivation and continued on and on;

CULTIVATION 1968
CULTIVATION 1969
CULTIVATION 1973
CULTIVATION 1974
CULTIVATION 1978
There was a brief hiatus until-
CULTIVATION 1986
CULTIVATION 1988
and so on...

I was appalled! Here my friend Bob the revolucionísta look-alike was a hardened criminal type, and I had no idea! "What were you up to between 1978 and 1986?" I queried him. "Working in community service?"

Oh that? Those were the Gerry Brown years," replied Bob. "Tolerance was the rule back then. They kept busting me and then throwing the charges out. I only grow for my own usage, I've never done any time."

I remained distressed and began to contemplate the solo journey ahead of me. Surely if the Salvadoran embassy demanded a review of our criminal records before granting us entry visas, then they would not allow this unsavory dope fiend to sully their sacred soil? I was wishing Bob had cut his hair and shaved too, instead of showing up looking like Phineas Phreak, when a door off the waiting room was suddenly thrown open and we were summoned into the inner sanctum of the embassy. We were seated before a clerk who glanced only briefly through bifocals at our paper work. In a flash he had typed up the official documents, stapled our photos thereon and placed the official stamp with a loud thump.

"Buen viaje señores," he offered with a yawn. *Have a nice trip.* And then, "Próximo!" It looked as though we were both in!

To my considerable surprise Bob and I were going hang gliding in war torn El Salvador! "Kind of makes you wonder what types of criminal acts you must perpetrate to be denied entry into El Salvador, huh amigo?" I asked Pancho as we made our exit. He didn't swallow the bait.

Our flight touched down on the tarmac with a squawk and a lurch. Pancho and I disembarked into the stifling heat and humidity of tropical sea level. The air hit us like a blast furnace and the white concrete of the airport glared back like a hot plate in Hell. I was immediately drenched with sweat.

Glancing upward I noticed the sky was really quite blue, and there were telltale wisps of water vapor topped with the first cumulus clouds of the day; certain signs of the necessary thermal activity we hoped would carry us high into the wild blue yonder. Better yet were the throngs of vultures that circled the Heavens. My spirits lifted after the long flight.

We were met there by Chito's sister Nancy and whisked into the mountains. Along the highway we passed many cane fields and I counseled Pancho against a landing in these fields. As a hang glider pilot I have mixed emotions for canefields. If faced with the choice of landing in a canefield or, say, a busy highway or a jungle forest, I would definitely opt for the cane.

But I had landed my glider in a cane field once outside of Colima, Mexico, and vowed to avoid that situation, if at all possible, in the future. I had flared just fine, and the tall cane had arrested my descent while my feet were still some inches off the ground. After some exertion I was able to unclip my harness and drop to what I figured would be terra firma. During the drop the cane slashed at my feet and poked at my eyes. The ground was not so firma after all but pure muck that sucked at my shoes. Glancing down I noticed a snake slithering off in fright. Then another. A rat scurried by and stared back boldly as though a gringo dropping down from the sky was not such an unusual annoyance. I'd yanked and tugged at my glider for some minutes to extricate it from the cane clutches and by then a small crowd of machete-wielding campesinos had gathered to see the gringo finally emerge, torn and bleeding from the struggle. It was not a beautiful moment from my flying career.

Now we drove up the highway towards the looming volcanic cone that towers over the capital city. We dropped into a valley of lush and chaotic jungle that holds San Salvador in its grasp. Nancy chatted pleasantly about what we could expect over the next two weeks in the way of flying. She pointed out that no one had flown in this country for the last twelve years, due to what she referred to euphemistically, as "las penas"- *the troubles.*

We drove past the city's most imposing edifice, a skyscraper by any standards, all steel-and-glass standing quite alone and forlorn amidst a tangle of single-level urban sprawl. Shot to Hell by the artillery fire the building had suffered from 'the troubles', several gaping holes yawned back at us from above, and there seemed to be no glass in the windows, at all. I wondered if there were people inside. Nancy explained that no one would work there because it made such tempting target practice for the Sandanistas. Finally, we were deposited at a pleasant hotel where we would spend a considerable amount of time languishing poolside and waiting for Chito.

The next day found us gathering at the hotel and meeting the local pilots. We were visibly distressed to learn that so little hang gliding, or any civil aviation for that matter, had been done prior to our arrival, or any flying at all since the war had begun more than a decade ago. Some of the locals were still in possession of ancient gliders that should have been retired years ago. Not to worry, Chito explained, as he would personally supervise our expedition.

We drove through the traffic of San Salvador to Chito's house that morning, to pick up the gliders. Pancho and I were not overjoyed to spot them hanging under the eaves where it looked as though they had been forever, or for twelve years at least: the wing bags were very faded on their bottoms, and covered with pigeon shit on their tops. I groaned inwardly at what I saw and I was tempted to order Chito back to the airport- chalk the whole trip up to a terrible mistake. Certainly, these gliders were not up to our lofty standards.

But Chito dropped first one wing and then the other at our feet, and swept the shit off with a broom. I timidly opened the zipper a few feet to see what was inside and was surprised to see fresh sailcloth. I unzipped the wing all the way and found a UP Axis 13 that had seen very little action. The cloth, anyway, was quite new. Pancho spoke first:

"Ahhh!" he exclaimed, "that's what I fly at home!" Pancho was essentially making 'dibs' on this wing. I turned my attention to the other bag- equally covered in shit, and with a bird's nest falling out of the nose plate.

We unzipped the bag to more fresh sailcloth and Chito explained: "I never flew the Axis. I only got a few hours on the Demon. Then I stuck them here, under the eves."

The gliders did, indeed, look to be in better shape than I had imagined at first glance. The Demon is a Comet clone- I had never flown a Demon, but I had lots of time on Comets. "I guess I'm stuck with the Demon," I said to Pancho, who was visibly relieved. He quickly shouldered the Axis and we totted our wings to Chito's truck. We were off to fly The Savior...

"¡Vamanos!"

We were taken first to the village of Los Altos (The Heights) above the capital, an outpost apparently famous as a site where Sandanista soldiers had once lobbed grenades towards the government buildings some fifteen hundred feet below.

Chito Ulloa brandished his machete in a menacing fashion. Several meters distant stood two local farmers, campesino types, who also brandished their machetes in what looked to be a Salvadoran stand-off. Pancho and I meanwhile, were in the process of setting up the gliders that Chito was providing for us. We all had gathered atop a nearly vertical cliff that had been, many years ago, the official launch site for the Club de Vuelo Libre, San Salvador.

But the launch was now covered with a field of tall corn that stood in the way of our flying, and Chito had begun to hack away at the crop, looking very stylish and wildly out of place in Gucci loafers and gold chains. His Drakkar cologne was quickly weaning thin, his shoes were soon covered in dust and the chains swung wildly as he toiled. Sweat beaded his forehead and flew wildly in all directions, large wet circles formed at the armpits of his starched white shirt, and he generally contrasted sharply with the peasants, who glowered from the foreground in obvious disapproval but lifted not a finger to help. Below us lay the convoluted sprawl of suburban San Salvador and one small field that looked possible for a landing, but was surrounded by houses, cardboard shacks, power lines and numerous small barrancas. As a landing field it was marginal at best.

Thermal cycles were blowing up the ridge however, and buzzards and hawks were even now hooking into the lift and skying out with lazy circles, becoming tiny dots in the blue sky above. But an impasse had developed now over the usage of this particular patch of 'milpa' and things were about to become nasty. Chito hurled curses at the two farmers and insisted that this crop of food was being grown illegally, and that no 'pinche campesinos' could tell him, Chito Ulloa, Presidente of the Club de Vuelo Libre, what to do about it. He continued to swing the machete, quite red-in-the-face now, regardless of his Latino complexion.

One of the farmers held an old bolt-action 22-caliber rifle swung over his shoulder, and a scowl grew on his stoic face. Pancho and I were poised to run, we wondered if we had just met our first Sandinista? Pancho informed me that he didn't like the looks of the landing field below anyway, and would not fly until he could actually walk the field and get a better look at it. "Really, I don't think I'll fly here at all," he observed. "This is crazy."

At this I realized that all our effort may well be for naught and stepped in to offer a compromise.

"Parate un minuto, Chito," I suggested. *Stop a minute.* "Creo que asi es suficiente." *I think that's sufficient.* A regular dervish at work, Chito had already made quite a dent in the 'milpa' and we could likely get off in the space he had created, if we just had a nice cycle. "Ask them how many Corona to pay for the damage we've done." Chito continued to swing the machete as though he had not heard. "Come on Chito, I don't want to take the food out of these peoples' mouths, or the money from their pockets. This is just hang gliding for Chrissake. Let's negotiate." I would be soaring this ridge after all, it was my ass that would be hanging out there, quite literally a tempting target for any pot-shot.

A brief meeting ensued with both sides in negotiations. The peasant farmers wanted one hundred Corona- about twenty bucks- for the corn that lay scattered on the ground, a ridiculously large sum of money according to our host, but one that I was quite ready to pay, just to stop any bloodshed and be able to check out this ridge. We'd come a long way, after all. But Chito insisted on our behalf that fifty centavos- about ten cents- would cover the cost nicely, and they should be happy at that. "Cinquenta centavos, cinquenta centavos," he chanted as he continued to swing the machete and gold chains. In the end we settled on twenty Corona and I threw in two cold cervesas from the cooler, and now the farmers settled down to watch the proceedings. Pancho conceded that he was not about to fly this place anyway, due to the marginal landing area, and that we had two weeks of flying ahead of us. He too, relaxed with a beer.

Meanwhile Chito and I performed a pre-flight inspection on his old glider and then, with a run, I got a taste of Salvadoran skies.

The ridge was working well that day and I soared there above Los Altos for some two hours. I kept looking over the back towards the ocean for a more forgiving landing area, but seeing nothing but more forbidding foothills and miles and miles of canefields. In the most distant reaches of my vision the pale blue arc of the Mar Pacífico was only just visible. I soared the ridge in thermal lift while I watched Pancho and Chito drive down the mountain and arrive at the small landing area field. I tried to enjoy myself too, flying wing tip to wing tip with several hawks and an old buzzard that was hanging under my starboard tip and looking at me with what I can only describe as an amorous look. But it's not easy enjoying a flight when you know all along that you must land down there, amidst the arroyos and powerlines and other man-made obstacles.

When the time came I blazed in hot over top and parallel to the powerlines, sort of diving on them as it were. Then I made a hard right turn just as I got down close to the cables and made it into the small field with room to spare. Pancho ran over, trailing a small band of gleefully curious kids, to congratulate me.

"Well... you made that look easy," said Pancho. "I see you've got the landing technique down."

"I wouldn't want to make a regular thing outta that but now 'n then... good practice, keep me on my toes." Pancho nodded and grinned. "What say we hustle you back up there for a glass-off in the smooth evening air?" I inquired. Pancho always liked a good glass-off.

"Noooo Bwana," he said. "Now that I've seen this field I like it even less. Didn't you find anywhere better than this place to land?" It was pretty bad; tall electrical cables surrounded the field on three sides. The field was dissected by several gullies and looked from above much like a hand, with skinny little plateaus for fingers and treacherous ditches for spaces in between. No way would I bring bunches of gringos here. I could envision someone now, hanging from the power lines amid terrible arcs and flashes. "Maybe somewhere over the back," intoned Pancho. He was waving a hopeful hand in the general direction of the Pacific ocean.

"No amigo," I said. "Believe me, if I'd seen anywhere bigger I'd been there by now. The beach looks impossibly far away with nothing landable in between except canefields." Pancho shook his head in disbelief and dismay, and we began to dismantle the glider. Chito came along then and shook my hand.

"Bravo volador, bravo," he said. "You know that was the first flight from Los Altos in many years, verdad?" Chito was almost as excited as I was.

"Chito," I inquired, "were those powerlines here the last time this place was flown?"

"No amigo, no avia nada esto," he said with a wave of his hand. *No, there was none of this.* His look encompassed the surrounding cardboard and corrugated tin shacks as well. Many children had gathered by now. I noticed a fresh cow pie at my feet and I wondered how many of the beasts could occupy this field at once and how would I like to land here when the cows were home?

Bob and I bagged my glider and Chito dropped us off at our hotel. We would spend the next few days eating and drinking poolside, waiting for Chito, who would always arrive too late to accomplish anything. During the nights we would hit the streets in search of some culture and female companionship. We didn't find much of either. There were attractive girls, but they seemed to want nothing to do with us. We found a small club where they played folksy music at night, but nothing much happened there either.

Chito finally supplied us with a driver, Raul, who proceeded to tour us all over El Salvador in search of a hypothetical launch, mythical perhaps, one that also had a decent landing area.

We climbed the volcano over town that looked so promising, only to discover that the army held a tight reign over the peak and would not grant passage to a couple of gringos with gliders. In fact, they laughed at the notion, seemed to think that the gringos who appeared at the gate with long skinny bundles atop their vehicle were just plain loco. We visited another town in the highlands that was said to have been a rebel stronghold and that was indeed plastered with Sandanista propaganda and anti-government slogans, but here too the troops had arrived and held the mountain top. We ended up on the flanks of yet another volcano, far from the capital city. Here the former launch was overgrown by a tangle of jungle forest and Bob and I and Raul set to work with machetes, saws and an axe in an effort to make something happen. But there was no real landing area here either, and the wind blew very cross all the while, until we became so discouraged that we finally left, having made quite a dent in the trees on the side of the volcano- all for naught.

Day Nine of our journey found us back at our hotel in a foul mood. Bob had bought a bottle of aguardiente to take home as a gift but was threatening to drink away his flying blues. We decided to take one more shot at Los Altos. At least then Bob will have had some airtime in his logbook from El Salvador. If we were to give the subsequent flight a name, it might have been *When The Cows Come Home Grab Your Wallet*.

I wire-launched Bob, who sailed into quite reasonable lift, and then clipped in myself. This was our last chance to fly El Salvador, and it came down to a repeat performance from Los Altos. This time, Bob would fly as well, resigned to landing amidst the powerlines. He had walked the field to find the best approach, and stood under the cables to get a feel for their height. As he sailed away from launch, I knew he was nervous. He turned left into the lift band and thermals, and immediately started to circle out.

I followed and found abundant lift. This was good; it would give us both some airtime, for which we were desperate. We spent an hour or so topping-out at cloudbase and touring the capital. No one shot at us meanwhile. Well... if they did... at least they didn't hit us.

All the while, I was watching the field below which was becoming quite full of spectators- all the children who had been there the previous week, and their brothers, sisters, tías and tíos- the place was filling up pretty good. Now that they had seen where we would land, they wanted a better look, wanted to be part of the action. But then I saw something really frightening; the cattle were being set out in the field to graze! Bob had been worried about this. I had too. What rotten luck!

Shit!

Worse- the lift was slowly dying as the afternoon wore on. The sun was leaving the east slopes and moving around to the back side. Soon, we were working thermals that were drifting over from the back. The wind was switching, too. There was nothing left to do but go in for a landing.

I went first, indeed, it seemed that I was being flushed and had little choice. I flew out over the LZ and began to circle down. I was distressed to see Bob follow me out. There would be little opportunity for me to land and clear the field, or even chase off a few vacas, if he continued out now. I put him out of my mind and dove on in to land.

I pulled the nose down and dove at the wires, referencing them as though they were the ground: I dove parallel and directly over them until I had to pull up or hit them. I followed them along until my airspeed had moderated a little, cranked a hard right turn and lined up on the middle finger- the Bird you might say. I dropped right in to ground-effect and flared to a stop amongst a crowd of running, cheering kids, and a startled herd of cows.

I quickly carried my wing out of the field and dropped in beneath the powerlines. As I stripped off my harness I was surrounded by what seemed like an entire village. I had two thoughts; 1) my wallet is in the glovebox of my harness and, 2) I'd better scare off a few of those cows in a hurry- to make room for Pancho.

I dropped the harness- wallet and all- and made a mad dash for the cows. The bovines saw the gringo charging at them and cleared out, leaving a perfect runway for Pancho, who settled in behind them for a beautiful flare. I dashed back to my harness where the crowd was still gathered. I immediately flipped over my harness, unzipped the glovebox and looked for my wallet.

It was gone!

The children who had gathered at my harness must have been first delighted and then surprised by this chain of events. First: the winged gringo had dropped the strange outfit he was wearing and made a mad dash, arms waving wildly, at the herd of heifers. Next, someone had taken advantage of the gringo's careless stupidity, and unzipped the harness glovebox to find a wallet stashed there. *What else did the foreigner expect?* Whoever had done this had then re-zipped the harness and ran away. Finally, the gringo had returned at the same harried speed, dropped to his knees, and immediately checked the glovebox. They must all have understood that they shared the blame for what had come to pass. They could even be considered accomplices. For now, they all stood up from my harness, and began to back away from me. Their eyes got big, their mouths formed Os, and about then I began to howl.

"¡Ladron!" I yelled, stomping about. "¡Ladron! ¡Ladron!" *Thief! Thief!* THIEF!

I was immediately set into action as well. I grabbed the two nearest, or maybe slowest of the kids- it didn't matter WHO I grabbed- they must have all known who was the guilty 'ladron'. I held the kids by the scruff of their shirt collars and continued my harangue: "¡Pinches Ladrones!" I yelled again. "¡Quiero mi cartera!" *I want my wallet!* The two kids I was holding protested loudly, they took swats at my hand and tried to wiggle out of their shirts. But it was no good; I was not about to relinquish anything more. I wanted that wallet- not so much for the cash; it contained very little- but I needed my license, credit cards, entry visa, photos, etc... These little shits were my only hope.

The rest of the kids in the LZ were having a wonderful time at my expense. They seemed not to care that two of their own were being held for ransom. They pranced about the field, laughing and exhorting the big gringo to fly again. "Otra vez," they yelled. "¡Otra vez!"

Then Pancho came lugging his wing across the field, a big grin plastered all over his face. "Man!" he exclaimed. "That was great!"

"Not so great now," I advised. "Someone stole my wallet."

"When?" asked Pancho incredulously. He must have been quite confused; there just had been no time for thievery. "Where?"

"Right here!" I said. "Bunch of thieves, one stupid gringo."

"Whatdaya mean here?" asked Pancho. "You've only been here about a minute."

"When I ran after the cows like a dang fool," I explained. "My wallet was in the glovebox when I dropped my harness. I ran out in the field and scared off the cows, then I ran back to my harness and... GONE! That's why I've got these two sprouts. I'm holding them for ransom." I continued to rail at the injustice I had suffered, and at the perspicacity of Salvadoran thieves, when suddenly my attention was drawn towards one of the arroyos at the far end of the field. There, a teenage youth was scrambling along the gully and hollering at me. "¡Señor!" he yelled, "¡SEÑOR!" He held what looked like my wallet above his head but from such a distance I was not sure. But he ran directly at me, a big smile lighting his face.

It was my wallet, all right. The youth handed it over to me with great satisfaction.

Where had he found it?

How had he even known it was stolen?

Something was fishy here, but I didn't matter, I thanked the boy, and examined the contents. I had several types of currency in that wallet before it disappeared. There were US Dollars, Guatemalan Quetzals, Salvadoran Corona, and Mexican Pesos, all of which counted together didn't add up to fifty bucks. Now, opening the wallet, I discovered that the thieves had stolen the dollars, the Quetzals, and the Corona... But they had left the pesos.

"Anything left?" asked Pancho who was still in his harness.

"Oh yea," said I. "There's some left. Wait 'till I get back to Mexico next winter," I told Pancho. "I'm gonna tell those glideheads in Valle de Bravo to go fly Salvador. *The thieves here don't accept pesos.*" It was our Big Lesson from The Savior. That, and: *There just ain't many places to hang glide in El Salvador.*

Pancho dug into his stach of Corona and lent me ten to pay the reward for my wallet, and we called the airlines, switching our flights to depart sooner than planned.

Ants In His Pants or,
Terror In The Sky

Walter pulled up to the airstrip in the Texas hill country on a fair spring day. A gentle breeze was blowing down the runway and a crowd of hang gliding enthusiasts had gathered at one end of the piste. The visitor parked his truck just off the grass and hopped out to watch the proceedings. As he approached the group a DragonFly tug-plane touched down nearby and rolled past a glider that was all loaded up and ready for the string. The pilot was already proned-out in his harness, hanging suspended and relaxed, and ready for the fun. He was hang-checked and geared-up to give the magic signal for launch, he had only to hook up the string and put on his helmet.

Before much longer, that glidehead would be gliding.

The ground crew snagged the string from the passing tug and made the connection to the pilot and his wing. As a last detail the pilot, a good-ol' boy named "Rebel", reached over to grab his helmet and pulled it on over his head. He fastened the chin strap securely, and was ready for action.

"Flight speed!" he commanded. "Let's ROLL!"

In response, his launch crew gave the tug driver the go-ahead signal— a wind milling arm— and leaned into the tow dolly to get the show rolling with a gentle shove. Meanwhile, the tug pilot stepped on the gas and his tiny craft began to roll along the runway towing its colorful and willing burden behind.

Flight was about to be committed.

Walter watched the operation commence and had to pause in wonder. He held his breath while the tug rolled faster and faster and the glider approached lift-off speed, about 30 miles-an-hour. The wing obliged Walter and everyone else as well, by it lifting eagerly into the sky and staying wings-level and nicely lined-up behind the tug.

Now the DragonFly lifted off too, and together the winged pair headed off for the Wild Blue Yonder. It was truly a sight to behold, a spectacle Walter never tired of watching.

"Hey Walter," came a friendly greeting, "Are you ready for the string?" It was Greazy, one of the local glideheads, and he was pointing at the sky. "There goes the Rebel now," he continued.

Walter gazed up Greazy's finger at the glider that was slowly disappearing into the friendly skies when he saw... a funny movement. Not just a strange-looking movement, but an honest-to-God funny movement, and Walter had to blink to make sure he believed his eyes; it appeared that the Rebel had hauled off and whacked himself in the kisser, mid-flight! His own self! But why would he do that? Most glideheads would be holding that bar as though their life depended upon it, which, when you consider the situation, it clearly does. But Walter had a nice view of the Reb, he'd seen it with his own eyes, the Reb had whacked himself in the face.

And now- there he goes again, smack!

Others from the group had noticed the unlikely too now; "What the heck is that about?" one of them asked for all.

"Did you see that?"

"What the heck's he doing?"

"Has he lost his mind?"

But the unlikely now became the focus because as all of the grounded flyers watched, Reb began to smack himself about the head and face in a most demented manner. First only one hand was the culprit, it socked him in the face two or three times. But quickly both hands left the control bar and joined in a mutual and concerted smacking of their rightful owner in the face, in a manner that a glidehead's hands should definitely not.

Walter wasn't sure due to the ever lengthening distance between himself and the tow operation, but he thought he might have heard the Reb exclaim something as well, a curse perhaps? He sure was smacking himself around though, of that there was just no doubt. In fact, the glider went wildly off-tow, accelerated in the wrong direction for a moment, and then the tug pilot had to cut ol' Reb loose, giving him the tow string. Next thing Reb must have realized was that, while he was for some reason known only to himself smacking his own head, face and shoulders, now he was also dragging two-hundred feet of towline. This was not in the flight plan at all.

"WWWWAAAAAHHHHH!"

The glider wobbled along at a slow speed for a moment or two, and then a wing dropped and the nose did too. The glider picked up some speed in a shallow bank and revealed the pilot in a better, so to speak, light. Exposed in profile now, it was

clear to all the bystanders that Reb had plumb lost his mind...
It was crazy!

Next, an object was jettisoned from the wing- Reb's helmet came tumbling down from the Heavens, hit the hard ground, and bounced wildly off into the bushes.

What the beJeezus...!

The wing was flying downwind now, it was still banked-up and was about to start slipping to the ground when Reb ceased his lunatic behavior for a few exciting moments and clutched at the control bar with both hands long enough to shove the wing level. It was still headed downwind at a low altitude and marginal airspeed but Reb seemed not to care- he was back at whacking himself in the kisser with both hands.

The ground was rapidly approaching however, and it appeared likely that the madman in the sky was about to plow a deep and lengthy furrow in the hard Texas soil. It would not be pretty. As Walter grabbed his head in horror, the Reb regained his senses for another brief moment and grabbed the wing long enough to shove the bar with a giant HEAVE and more-or-less turn the thing around into the breeze for landing. Then, still connected to the dangling tow string, and not bothering to lower his landing gear or even grab the bar at all, Reb plowed into the ground as expected.

Miraculously, he plowed-in nice and slowly on his tiny control bar wheels, bounced a time or two, and rolled gently to a stop. It looked like Reb had survived his ordeal after all, and yet the moment the flight was over he recommenced his self-flagellation. As he pushed urgently off the ground and gathered his feet beneath himself, he let fly a curse that suddenly made everything quite clear to one and all;

"Gol' dang FIRE ANTS," he cried. "Gol' dang 'em to Hell! FIRE ANTS AAAHHHRRRGGG!"

Apparently, Reb had set his helmet down atop a nest of the horrible plague while he waited for his journey into the sky. The fire ants had climbed aboard Reb's brain bucket, and then gone hang gliding along with him. Perhaps they didn't like to hang glide. Perhaps they didn't like flying of any sort. Perhaps they had some other agenda for climbing on as they had... Maybe they just didn't like the Rebel?

Well, anyway, they'd let ol' Reb fly for a few moments and then they let 'er rip, all at once taking a bite out of the hapless aviator, stinging him senseless and leaving him in a helpless and defenseless condition. It was a wonder Reb had survived the incident at all, but it had not been one of his better flights.

It is a flight that does not end until Reb has dashed to the nearest hose bib while stripping off his harness and shirt, has plunged his head in the bucket of dog water sitting there, and has extinguished the fire with a snort and a whimper.

Louie Goes For The Goat or, Little Bo Peep

The Ford-From-Hell pulled off the road between Valle de Bravo and Temascaltepec and onto the dusty dirt trail through the pine forest leading to El Peñon del Diablo. As so often in Mexico, a herd of ten or twelve goats blocked the road. A tiny peasant girl, quite hidden by the forest, was guarding them from a distance. She wore patent-leather shoes, and white socks with lace around the ankles, a pink ribbon in her braids. An incredibly grubby gingham dress completed her goatherd ensemble. A Mexican Bo Peep, she held a stick in one grubby hand—her main line of defense. Back in the Ford, Lynrd Skynrd was screaming': Free Bird!

As Walter got out to lock the hubs for the ride up the rough road to launch, Louie scrambled out onto the back porch of the Ford and jumped down, unaware of the little girl's presence in the pines. "Wait a sec' while I piss." he said. Santiago jumped out after him. "Good idea." he agreed. But the little goatherd girl didn't like the looks of the Ford, or maybe the two gringos, or maybe she just didn't like the music. At any rate, she screwed her dirty face in a frown and began to cry, revealing her presence in the forest.

"Mommy!" she screamed. "Mommyyy!" She looked to the shack across the highway, apparently hoping for reinforcements, to better the odds.

"MOMMYYY!"

Startled and embarrassed, Louie quickly re-zipped his trousers as he suddenly noticed the little niña. She stood off the road, but stepped timidly from behind her tree. "What the heck?" he asked. "Where'd she come from?" Louie smiled sheepishly.

"Mommyyy!" screamed the little girl again. She broke from the cover of the woods and ran towards the shack, quite terrified by the spectacle of Louie, Santiago and the Ford-From-Hell. Santiago, being of course fluent in Spanish, hollered after her. "Que onda?" he asked. *What's the matter?*

Still in retreat she slowed somewhat at this query, although now tears streamed from her eyes. "Que no toman las chivas!" she cried. *Don't be taking our goats!*

She dropped the stick she carried to fend off wolves and gringos, but stood her ground just out of stones-throw. Santiago laughed at that notion, possibly at the image he had of the Ford-From-Hell arriving back in Valle with a load of gringo pilots and half a dozen goats. "No vamos a tomar chivas," he assured her. *We're not taking any goats.*

"What's she crying about?" asked Louie.

"She's afraid that we're goat thieves," explained Santiago.

"Goat thieves?" asked Louie, incredulously. He grinned at the idea too. "Goat thieves?" The flyers in back of the Ford launched several derogatory remarks about what Louie would actually do with his goat, if he found himself lucky enough to have one. "Ask her which one is fattest," he urged Santiago.

His amigo turned to the little girl and waved towards the goats, who were paying no attention at all to the proceedings. "Qual es lo mas sabroso?" he asked. *Which one is the tastiest?* The little goatherd girl covered her mouth with one hand, but pointed to a particularly fat, possibly pregnant critter that was grazing nearby. Her lip trembled and she began to sob again, redoubling her cries for help.

"Tomamos el," said Santiago. *We'll take him.*

"Mommyyy!"

"Get in the truck," ordered Walter.

"Wait a minute," replied Louie. "I like that goat stew stuff. What do they call it?"

"Birria," said Santiago, naming a delicious Mexican goathead stew. At the word 'birria' the little peasant girl screamed the more. It was her worst nightmare, the gringos had come to haul off the fattest, tastiest goat, turn him/her/it into lunch. A couple of other peasants from the nearby shack finally appeared across the road, peering over to see what the fuss was about.

"GET IN THE TRUCK!" implored Walter. Things were getting out of hand. Louie approached the fat goat, stalking it as though to grab it. The beast shied away from the gringo.

"WWAHH!" came the cry of protest. "WHAAA!" Santiago grinned all the while, and more rude comments were thrown at Louie. Walter got in the truck and dropped it in gear. If they didn't want to walk up to launch, they'd have to act now, he decided. Accelerating, and glancing in his rear view mirror, he saw Santiago turn and dash for the truck. Louie stopped pestering the goat and broke for the truck too. In the mirror, Walter could still see the little muchacha, rubbing the tears from her eyes in victory.

"Dope will get you through times with no money
better than money will get you through times with no dope."
-- Freewheelin' Franklin

Pedro's Pot or;
Quick Bring the Whiskey and Women

When Walter and Wayne finally drove the palm-lined and sandy dirt road leading out along the Pacific to the campground called Boca de Iguanas, they felt as though renewed from a long perilous journey. Starlight shone brightly over beautiful Bahia Tenacatíta, lingering in the pre-dawn darkness and, appropriately, the stereo rocked, playing The New Riders of the Purple Sage.

> *Now Henry got to Mexico and he*
> *turned his truck around.*
> *He's speakin' with the man who's got it*
> *growing from the ground.*
> *Henry tasted he got wasted*
> *couldn't even see.*
> *And how he plans to drive like that is*
> *not too clear to me!*
> *But now he's rollin' down the mountain goin'*
> *fast fast FAST!*
> *'Cause if he makes it this time*
> *it'll be his last,*
> *Run to Acapulco to turn the golden keys*
> *Henry put yer brakes on*
> *for this corner if you please!*

The last few meters of the journey required a maneuver through the axle-deep Rio de Iguanas and up the bank to Boca de Iguanas campground itself. The Ford swept across gracefully. No one was stirring in camp, but at the sound of the Ford's engine a light erupted in Pancho's cottage. The door swung open and Pancho himself stepped out from the mosquito netting. He yawned and stretched under the naked light bulb, and waved a greeting, a big smile brightening his face.

"¡Amigos!" he shouted. The gringos were back! Pancho bounded towards the truck and extended his hand.

"Bienvenidos!" he declared, scratching the sleep from his eyes. *Welcome back!*

Wayne and Walter exchanged greetings with Pancho, and then they all joyously dashed into the sea. There were thousands of lightning bugs in the palm trees and jungle. Delightful phosphor- escent algae glowed in the surf and left glowing sparkles beneath their feet. As they walked their footsteps glowed behind them for a moment, and then faded to darkness. Walter dove into the flashing surf and held his breath against the refreshing coolness of the salty brine. He surfaced and looked into the blackness above. A shooting star, the same color as the lightning bugs and the phosphorescence, streaked across the Heavens. Bahia Tenacatíta, he realized, is a truly magical place.

Pancho and the gringos frolicked in the surf and the gringos washed off the road grime and weariness. They rode a breaker into shore and sat where the foaming flashing waves could wash them clean. Pancho filled them in on the local 'chisme' (gossip) around the sleepy, idyllic bay. Who was screwing whom mostly. Then he swam out to Oyster Rock and brought back a Pacific lobster, caught somehow in the darkness with his bare hands. There would be a sumptuous breakfast, scrambled huevos y langosta, á la Pancho.

As the sun rose and over breakfast Pancho dropped a question: "Ustedes quieren la mota?" he asked. *Do you guys want some pot?* It was a rhetorical question, one that did not require an answer, really. He might have asked, "Does the Pope wear a funny hat?" or "Is nuestro Presidente a pinche ladron?" Pedro knew these gringos were a couple of potheads. So it was quickly agreed, and the three amigos jumped in the van, retracing their path through the stream and along the palm shrouded Pacific shore of Tenacatíta. They traveled only a short distance back towards the north and as Pancho signaled, they stopped beyond a highway bridge, pulled sharply off the highway and hid the van beneath the bridge for cover. They left the hidden van and began walking up a jungle path.

It was a lovely morning and Pancho whistled as they walked, the sun now angling through the foliage and casting mottled patterns of light and shade before them. Not wanting to surprise anyone, Pancho kept whistling his tune. Momentarily, they stepped into a jungle clearing.

A camp of sorts had been set up with some battered old trailers and a tent or two. A large shed-type building had been erected, or maybe commandeered, and there were many bales of hay piled in a disorderly manner under its roof. Suddenly Walter got a strong whiff of contraband, and came to a startling conclusion about those bales: they were not hay bales after all.

THEY WERE MARIJUANA BALES!

Dope!

Mary Jane!

Mota, herb, grass, reefer, ganja, hooch, Woweee Zowee... Stuff!

Pancho waved as they stepped from the jungle and kicked at a mangy dog who ran barking towards them. Several tough-hombre types, lounging in hammocks, started at the sudden unexpected appearance of Pancho and his gringos. One grabbed a rusty rifle and made as though to defend himself, it may have been his watch.

"¡Oye cabrones!" called Pancho. *Hey assholes!* When said with a smile, this can be translated into something like: 'Hey friends!' One man set down his weapon and stood from his rest. He smiled at Pancho and his gringos, a rotten grin showing few teeth. His face lit up though, and he shook hands all around and gave Pancho a big abrazo bear hug, lifting him on tiptoe. The dogs sniffed the gringos now, and one of them attempted to piss on Walter's leg. The marijuanístas welcomed the gringos and offered them a cervesa from a cardboard case sitting in the sun. It was a little early for Walter to be drinking warm beer, but he followed Pancho's and Wayne's lead and accepted the offering. When he tipped the brew into his mouth a bit too enthusiastically the contents foamed suddenly, squirted from between his lips, gushed halfway down his throat and exited his nasal passage.

"BGACK!"

Without further ado, Pedro opened the negotiations. "Quieren la yerba," he stated. *They want some herb.* This was good news for the traficántes. Perhaps they had been waiting a long time for this news, for these here gringos, who had finally arrived. There certainly was pot aplenty.

The man Pancho had greeted and introduced simply as Pedro spread his arms in gratitude. He waved his hand at the shed and its contents. "Cuanto quieren?" he asked magnanimously. *How many do they want?* He grabbed Wayne by the shirtsleeve and tugged him towards the bales of pot. Some of them had broken open, spilling their illegal contents on the dusty ground. "Tenemos mucho," he confessed. "Un chingo. Muy bueno." *We have fucking lots. Very good!*

The bales looked seedy and rotten to Walter. A strong smell of decomposing vegetable matter assailed his nostrils. The man produced a pipe that was nothing more than a rusty beer can crushed and shaped to make a bowl, he ripped a seedy bud off a bale with a twist of his fingers. He placed the bud over pinholes in the can and touched it with a lighter. He took a long toke, began a hacking gagging cough, and passed the pipe to Walter.

"¡Hic hic pruéba lo!" he ordered through gritted teeth. *Give it a try!*

Walter hesitated only slightly. He felt very foolish but he held the beer can to his lips and took a strong hopeful toke. The pot was harsh and bit into his lungs. The smoke expanded there and quickly gushed from his windpipe. He convulsed into yet another severe coughing bout, and reeled away from the pipe. Things were not going well for at least one gringo, and this seemed to please Pedro greatly. He smiled and laughed and passed the pipe on to Wayne, who hit it with more caution. He hicced and hacked a time or two also, but kept most of the smoke down. Pedro slapped Wayne on the back by way of congratulations and said, "¡Muy bueno!" *Very good!* "¿Cuanto quieren?" he inquired again. "¡Muy buen precio!" *How much you guys want? Great price!*

Wayne looked towards the shed again. There was so much dope here, they would need a fleet of those large coconut trucks, the kind with dual wheels and gate bed sides that you see rumbling slowly, painfully, along Mexican highways burdened with coconuts, if they ever hoped to move it all. He had a sudden distinct vision of themselves approaching the border in Nuevo Laredo in a caravan of such wagons, a tarp stretched over the bales and marijuana detritus streaming along behind. An automatic bust, a lifetime in prison. He could see the headlines now:

DOPER GRINGOS BUSTED 100 TONS OF POT CONFISCATED ON SOUTHERN BORDER

It would only happen in his nightmares.

"Queremos poquito," he said. *We only want a little.*

This news did not please the traficánte however, was not what he hoped to hear at all. Not for 'poquito' had they toiled and struggled, risked it all. His gruesome smile turned into a scowl. He looked askance at the gringo and spat a disgusting brown goober upon the ground. He turned his attention to Wayne who was cautiously taking another toke from the beer-can pipe. "Cuanto... quieren?" he asked again, as if confounded.

Wayne looked to the man. "Hic hic poquito," he confirmed through puffed cheeks. *A little.*

Pedro looked to Pancho, who stood grinning at his gringos. Pancho was fine with poquito, but Pedro was very unhappy with poquito. Here stood two quite obviously rich spoiled brat pot-head gringos, who should just load up the whole stinking reeking fermenting mess and drag it off to Hollywood or Las Vegas. Don't they realize the riches that could be made with such a haul?

Yet... they wanted... poquito? POQUITO?

There was poquito alright.

There was poquito pot just scattered around the perimeter of the chingada bodega.

There was poquito AND MAS!

In fact, there was a chingada TONELADA!

Pedro spat again at the ground. "¡Ptuui!" Not yet satisfied, he spun away from the gringos and lashed out at one of his mangy dogs, placing a well-aimed kick to the beast's rib cage. The varmint yelped and slunk off behind the mass of rotting marijuana. He lifted his leg and urinated on the mess with a bitter glance over his haunch, as if in revenge. Pedro turned on Pancho and expressed his dismay, his disbelief, his anger.

"¡Quieren POCO!" he scgrowled.

Pancho grinned and shrugged; he had tried, anyway. Maybe you can lead a gringo to mota, but you can't always make him compra... He took the pipe from Wayne and toked a little himself. He sucked on the pipe and his face showed the same grimace as his gringos. Smoke gushed from his lips and he coughed a cloudy spasm. "Que vendes poquito," he suggested through clenched teeth. *So sell 'em a little.*

Pedro sgrowled some more at this notion. Rudely, he snatched the pipe from Pancho and threw it to the ground, stomping on it. He launched it into the jungle with an impetuous kick and returned to his hammock where he flung himself down in disgust. "¡Chinga les!" he concluded. *Fuck 'em!*

The situation had deteriorated rapidly, and Walter was uncomfortable. This looked like a tough bunch of desperadoes indeed. Other traficántes had come upon the scene as if from hiding, and he wondered how life's events had led him here, to this ugly stinking clearing on this beautiful day, an ocean paradise beckoning beyond the jungle. The mean hombres lurked in the shadows and slouched around the camp- mean and desperate looking' *desperados.*

Pancho wouldn't let them just roll the gringos, would he? Maybe just hold a rusty pistol to their heads and... The image was too gruesome to explore.

Suddenly Wayne sprung into action. He held two fingers about an inch apart and waved them in Pancho's smiling face as if to say, *Just wait a minuto.* Then he dashed off down the jungle trail from whence they had come. In a flash he parted the jungle foliage and was gone, leaving Walter to fend for himself with this bunch of mean, dirty hombres. Walter sat down on a bale of pot to indicate how really cool he was with this situation.

This is okay.

This is all right.

I can handle this.

This is okay.

This is all right.

I can handle this.

Yet another Mexican mantra. What he really wanted was to jump up and follow Wayne down the path, to hide in the van and spin off out of there, never to be seen again. He could just give up the dope as of today, go hole up somewhere, straighten himself out, clean up his act. Maybe check in at the Betty Ford Clinic. But he didn't move... Maybe it was the sight of various small weapons at hand. Maybe it was the dark cloud of disappointment that hung over the camp. He sat and waited, wondering about his Destiny.

Meanwhile Pancho picked up the flattened pipe and re-shaped it a bit. He tore off another rotten bud and, borrowing a match from the nearest desperado, he toked on more of the foul vegetation. To his credit, he never stopped grinning.

Thankfully, they didn't have long to wait. Wayne reappeared huffing up the jungle trail. In his hands he held a mostly-full half-gallon jug of Kentucky sour mash whiskey and a stack of the glossy pornography that the Federáles back up the road had failed to appropriate. He burst upon the scene bearing these gifts, which he handed to Pedro. It was a pivotal moment.

Pedro sat up in his hammock and took notice.   He grudgingly accepted the offerings. He uncorked the bottle and took a hearty swig. He flipped open a Hustler magazine and admired the tasty flesh therein, wiping his chin with a shirtsleeve. A smile broke the scowl and, with a grunt of approval, he got to perusing the smut while taking another gulp of whiskey. With fine Kentucky bourbon dripping down his chin, Pedro handed the bottle off to a nearby compadre, who smothered the mouth of the bottle with his lips and suckled as though it were Mother's own milk.

Pancho handed off to Wayne and took another toke off the pipe, burst into another coughing jag. The traficántes seemed to relax in the early morning light. The pall that had hung over the camp lifted like morning fog. Better Times lay ahead...

"Hey Walter..." said Wayne, who spoke little Español. "Can you explain to our amigos that we just want something that will fit in the glove box?"

"I'll try," offered Walter.

The deal was quickly consumated. For a ridiculously small sum of pesos, the gringos had their dope. More than enough, actually. It looked as though it might weigh a kilo. It certainly wouldn't fit in the guantero, but it wouldn't require a coconut truck to move it, either. And the traficántes had made dinner money. They could look forward to some fresh camarónes and maybe some delicious pozóle. Afterwards, they would head for the cantina for some female fun.

Walter felt a bit conspicuous leaving the dope camp with a kilo of pot tucked under his arm.

This is just like in the song, he decided. Henry!

But they slapped hands and promised to return, promised to spread the word meanwhile, among all those dope-crazed pot-head hippies throughout America, Land of the Libre, about the large stash of tasty buds, and the fortune to be had for the hauling, just a stone-throw up the Rio de Iguánas, down Old Mexico way.

Sunday afternoon Tijuana is a lovely town.
The bullfight brings the tourists in
Their money flowing down.
The border guards are much too busy
There at five o' clock.
Henry's truckin' right on through
He hardly even stopped!

Ole's Patented Hole In The Ground or, A True Gruesome Story

I was hospitalized when I heard the news. In fact, I could barley move. I'd spent the morning trying to lift a finger, and the afternoon trying to wiggle a toe. This was agony enough. But when I heard what Jeff had done, I was miffed, too. Could he really be that obtuse?

It was Will who had told me. He said that Jeff seemed quite gleeful that I had stacked up the trike, creating widespread wreckage. I was not surprised by this, Jeff always had been jealous that I had more experience than he- so, there would be little doubt he'd find some twisted satisfaction and joy in my disaster. But when Will told me that Jeff had added a little extra to his computer flight-simulator that he'd set up in the hangar, that was what really hurt. The program was set up to show our little airfield, quite realistically, and an assortment of the aircraft we had to fly that included trikes.

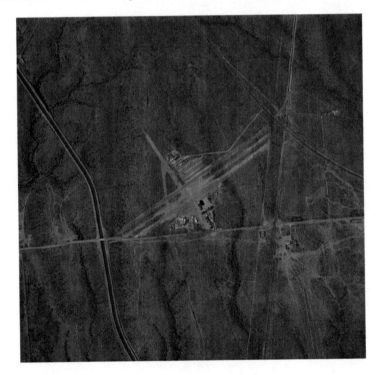

One day, as Will was passing through the hangar while Jeff was at the helm of his flight-simulator, Jeff's own voice recording came over the speakers and exclaimed: "Watch out! There's Ole's patented hole-in-the-ground!"

Startled, Will stopped and asked, "What was THAT?"

"Cool huh?" replied Jeff gleefully. "I just put that in there. Like it?"

"Have you no respect?" asked Will.

"Whaddya mean?" asked Jeff. He was quite animated at the suggestion, but then Jeff was an animated sort anyway.

"Well fer Chrissake, the guy nearly died. He can barely move! He's all fucked-up! Show some kindness."

Jeff glanced at Will with a silly look. "If he's dumb enough to stack up a trike, he deserves what ever I can dish out."

It was some days later that Jake came along too, heard Jeff's voice through the speakers, and told him to get it the hell off the program. Jake said it wasn't in keeping with the image he wanted around the hangar. But I suppose Jake was pissed at me too. After all, it was his trike I destroyed, I had nearly killed one of his students too.

Some months passed. I finally learned to walk again, and I had driven up to the Navajo Reservation to visit with my sister who is a teacher up there. On my return I would be going past the hangar, so of course I wanted to stop. I might even get in a quick flight while I was visiting. As I turned off I-10 at Biscuit Flats and headed west on the Carefree Highway I noticed a column of smoke rising from the desert out by the airfield. I thought that was peculiar and I wondered what was burning. I was more and more perplexed the closer I came.

But when I turned off the road and into the driveway to the field it became obvious that something tragic had happened. I was shocked and dismayed by what I saw: emergency medical vehicles and fire trucks were everywhere. Cops were directing traffic, and they waved me past an accident scene that was still smoldering. I assumed the tragedy- and that's clearly what it was- had happened to someone from across the runway at the soaring school. This was not a trike burning, not someone from our side of the field; an aircraft tail fin was sticking up out of the desert. I raced for the hangar, where I encountered Greg, who sat in the hangar wearing a long face.

"What happened?" I asked.

Greg spoke but one word: "Jeff," he said. But Jeff's trike was in the hangar. How could that be? Confused, I pointed at the trike. "But...?" was all I could say. Greg shrugged, turned away, and disappeared out the door.

I soon learned that Jeff had shown up at the hangar in a Varga- an experimental aircraft owned by Ron, from Ron's Desert Valley Aircraft Parts. By all accounts Ron was Old Leather. They had come to offer Jake a ride in the Varga, since the Varga was a machine that could be set up to fly solely with hand controls. It should be easy for a triker to fly. But Jake had been busy with customers and declined the offer.

As Jeff and Ron climbed back in that plane they were talking about doing a "performance take-off", whatever that was. Then they'd taxied out to mid-field, gave 'er the gun and popped off the runway. They held the Varga down low on the runway gathering speed for a few moments, and then someone hauled back on the stick. We'll never know who was in command- Ron the owner? Jeff the hotshot?

Maybe the both of them are to blame?

In any event, that Varga stood up on its tail and quickly shed its airspeed. Under full power, the plane had stalled, rotated and spun straight into the ground. It hit, burst into flames, and that was the tragic end of Ron and Jeff.

Jake and Greg didn't want to believe their eyes. "Holy shit!" They jumped in the golf cart, and sped to the scene. They watched a gruesome horror show, as Jeff and Ron burned to death before their eyes.

Soon the remains of our friends were hauled away, the fire trucks and ambulances left the scene, and there was nothing left but the wreckage and the grieving. I loaded my sorry, aching carcass in the golf cart and went to have a look at the crash scene. It wasn't that I wanted to, you know? It was that I had to, I was compelled. I motored out the drive and veered left through the creosote and ocotillo to a place I'd been before. To the place where they'd loaded me, broken and dying, into a CareFlight helicopter for a flight to my resurrection, a modern medical miracle.

But there would be no resurrection for Jeff.

I sat there and wondered why? WHY? What was it about this spot that hurt so damn much? Was it some sort of dastardly plot? Was it a magnet for fools and hapless flyers? Was it Hell On Earth?

Naw, it was just damn lousy luck, that's all...

One fact dawned crystal clear to me as I sat there in the desert: the last thing Jeff must have seen on the way to meet his maker was...

Ole's Patented Hole in the Ground.

He must have been horribly astonished for a second or two, watching it come up at him. *Watch out!* Wreckage, broken glass, a small crater and a scorched circle of burned desert marked the spot where that Varga went in, obliterating all signs of my disaster, but leaving no doubt about Jeff's.

Grandma's Farm or, My Journey Home

I traveled to Argos, Indiana, working with Buckeye Powered Parachutes on their trike project. From the first moment that I looked at a road map, I reflected on how close I would be to my hometown, a tiny burg in southern Michigan named Goodells. Goodells was a good place to grow up, a farm town, with lots of fields and creeks and woods. But as an adult it held little attraction for me. Except for one short visit when my mother was laid to rest, I had not returned in twenty-five years.

So as I traveled east towards Indiana that spring, I determined to return for a visit, but to return from the sky. The thought stayed with me through the summer, and so I was hopeful when I asked Buckeye Ralph to help me fulfill my dream.

"Ralph", says I, "I'd like to borrow your plane."

"Uh... oh yea?" asked Ralph.

"I'll pay the rental rate, of course."

"What you got in mind?" he questioned.

"I'm going home Ralph. Visit my kinfolk. They live in Goodells, Michigan, about six hours from here. I'm gonna drop in on their farms."

Ralph grinned and nodded his head. "You flyin' there or what?" he asked, a reasonable question.

"I dunno, yet. Maybe I'll just drag the trike behind my motorhome. Put less hours on it like that."

Ralph is an agreeable sort. "When you leaving?" he asked.

I took my motorhome and Ralph's Cosmos Phase II and one of his trailers, and drove through a hot summer night to Goodells. I remembered the giant farm that had once been the county poor farm where I had volunteered as a Boy Scout, which was located within the County Park. I thought I'd camp the night there, but a new highway, built since my departure, confused me greatly. Nothing seemed the same. Goodells is a tiny town of a thousand souls, if that, yet I drove the wrong way looking for the park. It was 4AM before I finally found my way. I pulled in past a sign that read:

Goodells County Park Open 8AM to 10PM daily.

I slept hard that night, for a few hours. Then I awoke and set about my task. I drove on to the closest public airstrip I could locate on the chart, in the more substantial town of Yale, Michigan. Here I found a beautiful grass strip amidst the cornfields, with a couple of planes tied under a roof and one locked hangar. The wind sock hung limp in the sultry midwestern air. It was a very quiet place.

I downloaded the Ghost 14 wing from the roof of my motorhome and unloaded the trike. I assembled the whole wagon single-handedly. The trike went together easily, and at a leisurely pace and within an hour I was set up and preflighted. By then the sky was a beautiful blue with shapely cumulus clouds and light winds blowing from the south. I would have a slight head wind, but even so, my destination would be but a few minutes flight. I eagerly slipped into my flight suit.

The 582 made a very satisfying racket as Ralph's trike climbed on out. I would head south until I found the old highway- with which I was more familiar, and then turn east. I was in search of three farms nestled beside Pine Creek, the ancestral home of the Quinn clan. My mother is a Quinn. Back in the 1850s, the Federal Government offered 80 acres of turf to anyone willing to make improvements. Homesteading, it was called, and my ancestors took them up on it. Since those first farms my kin have scattered and gone far and wide. Some still remain and there are lots of Quinns left there, but the Olsons have all gone.

The old farms were my destination, since my own childhood house was sold years ago. But the farms have been in the family from as long ago as 1858. I figured one of them would have enough room to land a trike.

I glanced east from a thousand feet and saw the great curve of Lake Huron, in the distance. It would provide a good landmark to judge the other distances. I figured I must look at least ten miles from the lake, and stay north of old highway M-21. The ground below was typically midwestern with a patchwork quilt of farms and villages. I worried for just a moment that I wouldn't be able to locate my goal when suddenly I spotted my Uncle Herb Quinn's place. It was quickly followed by my Uncle Bob's to the west and the Cribbins farm to the east. Warren Cribbins is my second cousin, whom I hadn't seen in a coon's age.

I cruised the farms for a few minutes and examined the situation, enjoyed the moment. Nothing, of course, looked the same: my perspective didn't help. Everything looked so miniature and had such a small scale. As a child it had all looked so big. It had been my whole world.

Here was Uncle Herb's giant red barn? So small... almost humble.

And Bob's barn? The one where I spent one whole summer helping him prepare for a big auction when he retired from farming? It looked more like a shed to me now.

And Pine Creek? We used to ice skate from my home all the way upstream to Grandma's farm for her good cinnamon buns, getting 'soakers' along the way. I could feel the sting of frozen toes and I could smell the warm buns, but I could barely make out the creek shrouded in trees; it was more like a trickle really. And neither Uncle Bob's or Uncle Herb's farm offered so much as a sketchy place to land. Even the dirt road out front was hemmed with powerlines and phone cables.

The Cribbins farm did have a short narrow grass lane. It was clean, though, with a good approach and bean fields under each wingtip. It would be there I would land, or not at all. I chopped the throttle and went down over Uncle Herb's place first. I strafed the rooftop, staying just off to one side. It would do no good at all to have the prodigal kid return as a bloody splotch on the barn door. I cranked a turn and circled the farmhouse. There were cars in the driveway and a couple of dogs barking out front, but no sign of human activity. I guess I expected a welcoming committee.

I climbed out and dove on in to Uncle Bob's. Bob lives in California now, a retiree. His house is occupied by his son Frankie. I tried to get a rise out of Frankie, too, but after several passes, he was a no-show.

So I headed over to cousin Warren's and made a spectacle of myself. Later I was to learn that their conversation went something like this;

Warren, through the pantry window: "Who is that dang fool in that funny-looking machine up there ma?"

Judy, his wife, from the front porch "I don't know, Pa... but whoever it is, he's waving at us like a darn fool."

I lined up on the grass lane and came in low over some pine trees. The Phase II touched easily and braked with room to spare. I taxied past the corncrib and around some lilac bushes, not stopping until I was parked in front of the old place. Everything looked good, from down here it was much as I had remembered it. Cousin Warren was standing on the porch now too. "What the..." he began. He'd never seen such a funny looking plane.

"Is that you Warren?" I asked.

"Who the heck are you?" he replied.

I took off the full-face helmet. "I'm yer long-lost cousin," I said. "Got any cinnamon buns?"

"Well I'll be darned," said Warren. "John Olson?" I laughed a confirmation. "Why, last I heard about you, you were laid up in a wheelchair. They said you'd maybe never walk again."

"Well, they were wrong, Warren. And I can still fly, too," Warren was happy as a little kid to see me.

"Come on in," he said. "Let's see what Ma's cookin' up."

I spent two days with the Cribbinses. They fed me fresh fruit and vegetables from their garden. We stayed up late each night drinking Stroh's beer and talking of old times, eating fresh rhubarb pie. Warren told me stories that I had never heard about my parents, including the New Year's when my Pa apparently got drunk. I'd never seen my father have more than one beer. He was a temperate sort, and it must have made my mother very angry. We talked about the traveling I had done. They told of plans to hit the road in their new motorhome.

Other kin got the news of my visit and came to see me and the funny-looking plane. Brian Quinn, a few years younger than me, brought his children. They were delighted to discover that I was flying the same plane as seen in Fly Away Home, his daughter's favorite movie. "You've got a Cosmos!" she said with obvious excitement- she even knew the brand.

Would they like to take a spin?

The daughter, yes. Everyone else, no. These were farm folk. Salt of the Earth. Feet firmly planted in the soil. "Take my daughter," said Brian. "The rest of us will watch."

It wasn't a particularly action-packed weekend. In fact, it was pretty laid-back, almost boring. But, in a way, it was one of the best I'd ever spent. The plane stayed tied to the ground, mostly. I took it out to fly over my old home, the house that my father had built with his own hands. I hooked up with an old high school friend, Walter Badgerow, and we went for a spin.

But mostly we just relaxed.

Sunday afternoon Warren and I loaded the trike back on my motorhome, and I said my farewells. We made plans to get together this winter in Florida. They stocked my motorhome refrigerator with goodness from the garden and I fired her up. When I left, there were several Quinns and Cribbinses, standing in the front hard, waving. It had been a great trip.

Who says you can't go home?

Stay tuned for more wild adventures from the Wild Blue at www.LearnToHangGlide.com

Hangbabble or,
The Glidehead Glossary

What is hang gliding all about and what are some of the terms and expressions that have evolved with it? Sometimes it's difficult to understand unless you have grown up with the sport and the slang. My sister says she loves the glossary, and I'm sure some of you are wondering what the heck I'm talking about. So I have listed here most of the stuff that I know about hang gliding- "hangbabble", if you will. Not all of it is pretty and some of it is downright vicious, but then- so is hang gliding. Some of this colorful lingo is not encountered in my book, but will no doubt come in handy if you meet a bunch of glideheads.

Accidental deployment- to deploy the on-board recovery system, inadvertently. This is very dangerous, since you have just relinquished all control. This is just about the worst thing that might happen to you in the sky.

AIDS- long before there was any such thing as the human immuno virus, there was AIDS, short for Aviation Induced Divorce Syndrome. Many a poor glidehead, including myself, has succumbed. It's also why we all have dogs.

bag- a paraglider. They resemble nothing so much as colorful bags in the sky. Also, pair-a-panties (from the French 'parapente') and, (because of their tendancy to not make it out to the landing field: tree condom.

bail off- to dive off the cliff, to launch.

bail out- to dive for safety. Usually a friendly field somewhere, but any safe place will do, even a safer place in the sky. Example: "I was so puckered I bailed out."

battens- aluminum ribs, in the shape of an air foil, which are inserted into skinny pockets in the sail, to give a hang glider wing its shape.

beener- from the French 'carabineer', the simple, strong, locking ring that connects the glidehead to his glider. This is a piece of climbing gear, usually, that facilitates the 'hang' in hang gliding.

clip in- to connect the harness to the glider using the 'beener'. For many years a major cause of death in hang gliding was failure to clip in. If you approach the sport in this way (carelessly) you are not likely be an old glidehead.

circle out- to climb in a thermal. For most glideheads this is the most fun you can have.

cycle- how thermals behave at launch. First they cycle in, then the cycle dies until more hot air is produced by the sun, and the cycle repeats itself. A glidehead learns to recognize cycles, tries to launch as the cycle is building, and circles out with it.

cummies- short for cumulus cloud. Cummies are made by thermals, and are a sign of good soaring. Many glideheads have quit their jobs at the first sigh of shapely, high cummies.

dead cloud- a cloud that is no longer being fed with thermal heating

deploy- to throw or fire the emergency recovery system (parachute). No guarantees.

dust devil- a thermal current that is strong enough to pick up dust, which makes it visible to the human eye. These currents may be weak, if the dust is light such as volcanic ash, but more likely this is a strong thermal. Dust devils are strong enough to pick up glideheads too, maybe too strong for safety. They appear much like a miniature tornado.

driver- someone who the glideheads have convinced to chase off after them with the 'retrieve' vehicle. This person usually, though not always, is in possession of a valid driver's license, a map, and good common sense.

factory- where the gliders are made. As in: "factory pilot" or "Check out what the factory sent me."

Feds- pathetic bureaucrats from the Federal Aviation Administration. These are the guy and gals who would like to shut down all the fun, so they can just sit back and collect their salary and count the years, months, days and minutes to retirement, whihout having to do any real work. Not long ago the FAA motto was: "To support and regulate aviation." Then, they dropped the "support" part. Now, there is a new motto: "We ain't happy 'till you ain't happy!" For Sport Flight there is yet another: "We ain't havin' fun 'till you ain't havin' fun!"

flight deck- a flight instrument essential for most soaring pilots. The most necessary instrument is the variometer with an audio readout. The variometer beeps happy as you climb and sad as you descend. As you begin to climb the "vario" begins to beep. The faster your rate of climb, the faster the beeps. When you reach the maximum rate that the vario can register, the beeps go constant. See: pegged. Also likely to include: altimeter, chronometer, thermometer, barometer, baroset, and lately GPS.

glass off- super smooth air, slowly rising. This usually happens in the evening, as the sun is setting, and hot air from the valley below is gently rising. This is how you might end up skyed-out at sunset.

glidehead- a pilot who lives to fly gliders. He don't want no stinking motors, he don't make no stinkin' noise!

grease- to land gently and smoothly.

harness- any of a variety of devices, usually made of fabric and flat webbing, designed to hold a hang glider pilot safely suspended in his wing. This harness is likely to hold your body weight to a factor of ten and still not fail.

HAND gliding- what you did when you were driving down the road with your mom and you rolled down the window, stuck out your hand like a plane, and said, "Wheee!" Many people confuse hand gliding with hang gliding.

HANG gliding- the most awesome sport ever invented by man, and much of it was developed by hippies. You pilot a glider while HANGING in a harness. You let go of the glider and you're STILL HANGING.

hang check- to check your connection before launching. (see: hang loop and clip-in)

hang loop- an essential piece of flat or tubular webbing, used to connect the pilot's harness to the glider. There are usually two hang loops; the main loop and a back-up loop that is about an inch longer.

hangbabble- to speak in terms only another glidehead might interpret without help.

hook in- to connect the harness to the glider. This is essential, because if you launch without first making the connection, you will be hand gliding, instead of hang gliding. Failure to hook in is still a major cause of accidents.

house thermal- a specific location that has a thermal that can usually be counted on, like a house wine.

hypothermic- too cold to function, and make judgments properly.

hypoxic- deprived of oxygen to the point where function and judgment are impaired. Sometimes accompanied by hypothermia. This is Rapture Of The Deep, in reverse.

lift- rising air. Usually rising fast enough that a glidehead gets a free ride up, or at least he does not go down (zero sink).

LZ- glidehead slang for "landing zone".

papalote- Spanish for 'kite'. This is widely used in Latin America as a term for 'hang glider'.

paraglider- (See: bag) a parachute that is foot-launched, sort of (but not exactly)like a hang glider. Paragliders are proliferating, probably because they are comparatively easy to learn to fly, unlike a hang glider, which is more difficult. This is for a number of reasons, but mostly because a hang glider has a wide speed range, and a paraglider has but one speed- slow.

pegged- your vario is registering maximum value up or down. If your vario is pegged up, you are usually a happy camper. If your vario is pegged down, you are usually a scared camper. Note: when you are pegged UP in a thermal, your glider is at a most unusual attitude- with the nose pointed at the Heavens, and you are climbing at one- or two- thousand feet per minute.

piano- noun: a large heavy object
verb: used in Latin America instead of 'sled ride' and it means to go down, rapidly, as might a large heavy object.
"What happened to Pedro?"
"He pianoed."

pocket thermal- **a marijuana cigarette. You keep it in your pocket and it gets you high.**

popcorn fart- very small thermal, difficult to work, but not necessarily stinky.

retrieve- whatever vehicle is sent to pick up a glidehead and his wing. Usually equipped to carry a number of both, and some refreshing beverages.

ridge lift- wind that is forced up by a hill or cliff or mountain and has nowhere else to go but up. This is the easiest type of lift to work for new pilots.

recovery system- a parachute, and more. A recovery system is a parachute and long bridle and a grip. The idea is to throw the parachute away from a broken glider, and when it opens the long bridle and the grip lower the glider and the glidehead. An optional piece of equipment that has made the sport safer, at the cost of other hazards. (see accidental deployment) I might add that personally, in a quarter-century of flying, I have never needed to deploy my recovery system.

safety meeting- a gathering of glideheads, usually before and after the day's flying, where large amounts of pot are consumed. This term originated at launches where there were large gatherings of tourists. (see: wuffo) and hippie pilots. Pilots could safely yell 'Safety meeting!' and the tourists were no wiser.

sailcloth- 1) the cloth use to make hang gliders 2) lots of hang gliders, as in: "That guy sure had a stack of sailcloth."

shoot-the-hoop - an often painful and sometimes dangerous maneuver, that usually results from a bad landing. First, the glidehead cannot run fast enough to hold up the glider. Next the basetube contacts the ground and stops instantly while the pilot is still running. Immediately after, the nose whacks the ground and the glidehead is sent swinging through the control bar at the end of his suspension. Often the pilot smacks his head on the keel. The pain usually comes from the keel, a hard aluminum tube that runs along the center of the wing, which is what the pilot's head smacks, and is harder than most heads. This is why no glidehead should EVER clip-in to a hang glider without a helmet that is harder than his head.

sink- descending air. Usually what a glidehead wants to avoid, unless he is frozen, hypothermic, has to urinate, or his wife is threatening him with AIDS if he doesn't take the sink, NOW!

Site Nazi- The guy who either enforces the rules or creates the rules at a flying site and who may or may not have 'em right or have the right but who does this anyway. Many sites have Site Nazis.

sled ride- to have a flight where you just glide to the LZ below. For most glideheads, this is about as disappointing as it gets. (See: piano)

soaring- the art of extending flight duration and distance, by using skill and the naturally-occurring rising air currents. This is an exciting three-dimensional game you play with Mother nature.

skyed out- 1)Very high 2)a little speck in the sky 3)to feel really good as in: "I was really skyed out!"

stuff the bar- to hold the bar as far back as possible, maybe even balling up with your legs tucked into your chest. This will make the glider go as fast as possible, in a vertical dive.

stunch- a contraction of "stuff" and "launch": "Did you see what happened to Ralph? He stunched it!" Usually when you stunch you also shoot the hoop.

tandem- to fly with two occupants, each in their own harness, in one hang glider. Usually an advanced flyer and a passenger/student

thermal- a rising column of air. If a soaring pilot is skillful enough, if he has the right equipment and a little luck, he can ride these currents to incredible heights.

tree condom- a paraglider that has failed to glide out and ended up draped over a tree.

trike- a three wheel powerpack that hangs below a hang glider and allows the pilot to take off from level flat ground by stepping on the gas... WAGONS HO!

variometer- (vario for short) the most important instrument in a flight deck, a variometer is an extremely sensitive rate-of-climb indicator, that usually has an audio readout. In other words, as the pilot begins to climb, the vario begins to sing a happy song. The faster the pilot climbs, the happier the vario sings, and he just needs to listen to understand his progress.

wagon- a trike. This appellation derives from an article that appeared in some long-forgotten flying publication which claimed that trikes are to flying what Conestoga wagons are to travel. We knew a good thing when we heard it... WAGONS HO!

washout- built-in dive-recovery, designed into all modern hang gliders. This is what causes the nose to pitch up when the pilot forces the wing into a dive. A necessary and noteworthy design characteristic.

wave lift- air that rises in the middle of nowhere, because it has previously struck a hill or mountain far upwind. Only stable air will act like this, and it may rise and fall in a wave like shape, many miles downwind of the original uplifting.

whack- to land hard, usually nose first. This comes from the sound a glider makes at the moment of impact, and what all the other glideheads who are watching yell with glee. The most impressive whacks are also shoot-the-hoops.

wuffo- a bystander. As in: "Wuffo you wanna jump the cliff huh? Wuffo?"

XC- short for 'cross-country', to fly somewhere far. Not literally across the country, just far. This is what most glideheads want to do after they have hooked-in, bailed-off, climbed-out and skyed-out. So far, the longest XC flight in a hang glider is 442 miles!

Announcing: Bad SPANISH Class

Everything you've always wanted to know about Spanish
but were afraid to ask.
Español con Olé!
Thirty years of street Español, Mexicaníto style!
Study with a maestro
Improve your vocabularyo
Polish your ackcento
Impress your amigos
¡Fightin' words!
¡Lovin' words!
¡"F" words!
Get really, really embarrassed!
¡Go to %^*!
¡You little mother!
¡#$*^ your mother!
¡You son of a whore!
¡You son of a raped woman!
¡Smack you in the face!
¡Smack you worse in the face!
¡Muffin! ¡Goater! ¡Cuckold!
¡Ox!

¡Dirty trick! ¡I don't give a damn!
And worse- much, much worse!
**Stuff you'll never learn in any other Spanish class
(and are glad you did!)**
A steal at N$1000
(those are pesos you pendejo!)
Adults only North hangar, Amigos del Cielo
Saturday January 12 at 1PM
Bring a notepad and chair
Also available to come to YOUR casa for special private
tutoring!
Special assistant Goldy Ivashkov

¡NO MAMES BUEY!

WAGONS HO! Across the Great Divide

Launching Vista Point

Damn big hole in the ground- Meteor Crater Arizona

Gordon Stitt landing at Lake Tahoe
Thanks for the bitchin' photos Gordy!

The kids love us!

¡Hasta la vista amigos!

3755451